Are There Ghosts
in Outer Space?

I was not alone. In that first heart-freezing moment **it** seemed that something was trying to get into my suit— something invisible, seeking shelter from the cruel and pitiless vacuum of space. I whirled madly in my harness, scanning the entire sphere of vision around me. There was nothing there, of course. There could not be—yet that purposeful scrabbling was clearer than ever.

I suddenly remembered how Bernie Summers had died, no farther from the station than I was at this very moment. I had never known Bernie, but suddenly his fate became of overwhelming importance to me— for a horrible idea had come into my mind.

What happens to the soul of a man who dies between the stars, far from his native world? Are you still there, Bernie, clinging to the last object that linked you to your lost and distant home?

It took me several tries before I could press the right button and switch my transmitter to the emergency wave length. "Station!" I gasped. "I'm in trouble. . . ."
from *WHO'S THERE?*

ARTHUR C. CLARKE

WITH A NEW INTRODUCTION BY THE AUTHOR

TALES OF TEN WORLDS

A SIGNET BOOK

NEW AMERICAN LIBRARY

SIGNET, SIGNET CLASSIC, MENTOR, ONYX, PLUME, MERIDIAN and NAL BOOKS are published by NAL PENGUIN INC., 1633 Broadway, New York, New York 10019

First Signet Printing, April, 1973

11   12   13   14   15   16   17   18   19

PRINTED IN THE UNITED STATES OF AMERICA

To the memory of my dear Mother
Nora Mary Clarke
who wrote her first book in her 84th year

Contents

Introduction to the 1987 Edition

Reading these stories has been like taking a time machine back to the beginning of the Space Age. Most of them were written while the human race was taking its first steps away from the planet of its birth, and reflect the hopes and fears of those days—now, incredibly, thirty years in the past. . . .

Although I am fond of quoting Sam Goldwyn's immortal: "If you've gotta message, use Western Union," I must admit that some of these tales contain a certain amount of propaganda. "I Remember Babylon" (original title, "Blue Network") was written in 1959 as a deliberate attempt to alert the public to the possibilities of communications satellites, by focusing on one of their more controversial uses. The story originally appeared in *Playboy* Magazine; well, twenty years later the Playboy Channel was making its predictions come true . . .

I certainly never imagined, in 1959, that one day I would have a five-meter dish on my own roof (courtesy of satellite promoter Bob Cooper and his friends in the TVRO industry), receiving a dozen channels from a whole constellation of Indian Ocean comsats. Alas, the program content, though of excellent technical quality, is not quite so stimulating as that promised in "Babylon." Shanghai, for example, beams out hours and hours of computer programming, electronics theory, structural engineering, chemistry, French and English lessons to its presumed millions of viewers. I applaud one of the greatest educational experiments in history (anticipated by the historic Indian/US SITE experiment of 1976), but sometimes I can't help feeling a little wistful . . .

"Death and the Senator" has not yet happened; there are still no hospitals in space. But there will be, and if it turns out that reduced gravity can increase the life-span, the slogan "Go West, young man!" may one day be replaced by "Go Up, old man!"

The event described in "Out of the Cradle . . ." also lies in the future, and it too will come. A couple of corrections, though, are now necessary. Yuri Gagarin was launched not from Kapustin Yar, but from the Baikonur Cosmodrome, near the town of Tyuratam. In 1982 I had the solemn privilege of visiting his little office at 'Star Village,' with the clock stopped and everything untouched, just as it was when his jet-trainer crashed. ("I heard the impact," Cosmonaut Alexei Leonov told me sadly. "We never found exactly what happened.")

And my friend Wernher von Braun, alas, never reached his eightieth birthday—still less the Moon. . . .

"Hate," of course, has also been bypassed by history; it was written before man or woman had entered space. But its message is even more urgent now that plans are afoot to take our terrestrial conflicts beyond the atmosphere.

The background of this story (originally published under the title "At the End of the Orbit") evokes nostalgic memories of the Great Barrier Reef. In 1955 I sailed from Thursday Island with Mike Wilson (see "I Remember Babylon") aboard the lugger *Galerhu*, to savor the unexciting—except during the hurricane season—life of a pearl diver in the Torres Straits. So I can assure you that the details are authentic; for further information, consult *The Coast of Coral*, available in the Rare Book Section of the New York Public Library.

Rereading "Into the Comet" while still suffering from a slight Halley Hangover has been rather an uncanny experience. (The fact that the spacecraft concerned is named *Challenger* now gives additional resonances.) When the story appeared in 1960, Fred Whipple thanked me for basing it on his "dirty snowball" theory of comets. I am delighted that Fred has now seen the dramatic confirmation of his ideas by the flotilla of European, Russian, and Japanese probes that encoutered Halley in 1986; the description of the core of "Randall's Comet" might be a preview of the VEGA findings a quarter of a century later. (By a happy coincidence, the December 1986 issue of the *National Geographic* showing Fred expounding them has just arrived on my desk, and the associated pictures would do nicely to illustrate this story.)

"Saturn Rising," I must confess, contains a couple of serious errors. Although everything I wrote in 1960 about that beautiful world has been more than justified by the stunning Voyager photographs, I'm afraid no one will ever see a Saturnrise from the surface of Titan, for two very good reasons. Titan's atmosphere has turned out to be so thick and cloudy that it probably blocks all view of the heavens. And as Titan (like our own Moon) keeps the same face always turned towards its primary, Saturn remains fixed in Titan's sky; it doesn't rise or set.

I put this right in *Imperial Earth* (1976), but got something else wrong. At that time, everyone thought there was lots of hydrogen in Titan's atmosphere; this now turns out to be incorrect. But it still remains one of the most interesting places in the Solar System, and the sooner we get there, the better . . .

"Let There be Light" really belongs, of course, in *Tales From the White Hart* (*q.v.*) and after all these years I've no idea how it got into *this* volume. "A

Slight Case of Sunstroke" (based on an idea from my old friend John R. Pierce) is a variation on the same theme, and both stories have been somewhat dated by the invention of the laser. If you want to kill anyone with light, there are now much better ways of going about it.

"Trouble With Time," my only detective story (later published in an Ellery Queen anthology as "Crime on Mars"), has a curious sequel. The discovery of a sculpted human head on Mars would seem to be an improbable enough prediction. Well, just such a phenomenon has now been reported by analysts of the Viking Orbiter photographs; its dimensions, however, are measured in miles rather than inches.

It's a quite startling likeness of a human face looking blankly up at the sky. But I have been unable to take it very seriously since the discovery of a formation in Canada that, viewed from the air, is a perfect profile of George Bernard Shaw. I await a headline in the *National Enquirer:* "What ancient race foresaw Ireland's literary sage?"*

"Dog Star" is a story I cannot bear to reread. My own Laika's bones have lain for twenty years in a garden I pass every day but have never revisited; son and grandson Sputnik and Rex sleep forever beneath my window, as does their successor Ravi. But now, I am happy to say, my four beloved Shepherds seem reincarnated in Rikki, the equally beautiful Ridgeback who is warming my feet at this very moment and who perfectly fulfills the story's closing paragraph.

Arthur C. Clarke

Colombo, Sri Lanka
January 14, 1987

*For my brief correspondence with GBS on the subject of space travel, see *1984: Spring.* Too bad he never knew about this really striking example of Nature's skill as a portrait artist.

I Remember Babylon

My name is Arthur C. Clarke, and I wish I had no connection with this whole sordid business. But as the moral—repeat, moral—integrity of the United States is involved, I must first establish my credentials. Only thus will you understand how, with the aid of the late Dr. Alfred Kinsey, I have unwittingly triggered an avalanche that may sweep away much of Western civilization.

Back in 1945, while a radar officer in the Royal Air Force, I had the only original idea of my life. Twelve years before the first Sputnik started beeping, it occurred to me that an artificial satellite would be a wonderful place for a television transmitter, since a station several thousand miles high could broadcast to half the globe. I wrote up the idea the week after Hiroshima, proposing a network of relay satellites twenty-two thousand miles above the Equator; at this height, they'd take exactly one day to complete a revolution, and so would remain fixed over the same spot on the Earth.

The piece appeared in the October 1945 issue of *Wireless World;* not expecting that celestial mechanics would be commercialized in my lifetime, I made no attempt to patent the idea, and doubt if I could have done so anyway. (If I'm wrong, I'd prefer not to know.) But I kept plugging it in my books, and today the idea of communications satellites is so commonplace that no one knows its origin.

I did make a plaintive attempt to put the record straight when approached by the House of Representatives Committee on Astronautics and Space Exploration; you'll find my evidence on page thirty-two of its report, *The Next Ten Years in Space.* And as you'll see in a moment, my concluding words had an irony I never appreciated at the time: "Living as I do in the Far East, I am constantly reminded of the struggle between the Western World and the USSR for the uncommitted millions of Asia . . . When line-of-sight TV transmissions become possible from satellites directly overhead, the propaganda effect may be decisive. . . ."

I still stand by those words, but there were angles I hadn't thought of—and which, unfortunately, other people have.

It all began during one of those official receptions which are such a feature of social life in Eastern capitals. They're even more common in the West, of course, but in Colombo there's little competing entertainment. At least once a week, if you are anybody, you get an invitation to cocktails at an embassy or legation, the British Council, the U.S. Operations Mission, L'Alliance Française, or one of the countless alphabetical agencies the United Nations has begotten.

At first, being more at home beneath the Indian Ocean than in diplomatic circles, my partner and I were nobodies and were left alone. But after Mike *compèred* Dave Brubeck's tour of Ceylon, people started to take notice of us—still more so when he married one of the island's best-known beauties. So now our consumption of cocktails and canapés is limited chiefly by reluctance to abandon our comfortable sarongs for such Western absurdities as trousers, dinner jackets, and ties.

It was the first time we'd been to the Soviet Embassy, which was throwing a party for a group of Russian oceanographers who'd just come into port. Beneath the inevitable paintings of Lenin and Marx, a couple of hundred guests of all colors, religions, and languages were milling around, chatting with friends, or single-mindedly demolishing the vodka and caviar. I'd been separated from Mike and Elizabeth, but could see them at the other side of the room. Mike was doing his "There was I at fifty fathoms" act to a fascinated audience, while Elizabeth watched him quizzically—and rather more people watched Elizabeth.

Ever since I lost an eardrum while pearl-diving on the Great Barrier Reef, I've been at a considerable disadvantage at functions of this kind; the surface noise is about twelve decibels too much for me to cope with. And this is no small handicap when being introduced to people with names like Dharmasiriwardene, Tissaveerasinghe, Goonetilleke, and Jayawickrema. When I'm not raiding the buffet, therefore, I usually look for a pool of relative quiet where there's a chance of following more than fifty per cent of any conversation in which I may get involved. I was standing in the acoustic shadow of a large ornamental pillar, surveying the scene in my detached or Somerset Maugham manner, when I noticed that someone was looking at me with that "Haven't we met before?" expression.

I'll describe him with some care, because there must be many people who can identify him. He was in the mid-thirties, and I guessed he was American; he had that well-scrubbed, crew-cut, man-about-Rockefeller-Center look that used to be a hallmark until the younger Russian diplomats and technical advisers started imitating it so successfully. He was about six feet in height, with shrewd brown eyes and black hair, prematurely gray at the sides. Though I was fairly certain we'd never met before, his face reminded me of someone. It took me a couple of days to work it out: remember the late John Garfield? That's who it was, as near as makes no difference.

When a stranger catches my eye at a party, my standard operating procedure goes into action automatically. If he seems a pleasant-enough person but I don't feel like introductions at the moment, I give him the Neutral Scan, letting my eyes sweep past him without a flicker of recognition, yet without positive unfriendliness. If he looks like a creep, he receives the *Coup d'oeil*, which consists of a long, disbelieving stare followed by an unhurried view of the back of my neck. In extreme cases, an expression of revulsion may be switched on for a few milliseconds. The message usually gets across.

But this character seemed interesting, and I was getting bored, so I gave him the Affable Nod. A few minutes later he drifted through the crowd, and I aimed my good ear toward him.

"Hello," he said (yes, he *was* American), "my name's Gene Hartford. I'm sure we've met somewhere."

"Quite likely," I answered, "I've spent a good deal of time in the States. I'm Arthur Clarke."

Usually that produces a blank stare, but sometimes it doesn't. I could almost see the IBM cards flickering behind those hard brown eyes, and was flattered by the brevity of his access time.

"The science writer?"

"Correct."

"Well, this is fantastic." He seemed genuinely astonished. "*Now* I know where I've seen you. I was in the studio once when you were on the Dave Garroway show."

(This lead may be worth following up, though I doubt it; and I'm sure that "Gene Hartford" was phony—it was too smoothly synthetic.)

"So you're in TV?" I said. "What are you doing here—collecting material, or just on vacation?"

He gave me the frank, friendly smile of a man who has plenty to hide.

"Oh, I'm keeping my eyes open. But this really is amazing; I read your *Exploration of Space* when it came out back in, ah—"

"Nineteen fifty-two; the Book-of-the-Month Club's never been quite the same since."

All this time I had been sizing him up, and though there was something about him I didn't like, I was unable to pin it down. In any case, I was prepared to make substantial allowances for someone who had read my books and was also in TV; Mike and I are always on the lookout for markets for our underwater movies. But that, to put it mildly, was not Hartford's line of business.

"Look," he said eagerly, "I've a big network deal cooking that will interest you—in fact, *you* helped to give me the idea."

This sounded promising, and my coefficient of cupidity jumped several points.

"I'm glad to hear it. What's the general theme?"

"I can't talk about it here, but could we meet at my hotel, around three tomorrow?"

"Let me check my diary; yes, that's O.K."

There are only two hotels in Colombo patronized by Americans, and I guessed right the first time. He was at the Mount Lavinia, and though you may not know it, you've seen the place where we had our private chat. Around the middle of *Bridge on the River Kwai*, there's a brief scene at a military hospital, where Jack Hawkins meets a nurse and asks her where he can find Bill Holden. We have a soft spot for this episode, because Mike was one of the convalescent naval officers in the background. If you look smartly you'll see him on the extreme right, beard in full profile, signing Sam Spiegel's name to his sixth round of bar chits. As the picture turned out, Sam could afford it.

It was here, on this diminutive plateau high above the miles of palm-fringed beach, that Gene Hartford started to unload—and my simple hopes of financial advantage started to evaporate. What his exact motives were, if indeed he knew them himself, I'm still uncertain. Surprise at meeting me, and a twisted feeling of gratitude (which I would gladly have done without) undoubtedly played a part, and for all his air of confidence he must have been a bitter, lonely man who desperately needed approval and friendship.

He got neither from me. I have always had a sneaking sympathy for Benedict Arnold, as must anyone who knows the full facts of the case. But Arnold merely betrayed his country; no one before Hartford ever tried to seduce it.

What dissolved my dream of dollars was the news that Hartford's connection with American TV had been severed, somewhat violently, in the early fifties. It was clear that he'd been bounced out of Madison Avenue for Party-lining, and it was equally clear that his was one case where no grave injustice had been done. Though he talked with a certain controlled fury of his fight against asinine censorship, and wept for a brilliant—but unnamed—cultural series he'd started before being kicked off the air, by this time I was beginning to smell so many rats that my replies were distinctly guarded. Yet as my pecuniary interest in Mr. Hartford diminished, so my personal curiosity increased. Who *was* behind him? Surely not the BBC . . .

He got round to it at last, when he'd worked the self-pity out of his system.

"I've some news that will make you sit up," he said

smugly. "The American networks are soon going to have some real competition. And it will be done just the way you predicted; the people who sent a TV transmitter to the Moon can put a much bigger one in orbit round the Earth."

"Good for them," I said cautiously. "I'm all in favor of healthy competition. When's the launching date?"

"Any moment now. The first transmitter will be parked due south of New Orleans—on the equator, of course. That puts it way out in the open Pacific; it won't be over anyone's territory, so there'll be no political complications on that score. Yet it will be sitting up there in the sky in full view of everybody from Seattle to Key West. Think of it—the only TV station the whole United States can tune in to! Yes, even Hawaii! There won't be any way of jamming it; for the first time, there'll be a clear channel into every American home. And J. Edgar's Boy Scouts can't do a thing to block it."

So that's your little racket, I thought; at least you're being frank. Long ago I learned not to argue with Marxists and Flat-Earthers, but if Hartford was telling the truth, I wanted to pump him for all he was worth.

"Before you get too enthusiastic," I said, "there are a few points you may have overlooked."

"Such as?"

"This will work both ways. Everyone knows that the Air Force, NASA, Bell Labs, I. T. & T., Hughes, and a few dozen other agencies are working on the same project. Whatever Russia does to the States in the propaganda line, she'll get back with compound interest."

Hartford grinned mirthlessly.

"Really, Clarke!" he said. (I was glad he hadn't first-named me.) "I'm a little disappointed. Surely you know that the United States is years behind in payload capacity! And do you imagine that the old T.3 is Russia's last word?"

It was at this moment that I began to take him very seriously. He was perfectly right. The T.3 could inject at least five times the pay load of any American missile into that critical twenty-two-thousand-mile orbit— the only one that would allow a satellite to remain fixed above the Earth. And by the time the U.S. could match that performance, heaven knows where the Russians would be. Yes, heaven certainly *would* know. . . .

"All right," I conceded. "But why should fifty million American homes start switching channels just as soon as they can tune in to Moscow? I admire the Russians, but their entertainment is worse than their politics. After the Bolshoi, what have you? And for me, a little ballet goes a long, long way."

Once again I was treated to that peculiarly humorless smile. Hartford had been saving up his Sunday punch, and now he let me have it.

"You were the one who brought in the Russians," he said. "They're involved, sure—but only as contractors. The independent agency I'm working for is hiring their services."

"That," I remarked dryly, "must be some agency."

"It is; just about the biggest. Even though the United States tries to pretend it doesn't exist."

"Oh," I said, rather stupidly. "So *that's* your sponsor."

I'd heard those rumors that the USSR was going to launch satellites for the Chinese; now it began to look as if the rumors fell far short of the truth. But how far short, I'd still no conception.

"You are so right," continued Hartford, obviously enjoying himself, "about Russian entertainment. After the initial novelty, the Nielson rating would drop to zero. But not with the program *I'm* planning. My job is to find material that will put everyone else out

of business when it goes on the air. You think it can't
be done? Finish that drink and come up to my room.
I've a highbrow movie about ecclesiastical art that I'd
like to show you."

Well, he wasn't crazy, though for a few minutes I
wondered. I could think of few titles more carefully
calculated to make the viewer reach for the channel
switch than the one that flashed on the screen: ASPECTS
OF THIRTEENTH-CENTURY TANTRIC SCULPTURE.

"Don't be alarmed," Hartford chuckled, above the
whirr of the projector. "That title saves me having
trouble with inquisitive Customs inspectors. It's perfectly accurate, but we'll change it to something with a
bigger box-office appeal when the time comes."

A couple of hundred feet later, after some innocuous architectural long shots, I saw what he meant.

You may know that there are certain temples in
India covered with superbly executed carvings of a
kind that we in the West scarcely associate with reli-
gion. To say that they are frank is a laughable under-
statement; they leave nothing to the imagination—*any*
imagination. Yet at the same time they are genuine
works of art. And so was Hartford's movie.

It had been shot, in case you're interested, at the
Temple of the Sun, Konarak. I've since looked it up;
it's on the Orissa coast, about twenty-five miles north-
east of Puri. The reference books are pretty mealy-
mouthed; some apologize for the "obvious" impossibility
of providing illustrations, but Percy Brown's *Indian
Architecture* minces no words. The carvings, it says
primly, are of "a shamelessly erotic character that
have no parallel in any known building." A sweeping
claim, but I can believe it after seeing that movie.

Camera work and editing were brilliant, the ancient
stones coming to life beneath the roving lens. There
were breath-taking time-lapse shots as the rising sun
chased the shadows from bodies intertwined in ec-

stasy; sudden startling close-ups of scenes which at first the mind refused to recognize; soft-focus studies of stone shaped by a master's hand in all the fantasies and aberrations of love; restless zooms and pans whose meaning eluded the eye until they froze into patterns of timeless desire, eternal fulfillment. The music—mostly percussion, with a thin, high thread of sound from some stringed instrument that I could not identify— perfectly fitted the tempo of the cutting. At one moment it would be languorously slow, like the opening bars of Debussy's "L'Après-midi"; then the drums would swiftly work themselves up to a frenzied, almost unendurable climax. The art of the ancient sculptors and the skill of the modern cameraman had combined across the centuries to create a poem of rapture, an orgasm of celluloid which I would defy any man to watch unmoved.

There was a long silence when the screen flooded with light and the lascivious music ebbed into exhaustion.

"My God!" I said, when I had recovered some of my composure. "Are you going to telecast *that?*"

Hartford laughed.

"Believe me," he answered, "that's nothing; it just happens to be the only reel I can carry around safely. We're prepared to defend it any day on grounds of genuine art, historic interest, religious tolerance—oh, we've thought of all the angles. But it doesn't really matter; no one can stop us. For the first time in history, any form of censorship's become utterly impossible. There's simply no way of enforcing it; the customer can get what he wants, right in his own home. Lock the door, switch on the TV set—friends and family will never know."

"Very clever," I said, "but don't you think such a diet will soon pall?"

"Of course; variety is the spice of life. We'll have

plenty of conventional entertainment; let *me* worry about that. And every so often we'll have information programs—I hate that word 'propaganda'—to tell the cloistered American public what's really happening in the world. Our special features will just be the bait."

"Mind if I have some fresh air?" I said. "It's getting stuffy in here."

Hartford drew the curtains and let daylight back into the room. Below us lay that long curve of beach, with the outrigger fishing boats drawn up beneath the palms, and the little waves falling in foam at the end of their weary march from Africa. One of the loveliest sights in the world, but I couldn't focus on it now. I was still seeing those writhing stone limbs, those faces frozen with passions which the centuries could not slake.

That lickerish voice continued behind my back.

"You'd be astonished if you knew just how much material there is. Remember, we've absolutely no taboos. If you can film it, we can telecast it."

He walked over to his bureau and picked up a heavy, dog-eared volume.

"This has been my Bible," he said, "or my Sears, Roebuck, if you prefer. Without it, I'd never have sold the series to my sponsors. They're great believers in science, and they swallowed the whole thing, down to the last decimal point. Recognize it?"

I nodded; whenever I enter a room, I always monitor my host's literary tastes.

"Dr. Kinsey, I presume."

"I guess I'm the only man who's read it from cover to cover, and not just looked up his own vital statistics. You see, it's the only piece of market research in its field. Until something better comes along, we're making the most of it. It tells us what the customer wants, and we're going to supply it."

"*All* of it?"

"If the audience is big enough, yes. We won't bother about feeble-minded farm boys who get too attached to the stock. But the four main sexes will get the full treatment. That's the beauty of the movie you just saw—it appeals to them all."

"You can say that again," I muttered.

"We've had a lot of fun planning the feature I've christened 'Queer Corner.' Don't laugh—no go-ahead agency can afford to ignore *that* audience. At least ten million, if you count the ladies—bless their clogs and tweeds. If you think I'm exaggerating, look at all the male art mags on the newsstands. It was no trick, blackmailing some of the daintier musclemen to perform for us."

He saw that I was beginning to get bored; there are some kinds of single-mindedness that I find depressing. But I had done Hartford an injustice, as he hastened to prove.

"Please don't think," he said anxiously, "that sex is our only weapon. Sensation is almost as good. Ever see the job Ed Murrow did on the late sainted Joe McCarthy? That was milk and water compared with the profiles we're planning in 'Washington Confidential.'

"And there's our 'Can You Take It?' series, designed to separate the men from the milksops. We'll issue so many advance warnings that every red-blooded American will feel he has to watch the show. It will start innocently enough, on ground nicely prepared by Hemingway. You'll see some bull-fighting sequences that will really lift you out of your seat—or send you running to the bathroom—because they show all the little details you never get in those cleaned-up Hollywood movies.

"We'll follow that with some really unique material that cost us exactly nothing. Do you remember the photographic evidence the Nuremburg war trials turned up? You've never seen it, because it wasn't publishable. There were quite a few amateur photographers in the concentration camps, who made the most of opportunities they'd never get again. Some of them were hanged on the testimony of their own cameras, but their work wasn't wasted. It will lead nicely into our series 'Torture Through the Ages'—very scholarly and thorough, yet with a remarkably wide appeal. . . .

"And there are dozens of other angles, but by now you'll have the general picture. The Avenue thinks it knows all about Hidden Persuasion—believe me, it doesn't. The world's best *practical* psychologists are in the East these days. Remember Korea, and brainwashing? We've learned a lot since then. There's no need for violence any more; people enjoy being brainwashed, if you set about it the right way."

"And you," I said, "are going to brainwash the United States. Quite an order."

"Exactly—and the country will love it, despite all the screams from Congress and the churches. Not to mention the networks, of course. They'll make the biggest fuss of all, when they find they can't compete with us."

Hartford glanced at his watch, and gave a whistle of alarm.

"Time to start packing," he said, "I've got to be at that unpronounceable airport of yours by six. There's no chance, I suppose, that you can fly over to Macao and see us sometime?"

"Not a hope; but I've got a pretty good idea of the picture now. And incidentally, aren't you afraid that I'll spill the beans?"

"Why should I be? The more publicity you can give us, the better. Although our advertising campaign doesn't go into top gear for a few months yet, I feel you've earned this advance notice. As I said, your books helped to give me the idea."

His gratitude was quite genuine, by God; it left me completely speechless.

"Nothing can stop us," he declared—and for the first time the fanaticism that lurked behind that smooth, cynical façade was not altogether under control. "History is on our side. We'll be using America's own decadence as a weapon against her, and it's a weapon for which there's no defense. The Air Force won't attempt space piracy by shooting down a satellite nowhere near American territory. The FCC can't even protest to a country that doesn't exist in the eyes of the State Department. If you've any other suggestions, I'd be most interested to hear them."

I had none then, and I have none now. Perhaps these words may give some brief warning before the first teasing advertisements appear in the trade papers, and may start stirrings of elephantine alarm among the networks. But will it make any difference? Hartford did not think so, and he may be right.

"History is on our side." I cannot get those words out of my head. Land of Lincoln and Franklin and Melville, I love you and I wish you well. But into my heart blows a cold wind from the past; for I remember Babylon.

Summertime on Icarus

When Colin Sherrard opened his eyes after the crash, he could not imagine where he was. He seemed to be lying, trapped in some kind of vehicle, on the summit of a rounded hill, which sloped steeply away in all directions. Its surface was seared and blackened, as if a great fire had swept over it. Above him was a jet-black sky, crowded with stars; one of them hung like a tiny, brilliant sun low down on the horizon.

Could it be the sun? Was he so far from Earth? No—that was impossible. Some nagging memory told him that the sun was very close—hideously close—not so distant that it had shrunk to a star. And with that thought, full consciousness returned. Sherrard knew exactly where he was, and the knowledge was so terrible that he almost fainted again.

He was nearer to the sun than any man had ever been. His damaged space-pod was lying on no hill, but on the steeply curving surface of a world only two miles in diameter. That brilliant star sinking swiftly in the west was the light of *Prometheus*, the ship that had brought him here across so many millions of miles of space. She was hanging up there among the stars,

wondering why his pod had not returned like a hom-
ing pigeon to its roost. In a few minutes she would
have passed from sight, dropping below the horizon in
her perpetual game of hide-and-seek with the sun.

That was a game that he had lost. He was still on
the night side of the asteroid, in the cool safety of its
shadow, but the short night would be ending soon.
The four-hour day of Icarus was spinning him swiftly
toward that dreaded dawn, when a sun thirty times
larger than ever shone upon Earth would blast these
rocks with fire. Sherrard knew all too well why everything around him was burned and blackened. Icarus
was still a week from perihelion but the temperature
at noon had already reached a thousand degrees
Fahrenheit.

Though this was no time for humor, he suddenly
remembered Captain McClellan's description of Icarus:
"The hottest piece of real estate in the solar system."
The truth of that jest had been proved, only a few
days before, by one of those simple and unscientific
experiments that are so much more impressive than
any number of graphs and instrument readings.

Just before daybreak, someone had propped a piece
of wood on the summit of one of the tiny hills. Sherrard
had been watching, from the safety of the night side,
when the first rays of the rising sun had touched the
hilltop. When his eyes had adjusted to the sudden
detonation of light, he saw that the wood was already
beginning to blacken and char. Had there been an
atmosphere here, the stick would have burst into flames;
such was dawn, upon Icarus. . . .

Yet it had not been impossibly hot at the time of
their first landing, when they were passing the orbit of
Venus five weeks ago. *Prometheus* had overtaken the
asteroid as it was beginning its plunge toward the sun,
had matched speed with the little world and had touched
down upon its surface as lightly as a snowflake. (A

snowflake on Icarus—*that* was quite a thought. . . .)
Then the scientists had fanned out across the fifteen
square miles of jagged nickle-iron that covered most
of the asteroid's surface, setting up their instruments
and check-points, collecting samples and making endless observations.

Everything had been carefully planned, years in advance, as part of the International Astrophysical Decade. Here was a unique opportunity for a research
ship to get within a mere seventeen million miles of
the sun, protected from its fury by a two-mile-thick
shield of rock and iron. In the shadow of Icarus, the
ship could ride safely round the central fire which
warmed all the planets, and upon which the existence
of all life depended. As the Prometheus of legend had
brought the gift of fire to mankind, so the ship that
bore his name would return to Earth with other
unimagined secrets from the heavens.

There had been plenty of time to set up the instruments and make the surveys before *Prometheus* had to
take off and seek the permanent shade of night. Even
then, it was still possible for men in the tiny self-
propelled spacepods—miniature space-ships, only ten
feet long—to work on the night side for an hour or so,
as long as they were not overtaken by the advancing
line of sunrise. That had seemed a simple-enough condition to meet, on a world where dawn marched forward at only a mile an hour; but Sherrard had failed to
meet it, and the penalty was death.

He was still not quite sure what had happened. He
had been replacing a seismograph transmitter at Station 145, unofficially known as Mount Everest because
it was a full ninety feet above the surrounding territory. The job had been a perfectly straightforward
one, even though he had to do it by remote control
through the mechanical arms of his pod. Sherrard was
an expert at manipulating these; he could tie knots

with his metal fingers almost as quickly as with his flesh-and-bone ones. The task had taken little more than twenty minutes, and then the radioseismograph was on the air again, monitoring the tiny quakes and shudders that racked Icarus in ever-increasing numbers as the asteroid approached the sun. It was small satisfaction to know that he had now made a king-sized addition to the record.

After he had checked the signals, he had carefully replaced the sun screens around the instrument. It was hard to believe that two flimsy sheets of polished metal foil, no thicker than paper, could turn aside a flood of radiation that would melt lead or tin within seconds. But the first screen reflected more than ninety per cent of the sunlight falling upon its mirror surface and the second turned back most of the rest, so that only a harmless fraction of the heat passed through.

He had reported completion of the job, received an acknowledgment from the ship, and prepared to head for home. The brilliant floodlights hanging from *Prometheus*—without which the night side of the asteroid would have been in utter darkness—had been an unmistakable target in the sky. The ship was only two miles up, and in this feeble gravity he could have jumped that distance had he been wearing a planetary-type space suit with flexible legs. As it was, the low-powered micro-rockets of his pod would get him there in a leisurely five minutes.

He had aimed the pod with its gyros, set the rear jets at Strength Two, and pressed the firing button. There had been a violent explosion somewhere in the vicinity of his feet and he had soared away from Icarus—but not toward the ship. Something was horribly wrong; he was tossed to one side of the vehicle, unable to reach the controls. Only one of the jets was firing, and he was pinwheeling across the sky, spinning faster and faster under the off-balanced drive. He tried to find the cutoff, but the spin had completely disorientated him. When he was able to locate the controls, his first reaction made matters worse—he pushed the throttle over to full, like a nervous driver stepping on the accelerator instead of the brake. It took only a second to correct the mistake and kill the jet, but by then he was spinning so rapidly that the stars were wheeling round in circles.

Everything had happened so quickly that there was no time for fear, no time even to call the ship and report what was happening. He took his hands away from the controls; to touch them now would only make matters worse. It would take two or three minutes of cautious jockeying to unravel his spin, and from the flickering glimpses of the approaching rocks it was obvious that he did not have as many seconds. Sherrard remembered a piece of advice at the front of the *Spaceman's Manual* "When you don't know what to do, *do nothing.*" He was still doing it when Icarus fell upon him, and the stars went out.

It had been a miracle that the pod was unbroken, and that he was not breathing space. (Thirty minutes from now he might be glad to do so, when the capsule's heat insulation began to fail. . . .) There had been some damage, of course. The rear-view mirrors, just outside the dome of transparent plastic that enclosed his head, were both snapped off, so that he could no longer see what lay behind him without twisting his neck. This was a trivial mishap; far more serious was the fact that his radio antennas had been torn away by the impact. He could not call the ship, and the ship could not call him. All that came over the radio was a faint crackling, probably produced inside the set itself. He was absolutely alone, cut off from the rest of the human race.

It was a desperate situation, but there was one faint ray of hope. He was not, after all, completely helpless.

Even if he could not use the pod's rockets—he guessed that the starboard motor had blown back and ruptured a fuel line, something the designers said was impossible—he was still able to move. He had his arms.

But which way should he crawl? He had lost all sense of location, for though he had taken off from Mount Everest, he might now be thousands of feet away from it. There were no recognizable landmarks in his tiny world; the rapidly sinking star of *Prometheus* was his best guide, and if he could keep the ship in view he would be safe. It would only be a matter of minutes before his absence was noted, if indeed it had not been discovered already. Yet without radio, it might take his colleagues a long time to find him; small though Icarus was, its fifteen square miles of fantastically rugged no man's land could provide an effective hiding place for a ten-foot cylinder. It might take an hour to locate him—which meant that he would have to keep ahead of the murderous sunrise.

He slipped his fingers into the controls that worked his mechanical limbs. Outside the pod, in the hostile vacuum that surrounded him, his substitute arms came to life. They reached down, thrust against the iron surface of the asteroid, and levered the pod from the ground. Sherrard flexed them, and the capsule jerked forward, like some weird, two-legged insect . . . first the right arm, then the left, then the right. . . .

It was less difficult than he had feared, and for the first time he felt his confidence return. Though his mechanical arms had been designed for light precision work, it needed very little pull to set the capsule moving in this weightless environment. The gravity of Icarus was ten thousand times weaker than Earth's: Sherrard and his space-pod weighed less than an ounce here, and once he had set himself in motion he floated forward with an effortless, dreamlike ease.

Yet that very effortlessness had its dangers. He had

traveled several hundred yards, and was rapidly over-hauling the sinking star of the *Prometheus*, when overconfidence betrayed him. (Strange how quickly the mind could switch from one extreme to the other; a few minutes ago he had been steeling himself to face death—now he was wondering if he would be late for dinner.) Perhape the novelty of the movement, so unlike anything he had ever attempted before, was responsible for the catastrophe; or perhaps he was still suffering from the after-effects of the crash.

Like all astronauts, Sherrard had learned to orientate himself in space, and had grown accustomed to living and working when the Earthly conceptions of up and down were meaningless. On a world such as Icarus, it was necessary to pretend that there was a real, honest-to-goodness planet "beneath" your feet, and that when you moved you were traveling over a horizontal plain. If this innocent self-deception failed, you were heading for space vertigo.

The attack came without warning, as it usually did. Quite suddenly, Icarus no longer seemed to be be-neath him, the stars no longer above. The universe tilted through a right angle; he was moving straight *up* a vertical cliff, like a mountaineer scaling a rock face, and though Sherrard's reason told him that this was pure illusion, all his senses screamed that it was true. In a moment gravity must drag him off this sheer wall, and he would drop down mile upon endless mile until he smashed into oblivion.

Worse was to come; the false vertical was still swing-ing like a compass needle that had lost the pole. Now he was on the *underside* of an immense rocky roof, like a fly clinging to a ceiling; in another moment it would have become a wall again—but this time he would be moving straight down it, instead of up. . . .

He had lost all control over the pod, and the clammy sweat that had begun to dew his brow warned him that he would soon lose control over his body. There was only one thing to do; he clenched his eyes tightly shut, squeezed as far back as possible into the tiny closed world of the capsule, and pretended with all his might that the universe outside did not exist. He did not even allow the slow, gentle crunch of his second crash to interfere with his self-hypnosis.

When he again dared to look outside, he found that the pod had come to rest against a large boulder. Its mechanical arms had broken the force of the impact, but at a cost that was more than he could afford to pay. Though the capsule was virtually weightless here, it still possessed its normal five hundred pounds of inertia, and it had been moving at perhaps four miles an hour. The momentum had been too much for the metal arms to absorb; one had snapped, and the other was hopelessly bent.

When he saw what had happened, Sherrard's first reaction was not despair, but anger. He had been so certain of success when the pod had started its glide across the barren face of Icarus. And now this, all through a moment of physical weakness! But space made no allowance for human frailties or emotions, and a man who did not accept that fact had no right to be here.

At least he had gained precious time in his pursuit of the ship; he had put an extra ten minutes, if not more, between himself and dawn. Whether that ten minutes would merely prolong the agony or whether it would give his shipmates the extra time they needed to find him, he would soon know.

Where were they? Surely they had started the search by now! He strained his eyes toward the brilliant star of the ship, hoping to pick out the fainter lights of space-pods moving toward him—but nothing else was visible against the slowly turning vault of heaven.

He had better look to his own resources, slender

though they were. Only a few minutes were left before the *Prometheus* and her trailing lights would sink below the edge of the asteroid and leave him in darkness. It was true that the darkness would be all too brief, but before it fell upon him he might find some shelter against the coming day. This rock into which he had crashed, for example. . . .

Yes, it would give some shade, until the sun was halfway up the sky. Nothing could protect him if it passed right overhead, but it was just possible that he might be in a latitude where the sun never rose far above the horizon at this season of Icarus' four-hundred-and-nine-day year. Then he might survive the brief period of daylight; that was his only hope, if the rescuers did not find him before dawn.

There went *Prometheus* and her lights, below the edge of the world. With her going, the now-unchallenged stars blazed forth with redoubled brilliance. More glorious than any of them—so lovely that even to look upon it almost brought tears to his eyes—was the blazing beacon of Earth, with its companion moon beside it. He had been born on one, and had walked on the other; would he see either again?

Strange that until now he had given no thought to his wife and children, and to all that he loved in the life that now seemed so far away. He felt a spasm of guilt, but it passed swiftly. The ties of affection were not weakened, even across the hundred million miles of space that now sundered him from his family. At this moment, they were simply irrelevant. He was now a primitive, self-centered animal fighting for his life, and his only weapon was his brain. In this conflict, there was no place for the heart; it would merely be a hindrance, spoiling his judgment and weakening his resolution.

And then he saw something that banished all thoughts of his distant home. Reaching up above the horizon behind him, speading across the stars like a milky mist, was a faint and ghostly cone of phosphorescence. It was the herald of the sun—the beautiful, pearly phantom of the corona, visible on Earth only during the rare moments of a total eclipse. When the corona was rising, the sun would not be far behind, to smite this little land with fury.

Sherrard made good use of the warning. Now he could judge, with some accuracy, the exact point where the sun would rise. Crawling slowly and clumsily on the broken stumps of his metal arms, he dragged the capsule round to the side of the boulder that should give the greatest shade. He had barely reached it when the sun was upon him like a beast of prey, and his tiny world exploded into light.

He raised the dark filters inside his helmet, one thickness after another, until he could endure the glare. Except where the broad shadow of the boulder lay across the asteroid, it was like looking into a furnace. Every detail of the desolate land around him was revealed by that merciless light; there were no greys, only blinding whites and impenetrable blacks. All the shadowed cracks and hollows were pools of ink, while the higher ground already seemed to be on fire, as it caught the sun. Yet it was only a minute after dawn.

Now Sherrard could understand how the scorching heat of a billion summers had turned Icarus into a cosmic cinder, baking the rocks until the last traces of gas had bubbled out of them. Why should men travel, he asked himself bitterly, across the gulf of stars at such expense and risk—merely to land on a spinning slag heap? For the same reason, he knew, that they had once struggled to reach Everest and the Poles and the far places of the Earth—for the excitement of the body that was adventure, and the more enduring excitement of the mind that was discovery. It was an answer that gave him little consolation, now that he was about to be grilled like a joint on the turning spit of Icarus.

Already he could feel the first breath of heat upon his face. The boulder against which he was lying gave him protection from direct sunlight, but the glare reflected back at him from those blazing rocks only a few yards away was striking through the transparent plastic of the dome. It would grow swiftly more intense as the sun rose higher; he had even less time than he had thought, and with the knowledge came a kind of numb resignation that was beyond fear. He would wait—if he could—until the sunrise engulfed him and the capsule's cooling unit gave up the unequal struggle; then he would crack the pod and let the air gush out into the vacuum of space.

Nothing to do but to sit and think in the minutes that were left to him before his pool of shadow contracted. He did not try to direct his thoughts, but let them wander where they willed. How strange that he should be dying now, because back in the nineteen-forties—years before he was born—a man at Palomar had spotted a streak of light on a photographic plate, and had named it so appropriately after the boy who flew too near the sun.

One day, he supposed, they would build a monument here for him on this blistered plain. What would they inscribe upon it? "Here died Colin Sherrard, astronics engineer, in the cause of Science." That would be funny, for he had never understood half the things that the scientists were trying to do.

Yet some of the excitement of their discoveries had communicated itself to him. He remembered how the geologists had scraped away the charred skin of the asteroid, and had polished the metallic surface that lay beneath. It had been covered with a curious pattern of lines and scratches, like one of the abstract paintings of the Post-Picasso Decadents. But these lines had some meaning; they wrote the history of Icarus, though only a geologist could read it. They revealed, so Sherrard had been told, that this lump of iron and rock had not always floated alone in space. At some remote time in the past, it had been under enormous pressure—and that could mean only one thing. Billions of years ago it had been part of a much larger body, perhaps a planet like Earth. For some reason that planet had blown up, and Icarus and all the thousands of other asteroids were the fragments of that cosmic explosion.

Even at this moment, as the incandescent line of sunlight came closer, this was a thought that stirred his mind. What Sherrard was lying upon was the core of a world—perhaps a world that had once known life. In a strange, irrational way it comforted him to know that his might not be the only ghost to haunt Icarus until the end of time.

The helmet was misting up; that could only mean that the cooling unit was about to fail. It had done its work well; even now, though the rocks only a few yards away must be glowing a sullen red, the heat inside the capsule was not unendurable. When failure came, it would be sudden and catastrophic.

He reached for the red lever that would rob the sun of its prey—but before he pulled it, he would look for the last time upon Earth. Cautiously, he lowered the dark filters, adjusting them so that they still cut out the glare from the rocks, but no longer blocked his view of space.

The stars were faint now, dimmed by the advancing glow of the corona. And just visible over the boulder whose shield would soon fail him was a stub of crimson flame, a crooked finger of fire jutting from the edge of the sun itself. He had only seconds left.

There was the Earth, there was the moon. Good-by to them both, and to his friends and loved ones on each of them. While he was looking at the sky, the sunlight had begun to lick the base of the capsule, and he felt the first touch of fire. In a reflex as automatic as it was useless, he drew up his legs, trying to escape the advancing wave of heat.

What was that? A brilliant flash of light, infinitely brighter than any of the stars, had suddenly exploded overhead. Miles above him, a huge mirror was sailing across the sky, reflecting the sunlight as it slowly turned through space. Such a thing was utterly impossible; he was beginning to suffer from hallucinations, and it was time he took his leave. Already the sweat was pouring from his body, and in a few seconds the capsule would be a furnace.

He waited no longer, but pulled on the Emergency Release with all his waning strength, bracing himself at the same moment to face the end.

Nothing happened; the lever would not move. He tugged it again and again before he realized that it was hopelessly jammed. There was no easy way out for him, no merciful death as the air gushed from his lungs. It was then, as the true terror of his situation struck home to him, that his nerve finally broke and he began to scream like a trapped animal.

When he heard Captain McClellan's voice speaking to him, thin but clear, he knew that it must be another hallucination. Yet some last remnant of discipline and self-control checked his screaming; he clenched his teeth and listened to that familiar, commanding voice.

"Sherrard! Hold on, man! We've got a fix on you—but keep shouting!"

"Here I am!" he cried, "but hurry, for God's sake! I'm burning!"

Deep down in what was left of his rational mind he realized what had happened. Some feeble ghost of a signal was leaking through the broken stubs of his antennas, and the searchers had heard his screams—as he was hearing their voices. That meant they must be very close indeed, and the knowledge gave him sudden strength.

He stared through the steaming plastic of the dome, looking once more for that impossible mirror in the sky. There it was again—and now he realized that the baffling perspectives of space had tricked his senses. The mirror was not miles away, nor was it huge. It was almost on top of him, and it was moving fast.

He was still shouting when it slid across the face of the rising sun, and its blessed shadow fell upon him like a cool wind that had blown out of the heart of winter, over leagues of snow and ice. Now that it was so close, he recognized it at once; it was merely a large metal-foil radiation screen, no doubt hastily snatched from one of the instrument sites. In the safety of its shadow, his friends had been searching for him.

A heavy-duty, two-man capsule was hovering overhead, holding the glittering shield in one set of arms and reaching for him with the other. Even through the misty dome and the haze of heat that still sapped his senses, he recognized Captain McClellan's anxious face, looking down at him from the other pod.

So this was what birth was like, for truly he had been reborn. He was too exhausted for gratitude—that would come later—but as he rose from the burning rocks his eyes sought and found the bright star of Earth. "Here I am," he said silently. "I'm coming back."

Back to enjoy and cherish all the beauties of the world he had thought was lost forever. No—not all of them.

He would never enjoy summer again.

Out of the Cradle,
Endlessly Orbiting ...

Before we start, I'd like to point out something that a good many people seem to have overlooked. The twenty-first century does *not* begin tomorrow; it begins a year later, on January 1, 2001. Even though the calendar reads 2000 from midnight, the old century still has twelve months to run. Every hundred years we astronomers have to explain this all over again, but it makes no difference. The celebrations start just as soon as the two zeros go up. . . .

So you want to know my most memorable moment in fifty years of space exploration . . . I suppose you've already interviewed von Braun? How is he? Good; I've not seen him since that symposium we arranged in Astrograd on his eightieth birthday, the last time he came down from the Moon.

Yes—I've been present at some of the biggest moments in the history of space flight, right back to the launching of the first satellite. I was only twenty-five then, and a very junior mathematician at Kapustin Yar—not important enough to be in the control center during the countdown. But I heard the take-off: it was the second most awe-inspiring sound I've heard in my entire life. (The first? I'll come to that later.) When we knew we'd hit orbit, one of the senior scientists called for his Zis, and we drove into Stalingrad for a real party. Only the very top people had cars in the Worker's Paradise, you know; we made the hundred-kilometer drive in just about the same time the Sputnik took for one circuit of Earth, and *that* was pretty good going. Someone calculated that the amount of vodka consumed the next day could have launched the satellite the Americans were building, but I don't think that was quite true.

Most of the history books say that the Space Age began then, on October 4, 1957; I'm not going to argue with them, but I think the really exciting times came later. For sheer drama you can't beat the U.S. Navy's race to fish Dimitri Kalinin out of the South Atlantic before his capsule sank. Then there was Jerry Wingate's radio commentary, with all the adjectives which no network dared to censor, as he rounded the Moon and became the first man to see its hidden face. And, of course, only five years later, that TV broadcast from the cabin of the *Hermann Oberth* as she touched down on the plateau in the Bay of Rainbows, where she still stands, an eternal monument to the men buried beside her.

Those were the great landmarks on the road to space, but you're wrong if you think I'm going to talk about them; for what made the greatest impact on me was something very, very different. I'm not even sure if I can share the experience, and if I succeed you won't be able to make a story out of it. Not a new one, anyway, for the papers were full of it at the time. But most of them missed the point completely; to them it was just good human-interest material, nothing more.

The time was twenty years after the launching of Sputnik I, and by then, with a good many other people, I was on the Moon . . . and too important, alas, to be a real scientist any more. It had been a dozen years since I'd programmed an electronic computer; now I had the slightly more difficult task of programming human beings, since I was Chief Co-ordinator of Project Ares, the first manned expedition to Mars.

We were starting from the Moon, of course, because of the low gravity; it's about fifty times easier, in terms of fuel, to take off from there than from the Earth. We'd thought of constructing the ships in a satellite orbit, which would have cut fuel requirements even further, but when we looked into it, the idea wasn't as good as it seemed. It's not easy to set up factories and machine shops in space; the absence of gravity is a nuisance rather than an advantage when you want things to stay put. By that time, at the end of the seventies, the First Lunar Base was getting well organized, with chemical processing plants and all kinds of small-scale industrial operations to turn out the things the colony needed. So we decided to use the exising facilities rather than set up new ones, at great difficulty and expense, out in space.

Alpha, Beta, and *Gamma,* the three ships of the expedition, were being built inside the ramparts of Plato, perhaps the most perfect of all the walled plains on this side of the Moon. It's so large that if you stand in the middle you could never guess that you were inside a crater; the ring of mountains around you is hidden far below the horizon. The pressure domes of the base were about ten kilometers from the launching site, connected to it by one of those overhead cable systems that the tourists love to ride on, but which have ruined so much of the lunar scenery.

It was a rugged sort of life, in those pioneering days, for we had none of the luxuries everyone now takes for granted. Central Dome, with its parks and lakes, was still a dream on the architects' drawing boards;

even if it had existed, we would have been too busy to enjoy it, for Project Ares devoured all our waking moments. It would be Man's first great leap into space; by that time we already looked on the Moon as no more than a suburb of Earth, a steppingstone on the way to places that really mattered. Our beliefs were neatly expressed by that famous remark of Tsiolkovsky's, which I'd hung up for everyone to see as they entered my office:

EARTH IS THE CRADLE OF THE MIND—BUT
YOU CANNOT LIVE IN THE CRADLE FOREVER

(What was that? No—of *course* I never knew Tsiolkovsky! I was only four years old when he died in 1936!)

After half a lifetime of secrecy, it was good to be able to work freely with men of all nations, on a project that was backed by the entire world. Of my four chief assistants, one was American, one Indian, one Chinese, and one Russian. We often congratulated ourselves on escaping from Security and the worst excesses of nationalism, and though there was plenty of good-natured rivalry between scientists from different countries, it gave a stimulus to our work. I sometimes boasted to visitors who remembered the bad old days, "There are no secrets on the Moon."

Well, I was wrong; there *was* a secret, and it was under my very nose—in my own office. Perhaps I might have suspected something if I hadn't been so immersed in the multitudinous details of Project Ares that I'd no opportunity of taking the wider view. Looking back on it afterward, of course, I knew there were all sorts of hints and warnings, but I never noticed any of them at the time.

True, I was vaguely aware that Jim Hutchins, my young American assistant, was becoming increasingly abstracted, as if he had something on his mind. Once or twice I had to pull him up for some minor ineffi- ciency; each time he looked hurt and promised it wouldn't happen again. He was one of those typical, clean-cut college boys the United States produces in such quantities—usually very reliable, but not excep- tionally brilliant. He'd been on the Moon for three years, and was one of the first to bring his wife up from Earth when the ban on nonessential personnel was lifted. I'd never quite understood how he'd man- aged that; he must have been able to pull some strings, but certainly he was the last person you'd expect to find at the center of a world-wide conspiracy. World- wide, did I say? No—it was bigger than that, for it extended all the way back to Earth. Dozens of people were involved, right up to the top brass of the Astronautics Authority. It still seems a miracle that they were able to keep the plot from leaking out.

The slow sunrise had been under way for two days, Earth time, and though the needle-sharp shadows were shortening, it was still five days to noon. We were ready to make the first static tests of *Alpha*'s motors, for the power plant had been installed and the frame- work of the ship was complete. It stood out there on the plain looking more like a half-built oil refinery than a space ship, but to us it was beautiful, with its promise of the future. It was a tense moment; never before had a thermonuclear engine of such size been operated, and despite all the safety precautions that had been taken, one could never be sure. . . . If anything went wrong now, it could delay Project Ares by years.

The countdown had already begun when Hutchins, looking rather pale, came hurrying up to me. "I have to report to Base at once," he said. "It's very impor- tant." "More important than *this?*" I retorted sarcasti- cally, for I was mighty annoyed. He hesitated for a moment, as if wanting to tell me something; then he replied, "I think so." "O.K.," I said, and he was gone in a flash. I could have questioned him, but one has to trust one's subordinates. As I went back to the central control panel, in rather a bad temper, I decided that I'd had enough of my temperamental young American and would ask for him to be transferred. It was odd, though—he'd been as keen as anybody on this test, and now he was racing back to Base on the cable car. The blunt cylinder of the shuttle was already halfway to the nearest suspension tower, sliding along its almost invisible wires like some strange bird skimming across the lunar surface.

Five minutes later, my temper was even worse. A group of vital recording instruments had suddenly packed up, and the whole test would have to be postponed for at least three hours. I stormed around the blockhouse telling everyone who would listen (and of course everyone had to) that we used to manage things much better at Kapustin Yar. I'd quietened down a bit and we were on our second round of coffee when the General Attention signal sounded from the speakers. There's only one call with a higher priority than that— the wail of the emergency alarms, which I've heard just twice in all my years in the Lunar Colony, and hope never to hear again.

The voice that echoed through every enclosed space on the Moon, and over the radios of every worker out on the soundless plains, was that of General Moshe Stein, Chairman of the Astronautics Authority. (There were still lots of courtesy titles around in those days, though they didn't mean anything any more.)

"I'm speaking from Geneva," he said, "and I have an important announcement to make. For the last nine months, a great experiment has been in progress. We have kept it secret for the sake of those directly involved, and because we did not wish to raise false hopes or fears. Not long ago, you will remember, many experts refused to believe that men could survive in space; this time, also, there were pessimists who doubted if we could take the next step in the conquest of the universe. We have proved that they were wrong; for now I would like to introduce you to George Jonathan Hutchins—first Citizen of Space."

There was a click as the circuit was rerouted, followed by a pause full of indeterminate shufflings and whisperings. And then, over all the Moon and half the Earth, came the noise I promised to tell you about— the most awe-inspiring sound I've ever heard in my life.

It was the thin cry of a newborn baby—the first child in all the history of mankind to be brought forth on another world than Earth. We looked at each other, in the suddenly silenced blockhouse, and then at the ships we were building out there on the blazing lunar plain. They had seemed so important, a few minutes ago. They still were—but not as important as what had happened over in Medical Center, and would happen again billions of times on countless worlds down all the ages to come.

For that was the moment, gentlemen, when I knew that Man had *really* conquered space.

Who's There?

When Satellite Control called me, I was writing up the day's progress report in the Observation Bubble—the glass-domed office that juts out from the axis of the Space Station like the hubcap of a wheel. It was not really a good place to work, for the view was too overwhelming. Only a few yards away I could see the construction teams performing their slow-motion ballet as they put the station together like a giant jigsaw puzzle. And beyond them, twenty thousand miles below, was the blue-green glory of the full Earth, floating against the raveled star clouds of the Milky Way.

"Station Supervisor here," I answered. "What's the trouble?"

"Our radar's showing a small echo two miles away, almost stationary, about five degrees west of Sirius. Can you give us a visual report on it?"

Anything matching our orbit so precisely could hardly be a meteor; it would have to be something we'd dropped—perhaps an inadequately secured piece of equipment that had drifted away from the station. So I assumed; but when I pulled out my binoculars and searched the sky around Orion, I soon found my mis-

take. Though this space traveler was man-made, it had
nothing to do with us.

"I've found it," I told Control. "It's someone's test
satellite—cone-shaped, four antennas, and what looks
like a lens system in its base. Probably U.S. Air Force,
early nineteen-sixties, judging by the design. I know
they lost track of several when their transmitters failed.
There were quite a few attempts to hit this orbit before they finally made it."

After a brief search through the files, Control was
able to confirm my guess. It took a little longer to find
out that Washington wasn't in the least bit interested
in our discovery of a twenty-year-old stray satellite,
and would be just as happy if we lost it again.

"Well, we can't do *that*," said Control. "Even if
nobody wants it, the thing's a menace to navigation.
Someone had better go out and haul it aboard."

That someone, I realized, would have to be me. I
dared not detach a man from the closely knit construction teams, for we were already behind schedule—and
a single day's delay on this job cost a million dollars.
All the radio and TV networks on Earth were waiting
impatiently for the moment when they could route
their programs through us, and thus provide the first
truly global service, spanning the world from Pole to
Pole.

"I'll go out and get it," I answered, snapping an
elastic band over my papers so that the air currents
from the ventilators wouldn't set them wandering around
the room. Though I tried to sound as if I was doing
everyone a great favor, I was secretly not at all displeased. It had been at least two weeks since I'd been
outside; I was getting a little tired of stores schedules,
maintenance reports, and all the glamorous ingredi-
ents of a Space Station Supervisor's life.

The only member of the staff I passed on my way to
the air lock was Tommy, our recently acquired cat. Pets

mean a great deal to men thousands of miles from Earth, but there are not many animals that can adapt themselves to a weightless environment. Tommy mewed plaintively at me as I clambered into my spacesuit, but I was in too much of a hurry to play with him.

At this point, perhaps I should remind you that the suits we use on the station are completely different from the flexible affairs men wear when they want to walk around on the moon. Ours are really baby space-ships, just big enough to hold one man. They are stubby cylinders, about seven feet long, fitted with low-powered propulsion jets, and have a pair of accordion-like sleeves at the upper end for the opera-tor's arms. Normally, however, you keep your hands drawn inside the suit, working the manual controls in front of your chest.

As soon as I'd settled down inside my very exclusive spacecraft, I switched on power and checked the gauges on the tiny instrument panel. There's a magic word, "FORB," that you'll often hear spacemen mutter as they climb into their suits; it reminds them to test fuel, oxygen, radio, batteries. All my needles were well in the safety zone, so I lowered the transparent hemi-sphere over my head and sealed myself in. For a short trip like this, I did not bother to check the suit's internal lockers, which were used to carry food and special equipment for extended missions.

As the conveyor belt decanted me into the air lock, I felt like an Indian papoose being carried along on its mother's back. Then the pumps brought the pressure down to zero, the outer door opened, and the last traces of air swept me out into the stars, turning very slowly head over heels.

The station was only a dozen feet away, yet I was now an independent planet—a little world of my own. I was sealed up in a tiny, mobile cylinder, with a superb view of the entire universe, but I had practically no freedom of movement inside the suit. The padded seat and safety belts prevented me from turning around, though I could reach all the controls and lockers with my hands or feet.

In space, the great enemy is the sun, which can blast you to blindless in seconds. Very cautiously, I opened up the dark filters on the "night" side of my suit, and turned my head to look out at the stars. At the same time I switched the helmet's external sunshade to automatic, so that whichever way the suit gyrated my eyes would be shielded from that intolerable glare.

Presently, I found my target—a bright fleck of silver whose metallic glint distinguished it clearly from the surrounding stars. I stamped on the jet-control pedal, and felt the mild surge of acceleration as the low-powered rockets set me moving away from the station. After ten seconds of steady thrust, I estimated that my speed was great enough, and cut off the drive. It would take me five minutes to coast the rest of the way, and not much longer to return with my salvage.

And it was at that moment, as I launched myself out into the abyss, that I knew that something was horribly wrong.

It is never completely silent inside a spacesuit; you can always hear the gentle hiss of oxygen, the faint whirr of fans and motors, the susurration of your own breathing—even, if you listen carefully enough, the rhythmic thump that is the pounding of your heart. These sounds reverberate through the suit, unable to escape into the surrounding void; they are the unnoticed background of life in space, for you are aware of them only when they change.

They had changed now; to them had been added a sound which I could not identify. It was an intermittent, muffled thudding, sometimes accompanied by a scraping noise, as of metal upon metal.

I froze instantly, holding my breath and trying to

locate the alien sound in my ears. The meters on the control board gave no clues; all the needles were rock-steady on their scales, and there were none of the flickerlng red lights that would warn of impending disaster. That was some comfort, but not much. I had long ago learned to trust my instincts in such matters; their alarm signals were flashing now, telling me to return to the station before it was too late. . . .

Even now, I do not like to recall those next few minutes, as panic slowly flooded into my mind like a rising tide, overwhelming the dams of reason and logic which every man must erect against the mystery of the universe. I knew then what it was like to face insanity; no other explanation fitted the facts.

For it was no longer possible to pretend that the noise disturbing me was that of some faulty mechanism. Though I was in utter isolation, far from any other human being or indeed any material object, I was not alone. The soundless void was bringing to my ears the faint but unmistakable stirrings of life.

In that first, heart-freezing moment it seemed that something was trying to get into my suit—something invisible, seeking shelter from the cruel and pitiless vacuum of space. I whirled madly in my harness, scanning the entire sphere of vision around me except for the blazing, forbidden cone toward the sun. There was nothing there, of course. There could not be—yet that purposeful scrabbling was clearer than ever.

Despite the nonsense that has been written about us, it is not true that spacemen are superstitious. But can you blame me if, as I came to the end of logic's resources, I suddenly remembered how Bernie Summers had died, no farther from the station than I was at this very moment?

It was one of those "impossible" accidents; it always is. Three things had gone wrong at once. Bernie's oxygen regulator had run wild and sent the pressure soaring, the safety valve had failed to blow—and a faulty joint had given way instead. In a fraction of a second, his suit was open to space.

I had never known Bernie, but suddenly his fate became of overwhelming importance to me—for a horrible idea had come into my mind. One does not talk about these things, but a damaged spacesuit is too valuable to be thrown away, even if it has killed its wearer. It is repaired, renumbered—and issued to someone else. . . .

What happens to the soul of a man who dies between the stars, far from his native world? Are you still here, Bernie, clinging to the last object that linked you to your lost and distant home?

As I fought the nightmares that were swirling around me—for now it seemed that the scratchings and soft fumblings were coming from all directions—there was one last hope to which I clung. For the sake of my sanity, I had to prove that this wasn't Bernie's suit— that the metal walls so closely wrapped around me had never been another man's coffin.

It took me several tries before I could press the right button and switch my transmitter to the emergency wave length. "Station!" I gasped. "I'm in trouble! Get records to check my suit history and—"

I never finished; they say my yell wrecked the microphone. But what man alone in the absolute isolation of a spacesuit would *not* have yelled when something patted him softly on the back of the neck?

I must have lunged forward, despite the safety harness, and smashed against the upper edge of the control panel. When the rescue squad reached me a few minutes later, I was still unconscious, with an angry bruise across my forehead.

And so I was the last person in the whole satellite relay system to know what had happened. When I came to my senses an hour later, all our medical staff was gathered around my bed, but it was quite a while before the doctors bothered to look at me. They were much too busy playing with the three cute little kittens our badly misnamed Tommy had been rearing in the seclusion of my spacesuit's Number Five Storage Locker.

Hate

Only Joey was awake on deck, in the cool stillness before dawn, when the meteor came flaming out of the sky above New Guinea. He watched it climb up the heavens until it passed directly overhead, routing the stars and throwing swift-moving shadows across the crowded deck. The harsh light outlined the bare rigging, the coiled ropes and air hoses, the copper diving helmets neatly snugged down for the night— even the low, pandanus-clad island half a mile away. As it passed into the southwest, out over the emptiness of the Pacific, it began to disintegrate. Incandescent globules broke off, burning and guttering in a trail of fire that stretched a quarter of the way across the sky. It was already dying when it raced out of sight, but Joey did not see its end. Still blazing furiously, it sank below the horizon, as if seeking to hurl itself into the face of the hidden sun.

If the sight was spectacular, the utter silence was unnerving. Joey waited and waited and waited, but no sound came from the riven heavens. When, minutes later, there was a sudden splash from the sea close at hand, he gave an involuntary start of surprise—then cursed himself for being frightened by a manta. (A mighty big one, though, to have made so much noise when it jumped.) There was no other sound, and presently he went back to sleep.

In his narrow bunk just aft of the air compressor, Tibor heard nothing. He slept so soundly after his day's work that he had little energy even for dreams— and when they came, they were not the dreams he wanted. In the hours of darkness, as his mind roamed back and forth across the past, it never came to rest amid memories of desire. He had women in Sydney and Brisbane and Darwin and Thursday Island—but none in his dreams. All that he ever remembered when he woke, in the fetid stillness of the cabin, was the dust and fire and blood as the Russian tanks rolled into Budapest. His dreams were not of love, but only of hate.

When Nick shook him back to consciousness, he was dodging the guards on the Austrian border. It took him a few seconds to make the ten-thousand-mile journey to the Great Barrier Reef; then he yawned, kicked away the cockroaches that had been nibbling at his toes, and heaved himself out of his bunk.

Breakfast, of course, was the same as always—rice, turtle eggs, and bully beef, washed down with strong, sweet tea. The best that could be said of Joey's cooking was that there was plenty of it. Tibor was used to the monotonous diet; he made up for it, and for other deprivations, when he was back on the mainland.

The sun had barely cleared the horizon when the dishes were stacked in the tiny galley and the lugger got under way. Nick sounded cheerful as he took the wheel and headed out from the island; the old pearling-master had every right to be, for the patch of shell they were working was the richest that Tibor had ever seen. With any luck, they would fill their hold in another day or two, and sail back to T. I. with half a

ton of shell on board. And then, with a little more
luck, he could give up this stinking, dangerous job and
get back to civilization. Not that he regretted anything; the Greek had treated him well, and he'd found
some good stones when the shells were opened. But
he understood now, after nine months on the Reef,
why the number of white divers could be counted on
the fingers of one hand. Japs and Kanakas and Island-
ers could take it—but damn few Europeans.

The diesel coughed into silence, and the *Arafura*
coasted to rest. They were some two miles from the
island, which lay low and green on the water, yet
sharply divided from it by its narrow band of dazzling
beach. It was no more than a nameless sand bar that a
tiny forest had managed to capture, and its only inhabitants were the myriads of stupid muttonbirds that
riddled the soft ground with their burrows and made
the night hideous with their banshee cries.

There was little talk as the three divers dressed;
each man knew what to do, and wasted no time in
doing it. As Tibor buttoned on his thick twill jacket,
Blanco, his tender, rinsed out the faceplate with vine-
gar so that it would not become fogged. Then Tibor
clambered down the rope ladder, while the heavy helmet and lead corselet were placed over his head. Apart
from the jacket, whose padding spread the weight
evenly over his shoulders, he was wearing his ordinary
clothes. In these warm waters there was no need for
rubber suits, and the helmet simply acted as a tiny
diving bell held in position by its weight alone. In an
emergency the wearer could—if he was lucky—duck
out of it and swim back to the surface unhampered.
Tibor had seen this done, but he had no wish to try
the experiment for himself.

Each time he stood on the last rung of the ladder,
gripping his shell bag with one hand and his safety line
with the other, the same thought flashed through Tibor's

mind. He was leaving the world he knew—but was it for an hour or was it forever? Down there on the seabed was wealth and death, and one could be sure of neither. The chances were that this would be another day of uneventful drudgery, as were most of the days in the pearl diver's unglamorous life. But Tibor had seen one of his mates die, when his air hose tangled in the *Arafura*'s prop—and he had watched the agony of another whose body twisted with the bends. In the sea, nothing was ever safe or certain. You took your chances with open eyes—and if you lost, there was no point in whining.

He stepped back from the ladder, and the world of sun and sky ceased to exist. Top-heavy with the weight of his helmet, he had to backpedal furiously to keep his body upright. He could see nothing but a featureless blue mist as he sank toward the bottom, and he hoped that Blanco would not play out the safety line too quickly. Swallowing and snorting, he tried to clear his ears as the pressure mounted; the right one "popped" quickly enough, but a piercing, intolerable pain grew rapidly in the left, which had bothered him for several days. He forced his hand up under the helmet, gripped his nose, and blew with all his might. There was an abrupt, soundless explosion somewhere inside his head, and the pain vanished instantly. He'd have no more trouble on this dive.

Tibor felt the bottom before he saw it. Since he was unable to bend over lest he risk flooding the open helmet, his vision in the downward direction was very limited. He could see around, but not immediately below. What he did see was reassuring in its drab monotony—a gently undulating, muddy plain that faded out of sight about ten feet ahead. A yard to his left a tiny fish was nibbling at a piece of coral the size and shape of a lady's fan. That was all; there was no beauty, no underwater fairyland here. But there was money, and that was what mattered.

The safety line gave a gentle pull as the lugger started to drift downward, moving broadside-on across the patch, and Tibor began to walk forward with the springy, slow-motion step forced on him by weightlessness and water resistance. As Number Two diver, he was working from the bow; amidships was Stephen, still comparatively inexperienced, while at the stern was the head diver, Billy. The three men seldom saw each other while they were working; each had his own lane to search as the *Arafura* drifted silently before the wind. Only at the extremes of their zigzags might they sometimes glimpse one another as dim shapes looming through the mist.

It needed a trained eye to spot the shells beneath their camouflage of algae and weeds, but often the mollusks betrayed themselves. When they felt the vibrations of the approaching diver, they would snap shut—and there would be a momentary, nacreous flicker in the gloom. Yet even then they sometimes escaped, for the moving ship might drag the diver past before he could collect the prize just out of reach. In the early days of his apprenticeship, Tibor had missed quite a few of the big silver lips—any one of which might have contained some fabulous pearl. Or so he had imagined, before the glamour of the profession had worn off, and he realized that pearls were so rare that you might as well forget them. The most valuable stone he'd ever brought up had been sold for fifty-six dollars, and the shell he gathered on a good morning was worth more than that. If the industry had depended on gems instead of mother-of-pearl, it would have gone broke years ago.

There was no sense of time in this world of mist. You walked beneath the invisible, drifting ship, with the throb of the air compressor pounding in your ears, the green haze moving past your eyes. At long intervals you would spot a shell, wrench it from the sea bed, and drop it in your bag. If you were lucky, you might gather a couple of dozen on a single drift across the patch; on the other hand, you might not find a single one.

You were alert for danger, but not worried by it. The real risks were simple, unspectacular things like tangled air hoses or safety lines—not sharks, groupers, or octopuses. Sharks ran when they saw your air bubbles, and in all his hours of diving Tibor had seen just one octopus, every bit of two feet across. As for groupers—well, *they* were to be taken seriously, for they could swallow a diver at one gulp if they felt hungry enough. But there was little chance of meeting them on this flat and desolate plain; there were none of the coral caves in which they could make their homes.

The shock would not have been so great, therefore, if this uniform, level grayness had not lulled him into a sense of security. At one moment he was walking steadily toward an unreachable wall of mist, which retreated as fast as he approached. And then, without warning, his private nightmare was looming above him.

Tibor hated spiders, and there was a certain creature in the sea that seemed deliberately contrived to take advantage of the phobia. He had never met one, and his mind had always shied away from the thought of such an encounter, but Tibor knew that the Japanese spider crab can span twelve feet across its spindly legs. That it was harmless mattered not in the least; a spider as big as a man simply had no right to exist.

As soon as he saw that cage of slender, jointed limbs emerge from the all-encompassing grayness, Tibor began to scream with uncontrollable terror. He never remembered jerking his safety line, but Blanco reacted with the instantaneous perception of the ideal tender. His helmet still echoing to his screams, Tibor felt himself snatched from the sea bed, lifted toward light and air—and sanity. As he swept upward, he saw both the strangeness and the absurdity of his mistake, and regained a measure of control. But he was still trembling so violently when Blanco lifted off his helmet that it was some time before he could speak.

"What the hell's going on here?" demanded Nick. "Everyone knocking off work early?"

It was then that Tibor realized that he was not the first to come up. Stephen was sitting amidships, smoking a cigarette and looking completely unconcerned. The stern diver, doubtless wondering what had happened, was being hauled up willy-nilly by his tender, since the *Arafura* had come to rest and all operations had been suspended until the trouble was resolved.

"There's some kind of wreck down there," said Tibor. "I ran right into it. All I could see were a lot of wires and rods."

To his annoyance and self-contempt, the memory set him trembling again.

"Don't see why *that* should give you the shakes," grumbled Nick. Nor could Tibor; here on this sun-drenched deck, it was impossible to explain how a harmless shape glimpsed through the mist could set one's whole mind jangling with terror.

"I nearly got hung up on it," he lied. "Blanco pulled me clear just in time."

"Hmm," said Nick, obviously not convinced. "Anyway, it ain't a ship." He gestured toward the midships diver. "Steve ran into a mess of ropes and cloth—like thick nylon, he says. Sounds like some kind of parachute." The old Greek stared in disgust at the soggy stump of his cigar, then flicked it overboard. "Soon as Billy's up, we'll go back and take a look. Might be worth something—remember what happened to Jo Chambers."

Tibor remembered; the story was famous the whole length of the Great Barrier Reef. Jo had been a lone-wolf fisherman who, in the last months of the war, had spotted a DC-3 lying in shallow water a few miles off the Queensland coast. After prodigies of singlehanded salvage, he had broken into the fuselage and started unloading boxes of taps and dies, perfectly protected by their greased wrappings. For a while he had run a flourishing import business, but when the police caught up with him he reluctantly revealed his source of sup-ply; Australian cops can be very persuasive.

And it was then, after weeks and weeks of backbreak-ing underwater work, that Jo discovered what his DC-3 had been carrying besides the miserable few hundred quid's worth of tools he had been flogging to garages and workshops on the mainland. The big wooden crates he'd never got round to opening held a week's payroll for the U.S. Pacific forces—most of it in twenty-dollar gold pieces.

No such luck here, thought Tibor as he sank over the side again; but the aircraft—or whatever it was—might contain valuable instruments, and there could be a reward for its discovery. Besides, he owed it to himself; he wanted to see exactly what it was that had given him such a fright.

Ten minutes later, he knew it was no aircraft. It was the wrong shape, and it was much too small—only about twenty feet long and half that in width. Here and there on the gently tapering body were access hatches and tiny ports through which unknown instru-ments peered at the world. It seemed unharmed, though one end had been fused as if by terrific heat. From the other sprouted a tangle of antennas, all of them bro-ken or bent by the impact with the water. Even now, they bore an incredible resemblance to the legs of a giant insect.

Tibor was no fool; he guessed at once what the

thing was. Only one problem remained, and he solved that with little difficulty. Though they had been partly charred away by heat, stenciled words could still be read on some of the hatch covers. The letters were Cyrillic, and Tibor knew enough Russian to pick out references to electrical supplies and pressurizing systems.

"So they've lost a sputnik," he told himself with satisfaction. He could imagine what had happened; the thing had come down too fast, and in the wrong place. Around one end were the tattered remnants of flotation bags; they had burst under the impact, and the vehicle had sunk like a stone. The *Arafura*'s crew would have to apologize to Joey; he hadn't been drinking grog. What he'd seen burning across the stars must have been the rocket carrier, separated from its pay load and falling back unchecked into the Earth's atmosphere.

For a long time Tibor hovered on the sea bed, knees bent in the diver's crouch, as he regarded this space creature now trapped in an alien element. His mind was full of half-formed plans, but none had yet come clearly into focus. He no longer cared about salvage money; much more important were the prospects of revenge. Here was one of the proudest creations of Soviet technology—and Szabo Tibor, late of Budapest, was the only man on earth who knew.

There must be some way of exploiting the situation —of doing harm to the country and the cause he now hated with such smoldering intensity. In his waking hours, he was seldom conscious of that hate, and still less did he ever stop to analyze its real cause. Here in this lonely world of sea and sky, of steaming mangrove swamps and dazzling coral strands, there was nothing to recall the past. Yet he could never escape it, and sometimes the demons in his mind would awake, lashing him into a fury of rage or vicious, wanton destructiveness. So far he had been lucky; he had not killed anyone. But some day . . .

An anxious jerk from Blanco interrupted his reveries of vengeance. He gave a reassuring signal to his tender, and started a closer examination of the capsule. What did it weigh? Could it be hoisted easily? There were many things he had to discover, before he could settle on any definite plans.

He braced himself against the corrugated metal wall, and pushed cautiously. There was a definite movement as the capsule rocked on the sea bed. Maybe it could be lifted, even with the few pieces of tackle that the *Arafura* could muster. It was probably lighter than it looked.

Tibor pressed his helmet against a flat section of the hull, and listened intently. He had half expected to hear some mechanical noise, such as the whirring of electric motors. Instead, there was utter silence. With the hilt of his knife, he rapped sharply on the metal, trying to gauge its thickness and to locate any weak spots. On the third try, he got results: but they were not what he had anticipated.

In a furious, desperate tattoo, the capsule rapped back at him.

Until this moment, Tibor had never dreamed that there might be someone inside; the capsule had seemed far too small. Then he realized that he had been thinking in terms of conventional aircraft; there was plenty of room here for a little pressure cabin in which a dedicated astronaut could spend a few cramped hours.

As a kaleidoscope can change its pattern completely in a single moment, so the half-formed plans in Tibor's mind dissolved and then crystallized into a new shape. Behind the thick glass of his helmet, he ran his tongue lightly across his lips. If Nick could have seen him now, he would have wondered—as he had sometimes done before—whether his Number Two diver was wholly sane. Gone were all thoughts of a remote and impersonal vengeance against something as abstract as a nation or a machine; now it would be man to man.

"Took your time, didn't you?" said Nick. "What did you find?"

"It's Russian," said Tibor. "Some kind of sputnik. If we can get a rope around it, I think we can lift it off the bottom. But it's too heavy to get aboard."

Nick chewed thoughtfully on his eternal cigar. The pearling master was worried about a point that had not occurred to Tibor. If there were any salvage operations around here, everyone would know where the *Arafura* had been drifting. When the news got back to Thursday Island, his private patch of shell would be cleaned out in no time.

They'd have to keep quiet about the whole affair, or else haul the damn thing up themselves and not say where they'd found it. Whatever happened, it looked like being more of a nuisance than it was worth. Nick, who shared most Australians' profound suspicion of authority, had already decided that all he'd get for his trouble would be a nice letter of thanks.

"The boys won't go down," he said. "They think it's a bomb. Want to leave it alone."

"Tell 'em not to worry," replied Tibor. "I'll handle it." He tried to keep his voice normal and unemotional, but this was too good to be true. If the other divers heard the tapping from the capsule, his plans would have been frustrated.

He gestured to the island, green and lovely on the skyline.

"Only one thing we can do. If we can heave it a couple of feet off the bottom, we can run for the shore. Once we're in shallow water, it won't be too hard to haul it up on the beach. We can use the boats, and maybe get a block and tackle on one of those trees."

Nick considered the idea without much enthusiasm. He doubted if they could get the sputnik through the reef, even on the leeward side of the island. But he was all in favor of lugging it away from this patch of shell; they could always dump it somewhere else, buoy the place, and still get whatever credit was going.

"O.K.," he said. "Down you go. That two-inch rope's the strongest we've got—better take that. Don't be all the bloody day; we've lost enough time already."

Tibor had no intention of being all day. Six hours would be quite long enough. That was one of the first things he had learned, from the signals through the wall.

It was a pity that he could not hear the Russian's voice; but the Russian could hear him, and that was what really mattered. When he pressed his helmet against the metal and shouted, most of his words got through. So far, it had been a friendly conversation; Tibor had no intention of showing his hand until the right psychological moment.

The first move had been to establish a code—one knock for "yes," two for "no." After that, it was merely a matter of framing suitable questions; given time, there was no fact or idea that could not be communicated by means of these two signals. It would have been a much tougher job if Tibor had been forced to use his indifferent Russian; he had been pleased, but not surprised, to find that the trapped pilot understood English perfectly.

There was air in the capsule for another five hours; the occupant was uninjured; yes, the Russians knew where it had come down. That last reply gave Tibor pause. Perhaps the pilot was lying, but it might very well be true. Although something had obviously gone wrong with the planned return to Earth, the tracking ships out in the Pacific must have located the impact point—with what accuracy, he could not guess. Still, did that matter? It might take them days to get here, even if they came racing straight into Australian territorial waters without bothering to get permission from Canberra. He was master of the situation; the entire might of the USSR could do nothing to interfere with his plans—until it was much too late.

The heavy rope fell in coils on the sea bed, stirring up a cloud of silt that drifted like smoke down the slow current. Now that the sun was higher in the sky, the underwater world was no longer wrapped in a gray, twilight gloom. The sea bed was colorless but bright, and the boundary of vision was now almost fifteen feet away. For the first time, Tibor could see the space capsule in its entirety. It was such a peculiar-looking object, being designed for conditions beyond all normal experience, that there was an eye-teasing wrongness about it. One searched in vain for a front or a rear; there was no way of telling in what direction it pointed as it sped along its orbit.

Tibor pressed his helmet against the metal and shouted.

"I'm back," he called. "Can you hear me?"

Tap

"I've got a rope, and I'm going to tie it on to the parachute cables. We're about three kilometers from an island, and as soon as we've made you fast we'll head toward it. We can't lift you out of the water with the gear on the lugger, so we'll try to get you up on the beach. You understand?"

Tap

It took only a few moments to secure the rope; now he had better get clear before the *Arafura* started to lift. But there was something he had to do first.

"Hello!" he shouted. "I've fixed the rope. We'll lift in a minute. D'you hear me?"

Tap

"Then you can hear this too. You'll never get there alive. I've fix *that* as well."

Tap, tap

"You've got five hours to die. My brother took longer than that, when he ran into your mine field. You understand? I'm from Budapest. I hate you and your country and everything it stands for. You've taken my home, my family, made my people slaves. I wish I could see your face now—I wish I could watch you die, as I had to watch Theo. When you're halfway to the island, this rope is going to break where I cut it. I'll go down and fix another—and that'll break, too. You can sit in there and wait for the bumps."

Tibor stopped abruptly, shaken and exhausted by the violence of his emotion. There was no room for logic or reason in this orgasm of hate; he did not pause to think, for he dared not. Yet somewhere far down inside his mind the real truth was burning its way up toward the light of consciousness.

It was not the Russians he hated, for all that they had done. It was himself, for he had done more. The blood of Theo, and of ten thousand countrymen, was upon his own hands. No one could have been a better Communist than he had been, or have more supinely believed the propaganda from Moscow. At school and college, he had been the first to hunt out and denounce "traitors." (How many had he sent to the labor camps or the AVO torture chambers?) When he had seen the truth, it was far, far too late; and even then, he had not fought—he had run.

He had run across the world, trying to escape his guilt; and the two drugs of danger and dissipation had helped him to forget the past. The only pleasures life gave him now were the loveless embraces he sought so feverishly when he was on the mainland, and his present mode of existence was proof that these were not enough. If he now had the power to deal out death, it was only because he had come here in search of it himself.

There was no sound from the capsule; its silence seemed contemptuous, mocking. Angrily, Tibor banged against it with the hilt of his knife.

"Did you hear me?" he shouted. "Did you hear me?"

No answer.

"Damn you! I know you're listening! If you don't answer, I'll hole you and let the water in!"

He was sure that he could, with the sharp point of his knife. But that was the last thing he wanted to do; that would be too quick, too easy an ending.

There was still no sound; maybe the Russian had fainted. Tibor hoped not, but there was no point in waiting any longer. He gave a vicious parting bang on the capsule, and signaled to his tender.

Nick had news for him when he broke the surface.

"T. I. radio's been squawking," he said. "The Ruskies are asking everyone to look out for one of their rockets. They say it should be floating somewhere off the Queensland coast. Sounds as if they want it badly."

"Did they say anything else about it?" Tibor asked anxiously.

"Oh yes—it's been round the moon a couple of times."

"That all?"

"Nothing else that I remember. There was a lot of science stuff I didn't get."

That figured; it was just like the Russians to keep as quiet as they could about an experiment that had gone wrong.

"You tell T. I. that we'd found it?"

"Are you crazy? Anyway, the radio's crook; couldn't if we wanted to. Fixed that rope properly?"

"Yes—see if you can haul her off the bottom."

The end of the rope had been wound round the

mainmast, and in a few seconds it had been drawn taut. Although the sea was calm, there was a slight swell, and the lugger was rolling ten or fifteen degrees. With each roll, the gunwales would rise a couple of feet, then drop again. There was a lift here of several tons, but one had to be careful in using it.

The rope twanged, the woodwork groaned and creaked, and for a moment Tibor was afraid that the weakened line would part too soon. But it held, and the load lifted. They got a further hoist on the second roll—and on the third. Then the capsule was clear of the sea bed, and the *Arafura* was listing slightly to port.

"Let's go," said Nick, taking the wheel. "Should be able to get her half a mile before she bumps again."

The lugger began to move slowly toward the island, carrying its hidden burden beneath it. As he leaned on the rails, letting the sun steam the moisture from his sodden clothing, Tibor felt at peace for the first time in—how many months? Even his hate had ceased to burn like fire in his brain. Perhaps, like love, it was a passion that could never be satisfied; but for the moment, at least, it was satiated.

There was no weakening of his resolve; he was implacably set upon the vengeance that had been so strangely—so miraculously—placed within his power. Blood called for blood, and now the ghosts that haunted him might rest at last. Yet he felt a strange sympathy, even pity, toward the unknown man through whom he could now strike back at the enemies who had once been his friends. He was robbing them of much more than a single life—for what was one man, even a highly trained scientist—to the Russians? What he was taking from them was power and prestige and knowledge, the things they valued most.

He began to worry when they were two thirds of the way to the island, and the rope had not parted. There

were still four hours to go, and that was much too
long. For the first time it occurred to him that his
entire plan might miscarry, and might even recoil on
his head. Suppose that, despite everything, Nick managed to get the capsule up on the beach before the
deadline?

With a deep "twang" that set the whole ship vibrat-
ing, the rope came snaking out of the water, scattering
spray in all directions.

"Might have guessed," muttered Nick. "She was
just starting to bump. You like to go down again, or
shall I send one of the boys?"

"I'll take it," Tibor hastily answered. "I can do it
quicker than they can."

That was perfectly true, but it took him twenty
minutes to locate the capsule. The *Arafura* had drifted
well away from it before Nick could stop the engine,
and there was a time when Tibor wondered if he
would ever find it again. He quartered the sea bed in
great arcs, and it was not until he had accidentally
tangled in the training parachute that his search was
ended. The shrouds lay pulsating slowly in the current
like some weird and hideous marine monster—but
there was nothing that Tibor feared now except frus-
tration, and his pulse barely quickened as he saw the
whitely looking mass ahead.

The capsule was scratched and stained with mud,
but appeared undamaged. It was lying on its side now,
looking rather like a giant milk churn that had been
tipped over. The passenger must have been bumped
around, but if he'd fallen all the way back from the
moon, he must have been well padded and was probably still in good shape. Tibor hoped so; it would be a
pity if the remaining three hours were wasted.

Once again he rested the verdigrised copper of his
helmet against the no-longer-quite-so-brightly-gleaming
metal of the capsule.

"Hello!" he shouted. "Can you hear me?"

Perhaps the Russian would try to balk him by remaining silent—but that, surely, was asking too much of any man's self-control. Tibor was right; almost at once there was the sharp knock of the reply.

"So glad you're there," he called back. "Things are working out just the way I said, though I guess I'll have to cut the rope a little deeper."

The capsule did not answer. It never answered again, though Tibor banged and banged on the next dive—and on the next. But he hardly expected it to then, for they'd had to stop for a couple of hours to ride out a squall, and the time limit had expired long before he made his final descent. He was a little annoyed about that, for he had planned a farewell message. He shouted it just the same, though he knew he was wasting his breath.

By early afternoon, the *Arafura* had come in as close as she dared. There were only a few feet of water beneath her, and the tide was falling. The capsule broke surface at the bottom of each wave trough, and was now firmly stranded on a sandbank. There was no hope of moving it any farther; it was stuck, until a high sea would dislodge it.

Nick regarded the situation with an expert eye.

"There's a six-foot tide tonight," he said. "The way she's lying now, she'll be in only a couple of feet of water at low. We'll be able to get at her with the boats."

They waited off the sandbank while the sun and the tide went down, and the radio broadcast intermittent reports of a search that was coming closer but was still far away. Late in the afternoon the capsule was almost clear of the water; the crew rowed the small boat toward it with a reluctance which Tibor, to his annoyance, found himself sharing.

"It's got a door in the side," said Nick suddenly. "Jeeze—think there's anyone in it?"

"Could be," answered Tibor, his voice not as steady as he thought. Nick glanced at him curiously. His diver had been acting strangely all day, but he knew better than to ask him what was wrong. In this part of the world, you soon learned to mind your own business.

The boat, rocking slightly in the choppy sea, had now come alongside the capsule. Nick reached out and grabbed one of the twisted antenna stubs; then, with catlike agility, he clambered up the curved metal surface. Tibor made no attempt to follow him, but watched silently from the boat as he examined the entrance hatch.

"Unless it's jammed," Nick muttered, "there must be some way of opening it from outside. Just our luck if it needs special tools."

His fears were groundless. The word "Open" had been stenciled in ten languages around the recessed door catch, and it took only seconds to deduce its mode of operation. As the air hissed out, Nick said "Phew!" and turned suddenly pale. He looked at Tibor as if seeking support, but Tibor avoided his eye. Then, reluctantly, Nick lowered himself into the capsule.

He was gone for a long time. At first, they could hear muffled bangings and bumpings from the inside, followed by a string of bilingual profanity. And then there was a silence that went on and on and on.

When at last Nick's head appeared above the hatchway, his leathery, wind-tanned face was gray and streaked with tears. As Tibor saw this incredible sight, he felt a sudden ghastly premonition. Something had gone horribly wrong, but his mind was too numb to anticipate the truth. It came soon enough, when Nick handed down his burden, no larger than an oversized doll.

Blanco took it, as Tibor shrank to the stern of the

boat. As he looked at the calm, waxen face, fingers of ice seemed to close not only upon his heart, but around his loins. In the same moment, both hate and desire died forever within him, and he knew the price of his revenge.

The dead astronaut was perhaps more beautiful in death than she had been in life; tiny though she was, she must have been tough as well as highly trained to qualify for this mission. As she lay at Tibor's feet, she was neither a Russian nor the first human being to have seen the far side of the moon; she was merely the girl that he had killed.

Nick was talking, from a long way off.

"She was carrying this," he said, in an unsteady voice. "Had it tight in her hand—took me a long time to get it out."

Tibor scarcely heard him, and never even glanced at the tiny spool of tape lying in Nick's palm. He could not guess, in this moment beyond all feeling, that the Furies had yet to close in upon his soul—and that soon the whole world would be listening to an accusing voice from beyond the grave, branding him more irrevocably than any man since Cain.

Into the Comet

"I don't know why I'm recording this," said George Takeo Pickett slowly into the hovering microphone. "There's no chance that anyone will ever hear it. They say the comet will bring us back to the neighborhood of Earth in about two million years, when it makes its next turn around the sun. I wonder if mankind will still be in existence then, and whether the comet will put on as good a display for our descendants as it did for us? Maybe they'll launch an expedition, just as we have done, to see what they can find. And they'll find us. . . .

"For the ship will still be in perfect condition, even after all those ages. There'll be fuel in the tanks, maybe even plenty of air, for our food will give out first, and we'll starve before we suffocate. But I guess we won't wait for that; it will be quicker to open the air lock and get it all over.

"When I was a kid, I read a book on polar exploration called *Winter Amid the Ice*. Well, that's what we're facing now. There's ice all around us, floating in great porous bergs. *Challenger*'s in the middle of a cluster, orbiting round one another so slowly that you have to wait several minutes before you're certain they've moved. But no expedition to Earth's poles ever faced *our* winter. During most of that two mlllion years, the temperature will be four hundred and fifty below zero. We'll be so far away from the sun that it'll give about as much heat as the stars. And who ever tried to warm his hands by Sirius on a cold winter night?"

That absurd image, coming suddenly into his mind, broke him up completely. He could not speak because of memories of moonlight upon snowfields, of Christmas chimes ringing across a land already fifty million miles away. Suddenly he was weeping like a child, his self-control dissolved by the remembrance of all the familiar, disregarded beauties of the Earth he had forever lost.

And everything had begun so well, in such a blaze of excitement and adventure. He could recall (was it only six months ago?) the very first time he had gone out to look for the comet, soon after eighteen-year-old Jimmy Randall had found it in his homemade telescope and sent his famous telegram to Mount Stromlo Observatory. In those early days, it had been only a faint polliwog of mist, moving slowly through the constellation of Eridanus, just south of the Equator. It was still far beyond Mars, sweeping sunward along its immensely elongated orbit. When it had last shone in the skies of Earth, there were no men to see it, and there might be none when it appeared again. The human race was seeing Randall's comet for the first and perhaps the only time.

As it approached the sun, it grew, blasting out plumes and jets, the smallest of which was larger than a hundred Earths. Like a great pennant streaming down some cosmic breeze, the comet's tail was already forty million miles long when it raced past the orbit of Mars. It was then that the astronomers realized that this might be the most spectacular sight ever to appear in the heavens; the display put on by Halley's comet, back in 1986, would be nothing in comparison. And it was then that the administrators of the International Astrophysical Decade decided to send the research ship *Challenger* chasing after it, if she could be fitted out in time; for here was a chance that might not come again in a thousand years.

For weeks on end, in the hours before dawn, the comet sprawled across the sky like a second but far brighter Milky Way. As it approached the sun, and felt again the fires it had not known since the mammoths shook the Earth, it became steadily more active. Gouts of luminous gas erupted from its core, forming great fans which turned like slowly swinging searchlights across the stars. The tail, now a hundred million miles long, divided into intricate bands and streamers which changed their patterns completely in the course of a single night. Always they pointed away from the sun, as if driven starward by a great wind blowing forever outward from the heart of the solar system.

When the *Challenger* assignment had been given to him, George Pickett could hardly believe his luck. Nothing like this had happened to any reporter since William Laurence and the atom bomb. The facts that he had a science degree, was unmarried, in good health, weighed less than one hundred and twenty pounds, and had no appendix undoubtedly helped. But there must have been many others equally qualified; well, their envy would soon turn to relief.

Because the skimpy pay load of *Challenger* could not accommodate a mere reporter, Pickett had had to double up in his spare time as executive officer. This meant, in practice, that he had to write up the log, act as captain's secretary, keep track of stores, and balance the accounts. It was very fortunate, he often thought, that one needed only three hours' sleep in every twenty-four, in the weightless world of space.

Keeping his two duties separate had required a great deal of tact. When he was not writing in his closet-sized office, or checking the thousands of items stacked away in stores, he would go on the prowl with his recorder. He had been careful, at one time or another, to interview every one of the twenty scientists and engineers who manned *Challenger*. Not all the recordings had been radioed back to Earth; some had been too technical, some too inarticulate, and others too much the reverse. But at least he had played no favorites and, as far as he knew, had trodden on no toes. Not that it mattered now.

He wondered how Dr. Martens was taking it; the astronomer had been one of his most difficult subjects, yet the one who could give most information. On a sudden impulse, Pickett located the earliest of the Martens tapes, and inserted it in the recorder. He knew that he was trying to escape from the present by retreating into the past, but the only effect of that self-knowledge was to make him hope the experiment would succeed.

He still had vivid memories of that first interview, for the weightless microphone, wavering only slightly in the draft of air from the ventilators, had almost hypnotized him into incoherence. Yet no one would have guessed: his voice had its normal, professional smoothness.

They had been twenty million miles behind the comet, but swiftly overtaking it, when he had trapped Martens in the observatory and thrown that opening question at him.

"Dr. Martens," he began, "just what *is* Randall's comet made of?"

"Quite a mixture," the astronomer had answered, "and it's changing all the time as we move away from the sun. But the tail's mostly ammonia, methane, carbon dioxide, water vapor, cyanogen—"

"Cyanogen? Isn't that a poison gas? What would happen if the Earth ran into it?"

"Not a thing. Though it looks so spectacular, by our normal standards a comet's tail is a pretty good vacuum. A volume as big as Earth contains about as much gas as a matchbox full of air."

"And yet this thin stuff puts on such a wonderful display!"

"So does the equally thin gas in an electric sign, and for the same reason. A comet's tail glows because the sun bombards it with electrically charged particles. It's a cosmic skysign; one day, I'm afraid, the advertising people will wake up to this, and find a way of writing slogans across the solar system."

"That's a depressing thought—though I suppose someone will claim it's a triumph of applied science. But let's leave the tail; how soon will we get into the heart of the comet—the nucleus, I believe you call it?"

"Since a stern chase always takes a long time, it will be another two weeks before we enter the nucleus. We'll be plowing deeper and deeper into the tail, taking a cross section through the comet as we catch up with it. But though the nucleus is still twenty million miles ahead, we've already learned a good deal about it. For one thing, it's extremely small—less than fifty miles across. And even that's not solid, but probably consists of thousands of smaller bodies, all milling round in a cloud."

"Will we be able to go into the nucleus?"

"We'll know when we get there. Maybe we'll play safe and study it through our telescopes from a few thousand miles away. But personally, I'll be disappointed unless we go right inside. Won't you?"

Pickett switched off the recorder. Yes, Martens had been right. He *would* have been disappointed, especially since there had seemed no possible source of danger. Nor was there, as far as the comet was concerned. The danger had come from within.

They had sailed through one after another of the huge but unimaginably tenuous curtains of gas that Randall's comet was still ejecting as it raced away from the sun. Yet even now, though they were approaching the densest regions of the nucleus, they were for all practical purposes in a perfect vacuum. The luminous fog that stretched around *Challenger* for so many millions of miles scarcely dimmed the stars; but directly ahead, where lay the comet's core, was a brilliant patch of hazy light, luring them onward like a will-o'-the-wisp.

The electrical disturbances now taking place around them with ever-increasing violence had almost completely cut their link with Earth. The ship's main radio transmitter could just get a signal through, but for the last few days they had been reduced to sending "O.K." messages in Morse. When they broke away from the comet and headed for home, normal communication would be resumed; but now they were almost as isolated as explorers had been in the days before radio. It was inconvenient, but that was all. Indeed, Pickett rather welcomed this state of affairs; it gave him more time to get on with his clerical duties. Though *Challenger* was sailing into the heart of a comet, on a course that no captain could have dreamed of before the twentieth century, someone still had to check the provisions and count the stores.

Very slowly and cautiously, her radar probing the whole sphere of space around her, *Challenger* crept into the nucleus of the comet. And there she came to rest—amid the ice.

Back in the nineteen-forties, Fred Whipple, of Harvard, had guessed the truth, but it was hard to believe it even when the evidence was before one's eyes. The comet's relatively tiny core was a loose cluster of icebergs, drifting and turning round one another as they moved along their orbit. But unlike the bergs that floated in polar seas, they were not a dazzling white, nor were they made of water. They were a dirty gray, and very porous, like partly thawed snow. And they were riddled with pockets of methane and frozen ammonia, which erupted from time to time in gigantic gas jets as they absorbed the heat of the sun. It was a wonderful display, but Pickett had little time to admire it. Now he had far too much.

He had been doing his routine check of the ship's stores when he came face to face with disaster—though it was some time before he realized it. For the supply situation had been perfectly satisfactory; they had ample stocks for the return to Earth. He had checked that with his own eyes, and now had merely to confirm the balances recorded in the pinhead-sized section of the ship's electronic memory which stored all the accounts.

When the first crazy figures flashed on the screen, Pickett assumed that he had pressed the wrong key. He cleared the totals, and fed the information into the computer once more.

Sixty cases of pressed meat to start with; 17 consumed so far; quantity left: 99999943.

He tried again, and again, with no better result. Then, feeling annoyed but not particularly alarmed, he went in search of Dr. Martens.

He found the astronomer in the Torture Chamber— the tiny gym, squeezed between the technical stores and the bulkhead of the main propellant tank. Each member of the crew had to exercise here for an hour a day, lest his muscles waste away in this gravityless environment. Martens was wrestling with a set of powerful springs, an expression of grim determination on his face. It became much grimmer when Pickett gave his report.

A few tests on the main input board quickly told them the worst. "The computer's insane," said Martens. "It can't even add or subtract."

"But surely we can fix it!"

Martens shook his head. He had lost all his usual cocky self-confidence; he looked, Pickett told himself, like an inflated rubber doll that had started to leak.

"Not even the builders could do that. It's a solid mass of microcircuits, packed as tightly as the human brain. The memory units are still operating, but the computing section's utterly useless. It just scrambles the figures you feed into it."

"And where does that leave us?" Pickett asked.

"It means that we're all dead," Martens answered flatly. "Without the computer, we're done for. It's impossible to calculate an orbit back to Earth. It would take an army of mathematicians weeks to work it out on paper."

"That's ridiculous! The ship's in perfect condition, we've plenty of food and fuel—and you tell me we're all going to die just because we can't do a few sums."

"A *few* sums!" retorted Martens, with a trace of his old spirit. "A major navigational change, like the one needed to break away from the comet and put us on an orbit to Earth, involves about a hundred thousand separate calculations. Even the computer needs several minutes for the job."

Pickett was no mathematician, but he knew enough of astronautics to understand the situation. A ship coasting through space was under the influence of many bodies. The main force controlling it was the gravity of the sun, which kept all the planets firmly chained in their orbits. But the planets themselves also tugged it this way and that, though with much feebler strength. To allow for all these conflicting tugs and pulls —above all, to take advantage of them to reach a desired goal scores of millions of miles away—was a problem of fantastic complexity. He could appreciate Martens' despair; no man could work without the tools of his trade, and no trade needed more elaborate tools than this one.

Even after the Captain's announcement, and that first emergency conference when the entire crew had gathered to discuss the situation, it had taken hours for the facts to sink home. The end was still so many months away that the mind could not grasp it; they were under the sentence of death, but there was no hurry about the execution. And the view was still superb. . . .

Beyond the glowing mists that enveloped them—and which would be their celestial monument to the end of time—they could see the great beacon of Jupiter, brighter than all the stars. Some of them might still be alive, if the others were willing to sacrifice themselves, when the ship went past the mightiest of the sun's children. Would the extra weeks of life be worth it, Pickett asked himself, to see with your own eyes the sight that Galileo had first glimpsed through his crude telescope four centuries ago—the satellites of Jupiter, shuttling back and forth like beads upon an invisible wire?

Beads upon a wire. With that thought, an all-but-forgotten childhood memory exploded out of his subconscious. It must have been there for days, struggling upward into the light. Now at last it had forced itself upon his waiting mind.

"No!" he cried aloud. "It's ridiculous! They'll laugh at me!"

So what? said the other half of his mind. You've nothing to lose; if it does no more, it will keep everyone busy while the food and the oxygen dwindle away. Even the faintest hope is better than none at all. . . .

He stopped fidgeting with the recorder; the mood of maudlin self-pity was over. Releasing the elastic webbing that held him to his seat, he set off for the technical stores in search of the material he needed.

"This," said Dr. Martens three days later, "isn't my

idea of a joke." He gave a contemptuous glance at the flimsy structure of wire and wood that Pickett was holding in his hand.

"I guessed you'd say that," Pickett replied, keeping his temper under control. "But please listen to me for a minute. My grandmother was Japanese, and when I was a kid she told me a story that I'd completely forgotten until this week. I think it may save our lives.

"Sometime after the Second World War, there was a contest between an American with an electric desk calculator and a Japanese using an abacus like this. The abacus won."

"Then it must have been a poor desk machine, or an incompetent operator."

"They used the best in the U.S. Army. But let's stop arguing. Give me a test—say a couple of three-figure numbers to multiply."

"Oh—856 times 437."

Pickett's fingers danced over the beads, sliding them up and down the wires with lightning speed. There were twelve wires in all, so that the abacus could handle numbers up to 999,999,999,999—or could be divided into separate sections where several independent calculations could be carried out simultaneously.

"374072," said Pickett, after an incredibly brief interval of time. "Now see how long *you* take to do it, with pencil and paper."

There was a much longer delay before Martens, who like most mathematicians was poor at arithmetic, called out "375072.' A hasty check soon confirmed that Martens had taken at least three times as long as Pickett to arrive at the wrong answer.

The astronomer's face was a study in mingled chagrin, astonishment, and curiosity.

"Where did you learn that trick?" he asked. "I thought those things could only add and subtract."

"Well—multiplication's only repeated addition, isn't

it? All I did was to add 856 seven times in the unit
column, three times in the tens column, and four times
in the hundreds column. You do the same thing when
you use pencil and paper. Of course, there are some
short cuts, but if you think *I'm* fast, you should have
seen my granduncle. He used to work in a Yokohama
bank, and you couldn't see his fingers when he was
going at speed. He taught me some of the tricks, but
I've forgotten most of them in the last twenty years.
I've only been practicing for a couple of days, so I'm
still pretty slow. All the same, I hope I've convinced
you that there's something in my argument."

"You certainly have: I'm quite impressed. Can you
divide just as quickly?"

"Very nearly, when you've had enough experience."

Martens picked up the abacus, and started flicking
the beads back and forth. Then he sighed.

"Ingenious—but it doesn't really help us. Even if
it's ten times as fast as a man with pencil and paper—
which it isn't—the computer was a million times faster."

"I've thought of that," answered Pickett, a little
impatiently.

(Martens had no guts—he gave up too easily. How
did he think astronomers managed a hundred years
ago before there were any computers?)

"This is what I propose—tell me if you can see any
flaws in it. . . ."

Carefully and earnestly he detailed his plan. As he
did so, Martens slowly relaxed, and presently he gave
the first laugh that Pickett had heard about *Challenger*
for days.

"I want to see the skipper's face," said the astronomer, "when you tell him that we're all going back to
the nursery to start playing with beads."

There was skepticism at first, but it vanished swiftly
when Pickett gave a few demonstrations. To men who

had grown up in a world of electronics, the fact that a simple structure of wire and beads could perform such apparent miracles was a revelation. It was also a challenge, and because their lives depended upon it, they responded eagerly.

As soon as the engineering staff had built enough smoothly operating copies of Pickett's crude prototype, the classes began. It took only a few minutes to explain the basic principles; what required time was practice—hour after hour of it, until the fingers flew automatically across the wires and flicked the beads into the right positions without any need for conscious thought. There were some members of the crew who never acquired both accuracy and speed, even after a week of constant practice: but there were others who quickly outdistanced Pickett himself.

They dreamed counters and columns, and flicked beads in their sleep. As soon as they had passed beyond the elementary stage they were divided into teams, which then competed fiercely against each other, until they had reached still higher standards of proficiency. In the end, there were men aboard *Challenger* who could multiply four-figure numbers on the abacus in fifteen seconds, and keep it up hour after hour.

Such work was purely mechanical; it required skill, but no intelligence. The really difficult job was Martens', and there was little that anyone could do to help him. He had to forget all the machine-based techniques he had taken for granted, and rearrange his calculations so that they could be carried out automatically by men who had no idea of the meaning of the figures they were manipulating. He would feed them the basic data, and then they would follow the program he had laid down. After a few hours of patient routine work, the answer would emerge from the end of the mathematical production line—provided that no mistakes had been made. And the way to guard against that was to have two independent teams working, cross-checking results at regular intervals.

"What we've done," said Pickett into his recorder, when at last he had time to think of the audience he had never expected to speak to again, "is to build a computer out of human beings instead of electronic circuits. It's a few thousand times slower, can't handle many digits, and gets tired easily—but it's doing the job. Not the whole job of navigating to Earth—that's far too complicated—but the simpler one of giving us an orbit that will bring us back into radio range. Once we've escaped from the electrical interference around us, we can radio our position and the big computers on Earth can tell us what to do next.

"We've already broken away from the comet and are no longer heading out of the solar system. Our new orbit checks with the calculations, to the accuracy that can be expected. We're still inside the comet's tail, but the nucleus is a million miles away and we won't see those ammonia icebergs again. They're racing on toward the stars into the freezing night between the suns, while we are coming home. . . .

"Hello, Earth . . . hello, Earth! This is *Challenger* calling, *Challenger* calling. Signal back as soon as you receive us—we'd like you to check our arithmetic—before we work our fingers to the bone!"

An Ape About the House

Granny thought it a perfectly horrible idea; but then, she could remember the days when there were *human* servants.

"If you imagine," she snorted, "that I'll share the house with a monkey, you're very much mistaken."

"Don't be so old-fashioned," I answered. "Anyway, Dorcas isn't a monkey."

"Then what is she—it?"

I flipped through the pages of the Biological Engineering Corporation's guide. "Listen to this, Gran," I said. " 'The Superchimp (Registered Trade-mark) *Pan Sapiens* is an intelligent anthropoid, derived by breeding and genetic modification from basic chimpanzee stock—' "

"Just what I said! A monkey!"

" '—and with a large-enough vocabulary to understand simple orders. It can be trained to perform all types of domestic work or routine manual labor and is docile, affectionate, housebroken, and particularly good with children—' "

"Children! Would you trust Johnnie and Susan with a—a *gorilla?*"

I put the handbook down with a sigh.

"You've got a point there. Dorcas *is* expensive, and if I find the little monsters knocking her about—"

At this moment, fortunately, the door buzzer sounded. "Sign, please," said the delivery man. I signed, and Dorcas entered our lives.

"Hello, Dorcas," I said. "I hope you'll be happy here."

Her big, mournful eyes peered out at me from beneath their heavy ridges. I'd met much uglier humans, though she was rather an odd shape, being only about four feet tall and very nearly as wide. In her neat, plain uniform she looked just like a maid from one of those early twentieth-century movies; her feet, however, were bare and covered an astonishing amount of floor space.

"Morning, Ma'am," she answered, in slurred but perfectly intelligible accents.

"She can speak!" squawked Granny.

"Of course," I answered. "She can pronounce over fifty words, and can understand two hundred. She'll learn more as she grows used to us, but for the moment we must stick to the vocabulary on pages forty-two and forty-three of the handbook." I passed the instruction manual over to Granny; for once, she couldn't find a single word to express *her* feelings.

Dorcas settled down very quickly. Her basic training —Class A Domestic, plus Nursery Duties—had been excellent, and by the end of the first month there were very few jobs around the house that she couldn't do, from laying the table to changing the children's clothes. At first she had an annoying habit of picking up things with her feet; it seemed as natural to her as using her hands, and it took a long time to break her of it. One of Granny's cigarette butts finally did the trick.

She was good-natured, conscientious, and didn't answer back. Of course, she was not terribly bright, and some jobs had to be explained to her at great length before she got the point. It took several weeks before I discovered her limitations and allowed for them; at first it was quite hard to remember that she was not exactly human, and that it was no good engaging her in the sort of conversations we women occupy ourselves with when we get together. Or not many of them; she did have an interest in clothes, and was fascinated by colors. If I'd let her dress the way she wanted, she'd have looked like a refugee from Mardi gras.

The children, I was relieved to find, adored her. I know what people say about Johnnie and Sue, and admit that it contains some truth. It's so hard to bring up children when their father's away most of the time, and to make matters worse, Granny spoils them when I'm not looking. So indeed does Eric, whenever his ship's on Earth, and I'm left to cope with the resulting tantrums. Never marry a spaceman if you can possibly avoid it; the pay may be good, but the glamour soon wears off.

By the time Eric got back from the Venus run, with three weeks' accumulated leave, our new maid had settled down as one of the family. Eric took her in his stride; after all, he'd met much odder creatures on the planets. He grumbled about the expense, of course, but I pointed out that now that so much of the housework was taken off my hands, we'd be able to spend more time together and do some of the visiting that had proved impossible in the past. I looked forward to having a little social life again, now that Dorcas could take care of the children.

For there was plenty of social life at Port Goddard, even though we were stuck in the middle of the Pacific. (Ever since what happened to Miami, of course, all major launching sites have been a long, long way from civilization.) There was a constant flow of distinguished visitors and travelers from all parts of the Earth—not to mention remoter points.

Every community has its arbiter of fashion and culture, its *grande dame* who is resented yet copied by all her unsuccessful rivals. At Port Goddard it was Christine Swanson; her husband was Commodore of the Space Service, and she never let us forget it. Whenever a liner touched down, she would invite all the officers on Base to a reception at her stylishly antique nineteenth-century mansion. It was advisable to go, unless you had a very good excuse, even though that meant looking at Christine's paintings. She fancied herself as an artist, and the walls were hung with multicolored daubs. Thinking of polite remarks to make about them was one of the major hazards of Christine's parties; another was her meter-long cigarette holder.

There was a new batch of paintings since Eric had been away: Christine had entered her "square" period. "You see, my dears," she explained to us, "the old-fashioned oblong pictures are terribly dated—they just don't go with the Space Age. There's no such thing as up or down, horizontal or vertical out *there*, so no really modern picture should have one side longer than another. And ideally, it should look *exactly* the same whichever way you hang it—I'm working on that right now."

"That seems very logical," said Eric tactfully. (After all, the Commodore was his boss.) But when our hostess was out of earshot, he added, "I don't know if Christine's pictures are hung the right way up, but I'm sure they're hung the wrong side to the wall."

I agreed; before I got married I spent several years at the art school and considered I knew something about the subject. Given as much cheek as Christine, I could have made quite a hit with my own canvases, which were now gathering dust in the garage.

"You know, Eric," I said a little cattily, "I could teach Dorcas to paint better than this."

He laughed and answered, "It might be fun to try it some day, if Christine gets out of hand." Then I forgot all about the matter—until a month later, when Eric was back in space.

The exact cause of the fight isn't important; it arose over a community development scheme on which Christine and I took opposing viewpoints. She won, as usual, and I left the meeting breathing fire and brimstone. When I got home, the first thing I saw was Dorcas, looking at the colored pictures in one of the weeklies—and I remembered Eric's words.

I put down my handbag, took off my hat, and said firmly: "Dorcas—come out to the garage."

It took some time to dig out my oils and easel from under the pile of discarded toys, old Christmas decorations, skin-diving gear, empty packing cases, and broken tools (it seemed that Eric never had time to tidy up before he shot off into space again). There were several unfinished canvases buried among the debris, which would do for a start. I set up a landscape which had got as far as one skinny tree, and said: "Now, Dorcas—I'm going to teach you to paint."

My plan was simple and not altogether honest. Although apes had, of course, splashed paint on canvas often enough in the past, none of them had created a genuine, properly composed work of art. I was sure that Dorcas couldn't either, but no one need know that mine was the guiding hand. She could get all the credit.

I was not actually going to lie to anyone, however. Though I would create the design, mix the pigments, and do most of the execution, I would let Dorcas tackle just as much of the work as she could handle. I hoped that she could fill in the areas of solid color, and perhaps develop a characteristic style of brush-work in the process. With any luck, I estimated, she might be able to do perhaps a quarter of the actual work. Then I could claim it was all hers with a reason-ably clear conscience—for hadn't Michelangelo and Leonardo signed paintings that were largely done by their assistants? I'd be Dorcas' "assistant."

I must confess that I was a little disappointed. Though Dorcas quickly got the general idea, and soon under-stood the use of brush and palette, her execution was very clumsy. She seemed unable to make up her mind which hand to use, but kept transferring the brush from one to the other. In the end I had to do almost all the work, and she merely contributed a few dabs of paint.

Still, I could hardly expect her to become a master in a couple of lessons, and it was really of no impor-tance. If Dorcas was an artistic flop, I would just have to stretch the truth a little farther when I claimed that it was all her own work.

I was in no hurry; this was not the sort of thing that could be rushed. At the end of a couple of months, the School of Dorcas had produced a dozen paintings, all of them on carefully chosen themes that would be familiar to a Superchimp at Port Goddard. There was a study of the lagoon, a view of our house, an impres-sion of a night launching (all glare and explosions of light), a fishing scene, a palm grove—clichés, of course, but anything else would rouse suspicion. Before she came to us, I don't suppose Dorcas had seen much of the world outside the labs where she had been reared and trained.

The best of these paintings (and some of them *were* good—after all, I should know) I hung around the house in places where my friends could hardly fail to notice them. Everything worked perfectly; admiring queries were followed by astonished cries of "You don't say!" when I modestly disclaimed responsibility. There was some skepticism, but I soon demolished that by letting a few privileged friends see Dorcas at work. I chose the viewers for their ignorance of art, and the picture was an abstraction in red, gold, and black which no one dared to criticize. By this time, Dorcas could fake it quite well, like a movie actor pretending to play a musical instrument.

Just to spread the news around, I gave away some of the best paintings, pretending that I considered them no more than amusing novelties—yet at the same time giving just the barest hint of jealousy. "I've hired Dorcas," I said testily, "to work for me—not for the Museum of Modern Art." And I was *very* careful not to draw any comparisons between her paintings and those of Christine: our mutual friends could be relied upon to do that.

When Christine came to see me, ostensibly to discuss our quarrel "like two sensible people," I knew that she was on the run. So I capitulated gracefully as we took tea in the drawing room, beneath one of Dorcas' most impressive productions. (Full moon rising over the lagoon—very cold, blue, and mysterious. I was really quite proud of it.) There was not a word about the picture, or about Dorcas; but Christine's eyes told me all I wanted to know. The next week, an exhibition she had been planning was quietly canceled.

Gamblers say that you should quit when you're ahead of the game. If I had stopped to think, I should have known that Christine would not let the matter rest there. Sooner or later, she was bound to counterattack.

She chose her time well, waiting until the kids were at school, Granny was away visiting, and I was at the shopping center on the other side of the island. Probably she phoned first to check that no one was at

home—no one human, that is. We had told Dorcas
not to answer calls; though she'd done so in the early
days, it had not been a success. A Superchimp on the
phone sounds exactly like a drunk, and this can lead to
all sorts of complications.

I can reconstruct the whole sequence of events:
Christine must have driven up to the house, expressed
acute disappointment at my absence, and invited herself in. She would have wasted no time in getting to
work on Dorcas, but luckily I'd taken the precaution
of briefing my anthropoid colleague. "Dorcas make,"
I'd said, over and over again, each time one of our
productions was finished. "Not Missy make—*Dorcas*
make." And, in the end, I'm sure she believed this
herself.

If my brainwashing, and the limitations of a fifty-
word vocabulary, baffled Christine, she did not stay
baffled for long. She was a lady of direct action, and
Dorcas was a docile and obedient soul. Christine, determined to expose fraud and collusion, must have
been gratified by the promptness with which she was
led into the garage studio; she must also have been
just a little surprised.

I arrived home about half an hour later, and knew
that there was trouble afoot as soon as I saw Christine's car parked at the curb. I could only hope I was
in time, but as soon as I stepped into the uncannily
silent house, I realized that it was too late. *Something*
had happened; Cristine would surely be talking, even
if she had only an ape as audience. To her, any silence
was as great a challenge as a blank canvas; it had to be
filled with the sound of her own voice.

The house was utterly still; there was no sign of life.
With a sense of mounting apprehension, I tiptoed
through the drawing room, the dining room, the kitchen,
and out into the back. The garage door was open, and
I peered cautiously through.

It was a bitter moment of truth. Finally freed from my influence, Dorcas had at last developed a style of her own. She was swiftly and confidently painting— but not in the way *I* had so carefully taught her. And as for her subject . . .

I was deeply hurt when I saw the caricature that was giving Christine so much obvious enjoyment. After all that I had done for Dorcas, this seemed sheer ingratitude. Of course, I know now that no malice was involved, and that she was merely expressing herself. The psychologists, and the critics who wrote those absurd program notes for her exhibition at the Guggenheim, say that her portraits cast a vivid light on man-animal relationships, and allow us to look for the first time at the human race from outside. But I did not see it *that* way when I ordered Dorcas back into the kitchen.

For the subject was not the only thing that upset me: what really rankled was the thought of all the time I had wasted improving her technique—and her manners. She was ignoring everything I had ever told her, as she sat in front of the easel with her arms folded motionless on her chest.

Even then, at the very beginning of her career as an independent artist, it was painfully obvious that Dorcas had more talent in either of her swiftly moving feet than I had in both my hands.

Saturn Rising

Yes, that's perfectly true. I met Morris Perlman when I was about twenty-eight. I met thousands of people in those days, from presidents downward.

When we got back from Saturn, everybody wanted to see us, and about half the crew took off on lecture tours. I've always enjoyed talking (don't say you haven't noticed it), but some of my colleagues said they'd rather go to Pluto than face another audience. Some of them did.

My beat was the Midwest, and the first time I ran into Mr. Perlman—no one ever called him anything else, certainly never "Morris"—was in Chicago. The agency always booked me into good, but not too luxurious, hotels. That suited me; I liked to stay in places where I could come and go as I pleased without running a gauntlet of liveried flunkies, and where I could wear anything within reason without being made to feel a tramp. I see you're grinning; well, I was only a kid then, and a lot of things have changed. . . .

It's all a long time ago now, but I must have been lecturing at the University. At any rate, I remember being disappointed because they couldn't show me the place where Fermi started the first atomic pile—they said that the building had been pulled down forty years before, and there was only a plaque to mark the spot. I stood looking at it for a while, thinking of all that had happened since that far-off day in 1942. I'd been born, for one thing; and atomic power had taken me out to Saturn and back. *That* was probably something that Fermi and Co. never thought of, when they built their primitive latticework of uranium and graphite.

I was having breakfast in the coffee shop when a slightly built, middle-aged man dropped into the seat on the other side of the table. He nodded a polite "Good morning," then gave a start of surprise as he recognized me. (Of course, he'd planned the encounter, but I didn't know it at the time.)

"This is a pleasure!" he said. "I was at your lecture last night. How I envied you!"

I gave a rather forced smile; I'm never very sociable at breakfast, and I'd learned to be on my guard against the cranks, bores, and enthusiasts who seemed to regard me as their legitimate prey. Mr. Perlman, however, was not a bore—though he was certainly an enthusiast, and I suppose you could call him a crank.

He looked like any average, fairly prosperous businessman, and I assumed that he was a guest like myself. The fact that he had attended my lecture was not surprising; it had been a popular one, open to the public, and of course well advertised over press and radio.

"Ever since I was a kid," said my uninvited companion, "Saturn has fascinated me. I know exactly when and how it all started. I must have been about ten years old when I came across those wonderful paintings of Chesley Bonestell's, showing the planet as it would look from its nine moons. I suppose you've seen them?"

"Of course," I answered. "Though they're half a

century old, no one's beaten them yet. We had a couple aboard the *Endeavour,* pinned on the plotting table. I often used to look at the pictures and then compare them with the real thing."

"Then you know how I felt, back in the nineteen-fifties. I used to sit for hours trying to grasp the fact that this incredible object, with its silver rings spinning around it, wasn't just some artist's dream, but actually existed—that it was a world, in fact, ten times the size of Earth.

"At that time I never imagined that I could see this wonderful thing for myself; I took it for granted that only the astronomers, with their giant telescopes, could ever look at such sights. But then, when I was about fifteen, I made another discovery—so exciting that I could hardly believe it."

"And what was that?" I asked. By now I'd become reconciled to sharing breakfast; my companion seemed a harmless-enough character, and there was something quite endearing about his obvious enthusiasm.

"I found that any fool could make a high-powered astronomical telescope in his own kitchen, for a few dollars and a couple of weeks' work. It was a revelation; like thousands of other kids, I borrowed a copy of Ingalls' *Amateur Telescope Making* from the public library, and went ahead. Tell me—have *you* ever built a telescope of your own?"

"No: I'm an engineer, not an astronomer. I wouldn't know how to begin the job."

"It's incredibly simple, if you follow the rules. You start with two disks of glass, about an inch thick. I got mine for fifty cents from a ship chandler's; they were porthole glasses that were no use because they'd been chipped around the edges. Then you cement one disk to some flat, firm surface—I used an old barrel, standing on end.

"Next you have to buy several grades of emery

powder, starting from coarse, gritty stuff and working down to the finest that's made. You lay a pinch of the coarsest powder between the two disks, and start rubbing the upper one back and forth with regular strokes. As you do so, you slowly circle around the job.

"You see what happens? The upper disk gets hollowed out by the cutting action of the emery powder, and as you walk around, it shapes itself into a concave, spherical surface. From time to time you have to change to a finer grade of powder, and make some simple optical tests to check that your curve's right.

"Later still, you drop the emery and switch to rouge, until at last you have a smooth, polished surface that you can hardly credit you've made yourself. There's only one more step, though that's a little tricky. You still have to silver the mirror, and turn it into a good reflector. This means getting some chemicals made up at the drugstore, and doing exactly what the book says.

"I can still remember the kick I got when the silver film began to spread like magic across the face of my little mirror. It wasn't perfect, but it was good enough, and I wouldn't have swapped it for anything on Mount Palomar.

"I fixed it at one end of a wooden plank; there was no need to bother about a telescope tube, though I put a couple of feet of cardboard round the mirror to cut out stray light. For an eyepiece I used a small magnifying lens I'd picked up in a junk store for a few cents. Altogether, I don't suppose the telescope cost more than five dollars—though that was a lot of money to me when I was a kid.

"We were living then in a run-down hotel my family owned on Third Avenue. When I'd assembled the telescope I went up on the roof and tried it out, among the jungle of TV antennas that covered every building in those days. It took me a while to get the

mirror and eyepiece lined up, but I hadn't made any
mistakes and the thing worked. As an optical instrument it was probably lousy—after all, it was my first
attempt—but it magnified at least fifty times and I
could hardly wait until nightfall to try it on the stars.

"I'd checked with the almanac, and knew that Saturn
was high in the east after sunset. As soon as it was
dark I was up on the roof again, with my crazy con-
traption of wood and glass propped between two chim-
neys. It was late fall, but I never noticed the cold, for
the sky was full of stars—and they were all mine.

"I took my time setting the focus as accurately as
possible, using the first star that came into the field.
Then I started hunting for Saturn, and soon discovered
how hard it was to locate anything in a reflecting
telescope that wasn't properly mounted. But presently
the planet shot across the field of view, I nudged the
instrument a few inches this way and that—and there
it was.

"It was tiny, but it was perfect. I don't think I
breathed for a minute; I could hardly believe my eyes.
After all the pictures, here was the reality. It looked
like a toy hanging there in space, with the rings slightly
open and tilted toward me. Even now, forty years
later, I can remember thinking 'It looks so *artificial*—
like something from a Christmas tree!' There was a
single bright star to the left of it, and I knew that was
Titan."

He paused, and for a moment we must have shared
the same thoughts. For to both of us Titan was no
longer merely the largest moon of Saturn—a point of
light known only to astronomers. It was the fiercely
hostile world upon which *Endeavour* had landed, and
where three of my crew-mates lay in lonely graves,
farther from their homes than any of Mankind's dead
had ever rested before.

"I don't know how long I stared, straining my eyes

and moving the telescope across the sky in jerky steps as Saturn rose above the city. I was a billion miles from New York; but presently New York caught up with me.

"I told you about our hotel; it belonged to my mother, but my father ran it—not very well. It had been losing money for years, and all through my boyhood there had been continuous financial crises. So I don't want to blame my father for drinking; he must have been half crazy with worry most of the time. And I had quite forgotten that I was supposed to be helping the clerk at the reception desk. . . .

"So Dad came looking for me, full of his own cares and knowing nothing about my dreams. He found me stargazing on the roof.

"He wasn't a cruel man—he couldn't have understood the study and patience and care that had gone into my little telescope, or the wonders it had shown me during the short time I had used it. I don't hate him any more, but I'll remember all my life the splintering crack of my first and last mirror as it smashed against the brickwork."

There was nothing I could say. My initial resentment at this interruption had long since changed to curiosity. Already I sensed that there was much more to this story than I'd heard so far, and I'd noticed something else. The waitress was treating us with an exaggerated deference—only a little of which was directed at me.

My companion toyed with the sugar bowl while I waited in silent sympathy. By this time I felt there was some bond between us, though I did not know exactly what it was.

"I never built another telescope," he said. "Something else broke, besides that mirror—something in my heart. Anyway, I was much too busy. Two things happened that turned my life upside down. Dad walked out on us, leaving me the head of the family. And then they pulled down the Third Avenue El."

He must have seen my puzzled look, for he grinned across the table at me.

"Oh, you wouldn't know about that. But when I was a kid, there was an elevated railroad down the middle of Third. It made the whole area dirty and noisy; the Avenue was a slum district of bars, pawnshops and cheap hotels—like ours. All that changed when the El went; land values shot up, and we were suddenly prosperous. Dad came back quickly enough, but it was too late; I was running the business. Before long I started moving across town—then across country. I wasn't an absent-minded stargazer any more, and I gave Dad one of my smaller hotels, where he couldn't do much harm.

"It's forty years since I looked at Saturn, but I've never forgotten that one glimpse, and last night your photographs brought it all back. I just wanted to say how grateful I am."

He fumbled in his wallet and pulled out a card.

"I hope you'll look me up when you're in town again; you can be sure I'll be there if you give any more lectures. Good luck—and I'm sorry to have taken so much of your time."

Then he was gone, almost before I could say a word. I glanced at the card, put it away in my pocket, and finished my breakfast, rather thoughtfully.

When I signed my check on the way out of the coffee shop I asked: "Who was that gentleman at my table? The boss?"

The cashier looked at me as if I were mentally retarded.

"I suppose you *could* call him that, sir," she answered. "Of course he owns this hotel, but we've never seen him here before. He always stays at the Ambassador, when he's in Chicago."

"And does he own *that?*" I said, without too much irony, for I'd already suspected the answer.

"Why, yes. As well as—" and she rattled off a whole string of others, including the two biggest hotels in New York.

I was impressed, and also rather amused, for it was now obvious that Mr. Perlman had come here with the deliberate intention of meeting me. It seemed a round-about way of doing it; I knew nothing then, of his notorious shyness and secretiveness. From the first, he was never shy with me.

Then I forgot about him for five years. (Oh, I should mention that when I asked for my bill, I was told I didn't have one.) During that five years, I made my second trip.

We knew what to expect this time, and weren't going completely into the unknown. There were no more worries about fuel, because all we could ever use was waiting for us on Titan; we just had to pump its methane atmosphere into our tanks, and we'd made our plans accordingly. One after another, we visited all the nine moons; and then we went into the rings. . . .

There was little danger, yet it was a nerve-racking experience. The ring system is very thin, you know— only about twenty miles in thickness. We descended into it slowly and cautiously, after having matched its spin so that we were moving at exactly the same speed. It was like stepping onto a carrousel a hundred and seventy thousand miles across. . . .

But a ghostly kind of carrousel, because the rings aren't solid and you can look right through them. Close up, in fact, they're almost invisible; the billions of separate particles that make them up are so widely spaced that all you see in your immediate neighbor-hood are occasional small chunks, drifting very slowly past. It's only when you look into the distance that the countless fragments merge into a continuous sheet, like a hailstorm that sweeps around Saturn forever.

That's not *my* phrase, but it's a good one. For when we brought our first piece of genuine Saturnian ring into the air lock, it melted down in a few minutes into a pool of muddy water. Some people think it spoils the magic to know that the rings—or ninety per cent of them—are made of ordinary ice. But that's a stupid attitude; they would be just as wonderful, and just as beautiful, if they were made of diamond.

When I got back to Earth, in the first year of the new century, I started off on another lecture tour—only a short one, for now I had a family and wanted to see as much of it as possible. This time I ran into Mr. Perlman in New York, when I was speaking at Columbia and showing our movie, "Exploring Saturn." (A misleading title, that, since the nearest we'd been to the planet itself was about twenty thousand miles. No one dreamed, in those days, that men would ever go down into the turbulent slush which is the closest thing Saturn has to a surface.)

Mr. Perlman was waiting for me after the lecture. I didn't recognize him, for I'd met about a million people since our last encounter. But when he gave his name, it all came back, so clearly that I realized he must have made a deep impression on my mind.

Somehow he got me away from the crowd; though he disliked meeting people in the mass, he had an extraordinary knack of dominating any group when he found it necessary—and then clearing out before his victims knew what had happened. Though I saw him in action scores of times, I never knew exactly how he did it.

At any rate, half an hour later we were having a superb dinner in an exclusive restaurant (his, of course). It was a wonderful meal, especially after the chicken and ice cream of the lecture circuit, but he made me pay for it. Metaphorically, I mean.

Now all the facts and photos gathered by the two expeditions to Saturn were available to everyone, in hundreds of reports and books and popular articles. Mr. Perlman seemed to have read all the material that wasn't too technical; what he wanted from me was something different. Even then, I put his interest down to that of a lonely, aging man, trying to recapture a dream that had been lost in youth. I was right; but that was only a fraction of the whole picture.

He was after something that all the reports and articles failed to give. What did it *feel* like, he wanted to know, to wake up in the morning and see that great, golden globe with its scudding cloud belts dominating the sky? And the rings themselves—what did they do to your mind when they were so close that they filled the heavens from end to end?

You want a poet, I said—not an engineer. But I'll tell you this; however long you look at Saturn, and fly in and out among its moons, you can never quite believe it. Every so often you find yourself thinking: "It's all a dream—a thing like that *can't* be real." And you go to the nearest view-port—and there it is, taking your breath away.

You must remember that, altogether apart from our nearness, we were able to look at the rings from angles and vantage points that are quite impossible from Earth, where you always see them turned toward the sun. We could fly into their shadow, and then they would no longer gleam like silver—they would be a faint haze, a bridge of smoke across the stars.

And most of the time we could see the shadow of Saturn lying across the full width of the rings, eclipsing them so completely that it seemed as if a great bite had been taken out of them. It worked the other way, too; on the day side of the planet, there would always be the shadow of the rings running like a dusky band parallel to the Equator and not far from it.

Above all—though we did this only a few times—we could rise high above either pole of the planet and look down upon the whole stupendous system, so that it was spread out in plan beneath us. Then we could see that instead of the four visible from Earth, there were at least a dozen separate rings, merging one onto the other. When we saw this, our skipper made a remark that I've never forgotten. "This," he said—and there wasn't a trace of flippancy in the words—"is where the angels have parked their halos."

All this, and a lot more, I told Mr. Perlman in that little but oh-so-expensive restaurant just south of Central Park. When I'd finished, he seemed very pleased, though he was silent for several minutes. Then he said, about as casually as you might ask the time of the next train at your local station: "Which would be the best satellite for a tourist resort?"

When the words got through to me, I nearly choked on my hundred-year-old brandy. Then I said, very patiently and politely (for after all, I'd had a wonderful dinner): "Listen, Mr. Perlman. You know as well as I do that Saturn is nearly a billion miles from Earth—more than that, in fact, when we're on opposite sides of the sun. Someone worked out that our round-trip tickets averaged seven and a half million dollars apiece—and, believe me, there was no first-class accommodation on *Endeavour I* or *II*. Anyway, no matter how much money he had, no one could book a passage to Saturn. Only scientists and space crews will be going there, for as far ahead as anyone can imagine."

I could see that my words had absolutely no effect: he merely smiled, as if he knew some secret hidden from me.

"What you say is true enough *now*," he answered,

"but I've studied history. And I understand people—
that's my business. Let me remind you of a few facts.

"Two or three centuries ago, almost all the world's
great tourist centers and beauty spots were as far away
from civilization as Saturn is today. What did—oh,
Napoleon, let's say—know about the Grand Canyon,
Victoria Falls, Hawaii, Mount Everest? And look at
the South Pole; it was reached for the first time when
my father was a boy—but there's been a hotel there
for the whole of your lifetime.

"Now it's starting all over again. *You* can appreciate
only the problems and difficulties, because you're too
close to them. Whatever they are, men will overcome
them, as they've always done in the past.

"For wherever there's something strange or beautiful or novel, people will want to see it. The rings of
Saturn are the greatest spectacle in the known universe: I've always guessed so, and now you've convinced me. Today it takes a fortune to reach them,
and the men who go there must risk their lives. So did
the first men who flew—but now there are a million
passengers in the air every second of the day and
night.

"The same thing is going to happen in space. It
won't happen in ten years, maybe not in twenty. But
twenty-five is all it took, remember, before the first
commercial flights started to the moon. I don't think it
will be as long for Saturn. . . .

"I won't be around to see it—but when it happens, I
want people to remember me. So—where should we
build?"

I still thought he was crazy, but at last I was beginning to understand what made him tick. And there
was no harm in humoring him, so I gave the matter
careful thought.

"Mimas is too close," I said, "and so are Enceladus
and Tethys." (I don't mind telling you, those names

were tough after all that brandy.) "Saturn just fills the sky, and you think it's falling on top of you. Besides, they aren't solid enough—they're nothing but over-grown snowballs. Dione and Rhea are better—you get a magnificent view from both of them. But all these inner moons are so tiny; even Rhea is only eight hundred miles across, and the others are much smaller.

"I don't think there's any real argument; it will have to be Titan. That's a man-sized satellite—it's a lot bigger than *our* moon, and very nearly as large as Mars. There's a reasonable gravity too—about a fifth of Earth's—so your guests won't be floating all over the place. And it will always be a major refueling point because of its methane atmosphere, which should be an important factor in your calculations. Every ship that goes out to Saturn will touch down there."

"And the outer moons?"

"Oh, Hyperion, Japetus, and Phoebe are much too far away. You have to look hard to see the rings at all from Phoebe! Forget about them. Stick to good old Titan. Even if the temperature is two hundred below zero, and ammonia snow isn't the sort of stuff you'd want to ski on."

He listened to me very carefully, and if he thought I was making fun of his impractical, unscientific notions he gave no sign of it. We parted soon afterward—I don't remember anything more of that dinner—and then it must have been fifteen years before we met again. He had no further use for me in all that time; but when he wanted me, he called.

I see now what he had been waiting for; his vision had been clearer than mine. He couldn't have guessed, of course, that the rocket would go the way of the steam engine within less than a century—but he knew *something* better would come along, and I think he financed Saunderson's early work on the Paragravity Drive. But it was not until they started building fusion plants that could warm up a hundred square miles of a world as cold as Pluto that he got in contact with me again.

He was a very old man, and dying. They told me how rich he was, and I could hardly believe it. Not until he showed me the elaborate plans and the beautiful models his experts had prepared with such remarkable lack of publicity.

He sat in his wheel chair like a wrinkled mummy, watching my face as I studied the models and blueprints. Then he said: "Captain, I have a job for you. . . ."

So here I am. It's just like running a spaceship, of course—many of the technical problems are identical. And by this time I'd be too old to command a ship, so I'm very grateful to Mr. Perlman.

There goes the gong. If the ladies are ready, I suggest we walk down to dinner through the Observation Lounge.

Even after all these years, I still like to watch Saturn rising—and tonight it's almost full.

Let There Be Light

The conversation had come around to death rays again, and some carping critic was poking fun at the old science-fiction magazines whose covers so often displayed multicolored beams creating havoc in all directions. "Such an elementary scientific blunder," he snorted. "All the visible radiations are harmless—we wouldn't be alive if they weren't. So anybody should have known that the green rays and purple rays and scots-tartan rays were a lot of nonsense. You might even make a rule—if you could see a ray, it couldn't hurt you."

"An interesting theory," said Harry Purvis, "but not in accordance with the facts. The only death ray that I, personally, have ever come across was perfectly visible."

"Indeed? What color was it?"

"I'll come round to that in a minute—if you want me to. But talking of rounds . . ."

We caught Charlie Willis before he could sneak out of the bar, and practiced a little jujitsu on him until all the glasses were filled again. Then that curious, suspenseful silence descended over the White Hart that all the regulars recognize as the prelude to one of Harry Purvis' improbable stories.

Edgar and Mary Burton were a somewhat ill-assorted pair, and none of their friends could explain why they had married. Perhaps the cynical explanation was the correct one; Edgar was almost twenty years older than his wife, and had made a quarter of a million on the stock exchange before retiring at an unusually early age. He had set himself this financial target, had worked hard to attain it—and when his bank balance had reached the desired figure had instantly lost all ambition. From now on he intended to live the life of a country gentleman, and to devote his declining years to his one absorbing hobby—astronomy.

For some reason, it seems to surprise many people that an interest in astronomy is compatible with business acumen or even with common sense. This is a complete delusion, said Harry with much feeling; I was once practically skinned alive at a poker game by a professor of astrophysics from the California Institute of Technology. But in Edgar's case, shrewdness seemed to have been combined with a vague impracticality in one and the same person; once he had made his money, he took no further interest in it, or indeed in anything else except the construction of progressively larger reflecting telescopes.

On his retirement, Edgar had purchased a fine old house high up on the Yorkshire moors. It was not as bleak and Wuthering-Heightsish as it may sound; there was a splendid view, and the Bentley would get you into town in fifteen minutes. Even so, the change did not altogether suit Mary, and it is hard not to feel rather sorry for her. There was no work for her to do, since the servants ran the house, and she had few intellectual resources to fall back on. She took up riding, joined all the book clubs, read the *Tatler* and

Country Life from cover to cover, but still felt that there was something missing.

It took her about four months to find what she wanted; and then she met it at an otherwise dismal village fete. It was six foot three, ex-Coldstream Guards, with a family that looked on the Norman Conquest as a recent and regrettable piece of impertinence. It was called Rupert de Vere Courtenay (we'll forget about the other six Christian names) and it was generally regarded as the most eligible bachelor in the district.

Two full weeks passed before Rupert, who was a high-principled English gentleman, brought up in the best traditions of the aristocracy, succumbed to Mary's blandishments. His downfall was accelerated by the fact that his family was trying to arrange a match for him with the Honorable Felicity Fauntleroy, who was generally admitted to be no great beauty. Indeed, she looked so much like a horse that it was risky for her to go near her father's famous stables when the stallions were exercising.

Mary's boredom, and Rupert's determination to have a last desperate fling, had the inevitable result. Edgar saw less and less of his wife, who found an amazing number of reasons for driving into town during the week. At first he was quite glad that the circle of her acquaintances was widening so rapidly, and it was several months before he realized that it was doing nothing of the sort.

It is quite impossible to keep any liaison secret for long in a small country town like Stocksborough, though this is a fact that every generation has to learn afresh, usually the hard way. Edgar discovered the truth by accident, but some kind friend would have told him sooner or later. He had driven into town for a meeting of the local astronomical society—taking the Rolls, since his wife had already gone with the Bentley—and was momentarily held up on the way home by the crowds emerging from the last performance at the local cinema. In the heart of the crowd was Mary, accompanied by a handsome young man whom Edgar had seen before but couldn't identify at the moment. He would have thought no more of the matter had not Mary gone out of her way the next morning to mention that she'd been unable to get a seat in the cinema and had spent a quiet evening with one of her women friends.

Even Edgar, engrossed though he now was in the study of variable stars, began to put two and two together when he realized that his wife was gratuitously lying. He gave no hint of his vague suspicions, which ceased to be vague after the local Hunt Ball. Though he hated such functions (and this one, by bad luck, occurred just when U Orionis was going through its minimum and he had to miss some vital observations), he realized that this would give him a chance of identifying his wife's companion, since everyone in the district would be there.

It proved absurdly easy to locate Rupert and to get into conversation with him. Although the young man seemed a little ill at ease, he was pleasant company, and Edgar was surprised to find himself taking quite a fancy to him. If his wife had to have a lover, on the whole he approved her choice.

And there matters rested for some months, largely because Edgar was too busy grinding and figuring a fifteen-inch mirror to do anything about it. Twice a week Mary drove into town, ostensibly to meet her friends or to go to the cinema, and arrived back at the lodge just before midnight. Edgar could see the lights of the car for miles away across the moor, the beams twisting and turning as his wife drove homeward with what always seemed to him excessive speed. That had been one of the reasons why they seldom went out together; Edgar was a sound but cautious driver, and his comfortable cruising speed was ten miles an hour below Mary's.

About three miles from the house the lights of the car would disappear for several minutes as the road was hidden by a hill. There was a dangerous hairpin bend here; in a piece of highway construction more reminiscent of the Alps than of rural England, the road hugged the edge of a cliff and skirted an unpleasant hundred-foot drop before it straightened out on the homeward stretch. As the car rounded this bend, its headlights would shine full on the house, and there were many evenings when Edgar was dazzled by the sudden glare as he sat at the eyepiece of his telescope. Luckily, this stretch of road was very little used at night; if it had been, observations would have been well-nigh impossible, since it took Edgar's eyes ten or twenty minutes to recover fully from the direct blast of the headlights. This was no more than a minor annoyance, but when Mary started to stay out four or five evenings a week it became a confounded nuisance. Something, Edgar decided, Would Have To Be Done.

It will not have escaped your notice, continued Harry Purvis, that throughout all this affair Edgar Burton's behavior was hardly that of a normal person. Indeed, anyone who could have switched his mode of life so completely from that of a busy London stockbroker to that of a near-recluse on the Yorkshire moors must have been a little odd in the first place. I would hesitate, however, to say that he was more than eccentric until the time when Mary's midnight arrivals started to interfere with the serious business of observation. And even thereafter, one must admit that there was a certain crazy logic in his actions.

He had ceased to love his wife some years earlier, but he did object to her making a fool of him. And Rupert de Vere Courtenay seemed a pleasant young chap; it would be an act of kindness to rescue him.

Well, there was a beautifully simple solution, which had come to Edgar in a literally blinding flash. And I literally mean literally, for it was while he was blinking in the glare of Mary's headlights that Edgar conceived the only really perfect murder I've ever encountered. It is strange how apparently irrelevant factors can determine a man's life; though I hate to say anything against the oldest and noblest of the sciences, it cannot be denied that if Edgar had never become an astronomer, he would never have become a murderer. For his hobby provided part of the motive, and a good deal of the means. . . .

He could have made the mirror he needed—he was quite an expert by this time—but astronomical accuracy was unnecessary in this case, and it was simpler to pick up a secondhand searchlight reflector at one of those war-surplus shops off Leicester Square. The mirror was about three feet across, and it was only a few hours' work to fix up a mounting for it and to arrange a crude but effective arc light at its focus. Getting the beam lined up was equally straightforward, and no one took the slightest notice of his activities, since his experimenting was now taken for granted by wife and servants alike.

He made the final brief test on a clear, dark night and settled down to await Mary's return. He did not waste the time, of course, but continued his routine observations of a group of selected stars. By midnight, there was still no sign of Mary, but Edgar did not mind, because he was getting a nicely consistent series of stellar magnitudes which were lying smoothly on his curves. Everything was going well, though he did not stop to wonder just why Mary was so unusually late.

At last he saw the headlights of the car flickering on the horizon, and rather reluctantly broke off his observations. When the car had disappeared behind the hill, he was waiting with his hand on the switch. His timing was perfect; the instant the car came around the curve and the headlights shone on him, he closed the arc.

Meeting another car at night can be unpleasant enough even when you are prepared for it and are driving on a straight road. But if you are rounding a hairpin bend, and *know* that there is no other car coming, yet suddenly find yourself staring directly into a beam fifty times as powerful as any headlight—well, the results are more than unpleasant.

They were exactly what Edgar had calculated. He switched off his beam almost at once, but the car's own lights showed him all that he wanted to see. He watched them swing out over the valley and then curve down, ever more and more swiftly, until they disappeared below the crest of the hill. A red glow flared for a few seconds, but the explosion was barely audible, which was just as well, since Edgar did not want to disturb the servants.

He dismantled his little searchlight and returned to the telescope; he had not quite completed his observations. Then, satisfied that he had done a good night's work, he went to bed.

His sleep was sound but short, for about an hour later the telephone started to ring. No doubt someone had found the wreckage, but Edgar wished they could have left it until morning, for an astronomer needed all the sleep he could get. With some irritation he picked up the phone, and it was several seconds before he realized that his wife was at the other end of the line. She was calling from Courtenay Place, and wanted to know what had happened to Rupert.

It seemed that they had decided to make a clean breast of the whole affair, and Rupert (not unfortified by strong liquor) had agreed to be a man and break the news to Edgar. He was going to call back as soon as he had done this, and tell Mary how her husband had received it. She had waited with mounting impatience and alarm as long as she could, until at last anxiety had got the better of discretion.

I need hardly say that the shock to Edgar's already somewhat unbalanced nervous system was considerable. After Mary had been talking to her husband for several minutes, she realized that he had gone completely round the bend. It was not until the next morning that she discovered that this was precisely what Rupert had failed to do, unfortunately for him.

In the long run, I think Mary came out of it rather well. Rupert wasn't really very bright, and it would never have been a satisfactory match. As it was, when Edgar was duly certified, Mary received power of attorney for the estate and promptly moved to Dartmouth, where she took a charming flat near the Royal Naval College and seldom had to drive the new Bentley for herself.

But all that is by the way, concluded Harry, and before some of you skeptics ask me how I know all this, I got it from the dealer who purchased Edgar's telescopes when they locked him up. It's a sad fact that no one would believe his confession; the general opinion was that Rupert had had too much to drink and had been driving too fast on a dangerous road. That may be true, but I prefer to think it isn't. After all, that is such a humdrum way to die. To be killed by a death ray would be a fate much more fitting for a de Vere Courtenay—and in the circumstances I don't see how anyone can deny that it *was* a death ray that Edgar had used. It was a ray, and it killed someone. What more do you want?

Death and the Senator

Washington had never looked lovelier in the spring; and this was the last spring, thought Senator Steelman bleakly, that he would ever see. Even now, despite all that Dr. Jordan had told him, he could not fully accept the truth. In the past there had always been a way of escape; no defeat had been final. When men had betrayed him, he had discarded them—even ruined them, as a warning to others. But now the betrayal was within himself; already, it seemed, he could feel the labored beating of the heart that would soon be stilled. No point in planning now for the Presidential election of 1976; he might not even live to see the nominations. . . .

It was an end of dreams and ambition, and he could not console himself with the knowledge that for all men these must end someday. For him it was too soon; he thought of Cecil Rhodes, who had always been one of his heroes, crying "So much to do—so little time to do it in!" as he died before his fiftieth birthday. He was already older than Rhodes, and had done far less.

The car was taking him away from the Capitol;

there was symbolism in that, and he tried not to dwell upon it. Now he was abreast of the New Smithsonian— that vast complex of museums he had never had time to visit, though he had watched it spread along the Mall throughout the years he had been in Washington. How much he had missed, he told himself bitterly, in his relentless pursuit of power. The whole universe of art and culture had remained almost closed to him, and that was only part of the price that he had paid. He had become a stranger to his family and to those who were once his friends. Love had been sacrificed on the altar of ambition, and the sacrifice had been in vain. Was there anyone in all the world who would weep at his departure?

Yes, there was. The feeling of utter desolation relaxed its grip upon his soul. As he reached for the phone, he felt ashamed that he had to call the office to get this number, when his mind was cluttered with memories of so many less important things.

(There was the White House, almost dazzling in the spring sunshine. For the first time in his life he did not give it a second glance. Already it belonged to another world—a world that would never concern him again.)

The car circuit had no vision, but he did not need it to sense Irene's mild surprise—and her still milder pleasure.

"Hello, Renee—how are you all?"

"Fine, Dad. When are we going to see you?"

It was the polite formula his daughter always used on the rare occasions when he called. And invariably, except at Christmas or birthdays, his answer was a vague promise to drop around at some indefinite future date.

"I was wondering," he said slowly, almost apologetically, "if I could borrow the children for an afternoon. It's a long time since I've taken them out, and I felt like getting away from the office."

"But of course," Irene answered, her voice warming with pleasure. "They'll love it. When would you like them?"

"Tomorrow would be fine. I could call around twelve, and take them to the Zoo or the Smithsonian, or anywhere else they felt like visiting."

Now she was really startled, for she knew well enough that he was one of the busiest men in Washington, with a schedule planned weeks in advance. She would be wondering what had happened; he hoped she would not guess the truth. No reason why she should, for not even his secretary knew of the stabbing pains that had driven him to seek this long-overdue medical checkup.

"That would be wonderful. They were talking about you only yesterday, asking when they'd see you again."

His eyes misted, and he was glad that Renee could not see him.

"I'll be there at noon," he said hastily, trying to keep the emotion out of his voice. "My love to you all." He switched off before she could answer, and relaxed against the upholstery with a sigh of relief. Almost upon impulse, without conscious planning, he had taken the first step in the reshaping of his life. Though his own children were lost to him, a bridge across the generations remained intact. If he did nothing else, he must guard and strengthen it in the months that were left.

Taking two lively and inquisitive children through the natural-history building was not what the doctor would have ordered, but it was what he wanted to do. Joey and Susan had grown so much since their last meeting, and it required both physical and mental alertness to keep up with them. No sooner had they entered the rotunda than they broke away from him, and scampered toward the enormous elephant dominating the marble hall.

"What's that?" cried Joey.

"It's an elephant, stupid," answered Susan with all the crushing superiority of her seven years.

"I know it's an effelant," retorted Joey. "But what's its name?"

Senator Steelman scanned the label, but found no assistance there. This was one occasion when the risky adage "Sometimes wrong, never uncertain" was a safe guide to conduct.

"He was called—er—Jumbo," he said hastily. "Just look at those tusks!"

"Did he ever get toothache?"

"Oh no."

"Then how did he clean his teeth? Ma says that if I don't clean mine . . ."

Steelman saw where the logic of this was leading, and thought it best to change the subject.

"There's a lot more to see inside. Where do you want to start—birds, snakes, fish, mammals?"

"Snakes!" clamored Susan. "I wanted to keep one in a box, but Daddy said no. Do you think he'd change his mind if you asked him?"

"What's a mammal?" asked Joey, before Steelman could work out an answer to that.

"Come along," he said firmly. "I'll show you."

As they moved through the halls and galleries, the children darting from one exhibit to another, he felt at peace with the world. There was nothing like a museum for calming the mind, for putting the problems of everyday life in their true perspective. Here, surrounded by the infinite variety and wonder of Nature, he was reminded of truths he had forgotten. He was only one of a million million creatures that shared this planet Earth. The entire human race, with its hopes and fears, its triumphs and its follies, might be no more than an incident in the history of the world. As he stood before the monstrous bones of Diplodocus (the children for once awed and silent), he felt the winds of Eternity blowing through his soul. He could no longer take so seriously the gnawing of ambition, the belief that he was the man the nation needed. *What* nation, if it came to that? A mere two centuries ago this summer, the Declaration of Independence had been signed; but this old American had lain in the Utah rocks for a hundred million years. . . .

He was tired when they reached the Hall of Oceanic Life, with its dramatic reminder that Earth still possessed animals greater than any that the past could show. The ninety-foot blue whale plunging into the ocean, and all the other swift hunters of the sea, brought back memories of hours he had once spent on a tiny, glistening deck with a white sail billowing above him. That was another time when he had known contentment, listening to the swish of water past the prow, and the sighing of the wind through the rigging. He had not sailed for thirty years; this was another of the world's pleasures he had put aside.

"I don't like fish," complained Susan. "When do we get to the snakes?"

"Presently," he said. "But what's the hurry? There's plenty of time."

The words slipped out before he realized it. He checked his step, while the children ran on ahead. Then he smiled, without bitterness. For in a sense, it was true enough. There *was* plenty of time. Each day, each hour could be a universe of experience, if one used it properly. In the last weeks of his life, he would begin to live.

As yet, no one at the office suspected anything. Even his outing with the children had not caused much surprise; he had done such things before, suddenly canceling his appointments and leaving his staff to pick up the pieces. The pattern of his behavior had not yet changed, but in a few days it would be obvious to all his associates that something had happened. He owed it to them—and to the party—to break the news as soon as possible; there were, however, many personal decisions he had to make first, which he wished to settle in his own mind before he began the vast unwinding of his affairs.

There was another reason for his hesitancy. During his career, he had seldom lost a fight, and in the cut and thrust of political life he had given quarter to none. Now, facing his ultimate defeat, he dreaded the sympathy and the condolences that his many enemies would hasten to shower upon him. The attitude, he knew, was a foolish one—a remnant of his stubborn pride which was too much a part of his personality to vanish even under the shadow of death.

He carried his secret from committee room to White House to Capitol, and through all the labyrinths of Washington society, for more than two weeks. It was the finest performance of his career, but there was no one to appreciate it. At the end of that time he had completed his plan of action; it remained only to dispatch a few letters he had written in his own hand, and to call his wife.

The office located her, not without difficulty, in Rome. She was still beautiful, he thought, as her features swam on to the screen; she would have made a fine First Lady, and that would have been some compensation for the lost years. As far as he knew, she had looked forward to the prospect; but had he ever really understood what she wanted?

"Hello, Martin," she said, "I was expecting to hear from you. I suppose you want me to come back."

"Are you willing to?" he asked quietly. The gentleness of his voice obviously surprised her.

"I'd be a fool to say no, wouldn't I? But if they

don't elect you, I want to go my own way again. You must agree to that."

"They won't elect me. They won't even nominate me. You're the first to know this, Diana. In six months, I shall be dead."

The directness was brutal, but it had a purpose. That fraction-of-a-second delay while the radio waves flashed up to the communication satellites and back again to Earth had never seemed so long. For once, he had broken through the beautiful mask. Her eyes widened with disbelief, her hand flew to her lips.

"You're joking!"

"About *this*? It's true enough. My heart's worn out. Dr. Jordan told me, a couple of weeks ago. It's my own fault, of course, but let's not go into that."

"So that's why you've been taking out the children: I wondered what had happened."

He might have guessed that Irene would have talked with her mother. It was a sad reflection on Martin Steelman, if so commonplace a fact as showing an interest in his own grandchildren could cause curiosity.

"Yes," he admitted frankly. "I'm afraid I left it a little late. Now I'm trying to make up for lost time. Nothing else seems very important."

In silence, they looked into each other's eyes across the curve of the Earth, and across the empty desert of the dividing years. Then Diana answered, a little unsteadily, "I'll start packing right away."

Now that the news was out, he felt a great sense of relief. Even the sympathy of his enemies was not as hard to accept as he had feared. For overnight, indeed, he had no enemies. Men who had not spoken to him in years, except with invective, sent messages whose sincerity could not be doubted. Ancient quarrels evaporated, or turned out to be founded on misunderstandings. It was a pity that one had to die to learn these things. . . .

He also learned that, for a man of affairs, dying was a full-time job. There were successors to appoint, legal and financial mazes to untangle, committee and state business to wind up. The work of an energetic lifetime could not be terminated suddenly, as one switches off an electric light. It was astonishing how many responsibilities he had acquired, and how difficult it was to divest himself of them. He had never found it easy to delegate power (a fatal flaw, many critics had said, in a man who hoped to be Chief Executive), but now he must do so, before it slipped forever from his hands.

It was as if a great clock was running down, and there was no one to rewind it. As he gave away his books, read and destroyed old letters, closed useless accounts and files, dictated final instructions, and wrote farewell notes, he sometimes felt a sense of complete unreality. There was no pain; he could never have guessed that he did not have years of active life ahead of him. Only a few lines on a cardiogram lay like a roadblock across his future—or like a curse, written in some strange language the doctors alone could read.

Almost every day now Diana, Irene, or her husband brought the children to see him. In the past he had never felt at ease with Bill, but that, he knew, had been his own fault. You could not expect a son-in-law to replace a son, and it was unfair to blame Bill because he had not been cast in the image of Martin Steelman, Jr. Bill was a person in his own right; he had looked after Irene, made her happy, and fathered her children. That he lacked ambition was a flaw—if flaw indeed it was—that the Senator could at last forgive.

He could even think, without pain or bitterness, of his own son, who had traveled this road before him and now lay, one cross among many, in the United Nations cemetery at Capetown. He had never visited Martin's grave; in the days when he had the time,

white men were not popular in what was left of South
Africa. Now he could go if he wished, but he was
uncertain if it would be fair to harrow Diana with such
a mission. His own memories would not trouble him
much longer, but she would be left with hers.

Yet he would like to go, and felt it was his duty.
Moreover, it would be a last treat for the children. To
them it would be only a holiday in a strange land,
without any tinge of sorrow for an uncle they had
never known. He had started to make the arrangements when, for the second time within a month, his
whole world was turned upside down.

Even now, a dozen or more visitors would be waiting for him each morning when he arrived at his office. Not as many as in the old days, but still a sizable
crowd. He had never imagined, however, that Dr.
Harkness would be among them.

The sight of that thin, gangling figure made him
momentarily break his stride. He felt his cheeks flush,
his pulse quicken at the memory of ancient battles
across committee-room tables, of angry exchanges that
had reverberated along the myriad channels of the
ether. Then he relaxed; as far as he was concerned, all
that was over.

Harkness rose to his feet, a little awkwardly, as he
approached. Senator Steelman knew that initial embarrassment—he had seen it so often in the last few
weeks. Everyone he now met was automatically at a
disadvantage, always on the alert to avoid the one
subject that was taboo.

"Well, Doctor," he said. "This is a surprise—I never
expected to see *you* here."

He could not resist the little jab, and derived some
satisfaction at watching it go home. But it was free
from bitterness, as the other's smile acknowledged.

"Senator," replied Harkness, in a voice that was
pitched so low that he had to lean forward to hear it,

"I've some extremely important information for you. Can we speak alone for a few minutes? It won't take long."

Steelman nodded; he had his own ideas of what was important now, and felt only a mild curiosity as to why the scientist had come to see him. The man seemed to have changed a good deal since their last encounter, seven years ago. He was much more assured and self-confident, and had lost the nervous mannerisms that had helped to make him such an unconvincing witness.

"Senator," he began, when they were alone in the private office, "I've some news that may be quite a shock to you. I believe that you can be cured."

Steelman slumped heavily in his chair. This was the one thing he had never expected; from the first, he had not encumbered himself with the burden of vain hopes. Only a fool fought against the inevitable, and he had accepted his fate.

For a moment he could not speak; then he looked up at his old adversary and gasped: "Who told you that? All my doctors—"

"Never mind them; it's not their fault they're ten years behind the times. Look at this."

"What does it mean? I can't read Russian."

"It's the latest issue of the USSR *Journal of Space Medicine*. It arrived a few days ago, and we did the usual routine translation. This note here—the one I've marked—refers to some recent work at the Mechnikov Station."

"What's that?"

"You don't *know?* Why, that's their Satellite Hospital, the one they've built just below the Great Radiation Belt."

"Go on," said Steelman, in a voice that was suddenly dry and constricted. "I'd forgotten they'd called it that." He had hoped to end his life in peace, but now the past had come back to haunt him.

"Well, the note itself doesn't say much, but you can read a lot between the lines. It's one of those advance hints that scientists put out before they have time to write a full-fledged paper, so they can claim priority later. The title is: 'Therapeutic Effects of Zero Gravity on Circulatory Diseases.' What they've done is to induce heart disease artificially in rabbits and hamsters, and then take them up to the space station. In orbit, of course, nothing has any weight; the heart and muscles have practically no work to do. And the result is exactly what I tried to tell you, years ago. Even extreme cases can be arrested, and many can be cured."

The tiny, paneled office that had been the center of his world, the scene of so many conferences, the birthplace of so many plans, became suddenly unreal. Memory was much more vivid: he was back again at those hearings, in the fall of 1969, when the National Aeronautics and Space Administration's first decade of activity had been under review—and, frequently, under fire.

He had never been chairman of the Senate Committee on Astronautics, but he had been its most vocal and effective member. It was here that he had made his reputation as a guardian of the public purse, as a hardheaded man who could not be bamboozled by utopian scientific dreamers. He had done a good job; from that moment, he had never been far from the headlines. It was not that he had any particular feeling for space and science, but he knew a live issue when he saw one. Like a tape-recorder unrolling in his mind, it all came back. . . .

"Dr. Harkness, you are Technical Director of the National Aeronautics and Space Administration?"

"That is correct."

"I have here the figures for NASA's expenditure over the period 1959–69; they are quite impressive. At the moment the total is $82,547,450,000, and the estimate for fiscal 69–70 is well over ten billions. Perhaps you could give us some indication of the return we can expect from all this."

"I'll be glad to do so, Senator."

That was how it had started, on a firm but not unfriendly note. The hostility had crept in later. That it was unjustified, he had known at the time; any big organization had weaknesses and failures, and one which literally aimed at the stars could never hope for more than partial success. From the beginning, it had been realized that the conquest of space would be at least as costly in lives and treasure as the conquest of the air. In ten years, almost a hundred men had died—on Earth, in space, and upon the barren surface of the Moon. Now that the urgency of the early sixties was over, the public was asking "Why?" Steelman was shrewd enough to see himself as mouthpiece for those questioning voices. His performance had been cold and calculated; it was convenient to have a scapegoat, and Dr. Harkness was unlucky enough to be cast for the role.

"Yes, Doctor, I understand all the benefits we've received from space research in the way of improved communications and weather forecasting, and I'm sure everyone appreciates them. But almost all this work has been done with automatic, unmanned vehicles. What I'm worried about—what many people are worried about—is the mounting expense of the Man-in-Space program, and its very marginal utility. Since the original Dyna-Soar and Apollo projects, almost a decade ago, we've shot billions of dollars into space. And with what result? So that a mere handful of men can spend a few uncomfortable hours outside the atmosphere, achieving nothing that television cameras and automatic equipment couldn't do—much better and cheaper. And the lives that have been lost! None of us will forget those screams we heard coming over the radio when the X-21 burned up on re-entry. What right have we to send men to such deaths?"

He could still remember the hushed silence in the committee chamber when he had finished. His questions were very reasonable ones, and deserved to be answered. What was unfair was the rhetorical manner in which he had framed them and, above all, the fact that they were aimed at a man who could not answer them effectively. Steelman would not have tried such tactics on a von Braun or a Rickover; they would have given him at least as good as they received. But Harkness was no orator; if he had deep personal feelings, he kept them to himself. He was a good scientist, an able administrator—and a poor witness. It had been like shooting fish in a barrel. The reporters had loved it; he never knew which of them coined the nickname "Hapless Harkness."

"Now this plan of yours, Doctor, for a fifty-man space laboratory—*how* much did you say it would cost?"

"I've already told you—just under one and a half billions."

"And the annual maintenance?"

"Not more than $250,000,000."

"When we consider what's happened to previous estimates, you will forgive us if we look upon these figures with some skepticism. But even assuming that they are right, what will we get for the money?"

"We will be able to establish our first large-scale research station in space. So far, we have had to do our experimenting in cramped quarters aboard unsuitable vehicles, usually when they were engaged on some other mission. A permanent, manned satellite labora-

tory is essential. Without it, further progress is out of
the question. Astrobiology can hardly get started—"

"Astro what?"

"Astrobiology—the study of living organisms in space.
The Russians really started it when they sent up the
dog Laika in Sputnik II and they're still ahead of us in
this field. But no one's done any serious work on
insects or invertebrates—in fact, on any animals except dogs, mice, and monkeys."

"I see. Would I be correct in saying that you would
like funds for building a zoo in space?"

The laughter in the committee room had helped to
kill the project. And it had helped, Senator Steelman
now realized, to kill him.

He had only himself to blame, for Dr. Harkness had
tried, in his ineffectual way, to outline the benefits
that a space laboratory might bring. He had particularly stressed the medical aspects, promising nothing
but pointing out the possibilities. Surgeons, he had
suggested, would be able to develop new techniques in
an environment where the organs had no weight; men
might live longer, freed from the wear and tear of
gravity, for the strain on heart and muscles would be
enormously reduced. Yes, he had mentioned the heart;
but that had been of no interest to Senator Steelman—
healthy, and ambitious, and anxious to make good
copy. . . .

"Why have you come to tell me this?" he said dully.
"Couldn't you let me die in peace?"

"That's the point," said Harkness impatiently.
"There's no need to give up hope."

"Because the Russians have cured some hamsters
and rabbits?"

"They've done much more than that. The paper I
showed you only quoted the preliminary results; it's

already a year out of date. They don't want to raise false hopes, so they are keeping as quiet as possible."

"How do you know this?"

Harkness looked surprised.

"Why, I called Professor Stanyukovitch, my opposite number. It turned out that he was up on the Mechnikov Station, which proves how important they consider this work. He's an old friend of mine, and I took the liberty of mentioning your case."

The dawn of hope, after its long absence, can be as painful as its departure. Steelman found it hard to breathe and for a dreadful moment he wondered if the final attack had come. But it was only excitement; the constriction in his chest relaxed, the ringing in his ears faded away, and he heard Dr. Harkness' voice saying: "He wanted to know if you could come to Astrograd right away, so I said I'd ask you. If you can make it, there's a flight from New York at ten-thirty tomorrow morning."

Tomorrow he had promised to take the children to the Zoo; it would be the first time he had let them down. The thought gave him a sharp stab of guilt, and it required almost an effort of will to answer: "I can make it."

He saw nothing of Moscow during the few minutes that the big intercontinental ramjet fell down from the stratosphere. The view-screens were switched off during the descent, for the sight of the ground coming straight up as a ship fell vertically on its sustaining jets was highly disconcerting to passengers.

At Moscow he changed to a comfortable but old-fashioned turboprop, and as he flew eastward into the night he had his first real opportunity for reflection. It was a very strange question to ask himself, but was he altogether glad that the future was no longer wholly certain? His life, which a few hours ago had seemed so

simple, had suddenly become complex again, as it
opened out once more into possibilities he had learned
to put aside. Dr. Johnson had been right when he said
that nothing settles a man's mind more wonderfully
than the knowledge that he will be hanged in the
morning. For the converse was certainly true—nothing
unsettled it so much as the thought of a reprieve.

He was asleep when they touched down at Astrograd,
the space capital of the USSR. When the gentle impact of the landing shook him awake, for a moment he
could not imagine where he was. Had he dreamed that
he was flying halfway around the world in search of
life? No; it was not a dream, but it might well be a
wild-goose chase.

Twelve hours later, he was still waiting for the answer. The last instrument reading had been taken; the
spots of light on the cardiograph display had ceased
their fateful dance. The familiar routine of the medical
examination and the gentle, competent voices of the
doctors and nurses had done much to relax his mind.
And it was very restful in the softly lit reception room,
where the specialists had asked him to wait while they
conferred together. Only the Russian magazines, and
a few portraits of somewhat hirsute pioneers of Soviet
medicine, reminded him that he was no longer in his
own country.

He was not the only patient. About a dozen men
and women, of all ages, were sitting around the wall,
reading magazines and trying to appear at ease. There
was no conversation, no attempt to catch anyone's
eye. Every soul in this room was in his private limbo,
suspended between life and death. Though they were
linked together by a common misfortune, the link did
not extend to communication. Each seemed as cut off
from the rest of the human race as if he was already
speeding through the cosmic gulfs where lay his only
hope.

But in the far corner of the room, there was an exception. A young couple—neither could have been more than twenty-five—were huddling together in such desperate misery that at first Steelman found the spectacle annoying. No matter how bad their own problems, he told himself severely, people should be more considerate. They should hide their emotions—especially in a place like this, where they might upset others.

His annoyance quickly turned to pity, for no heart can remain untouched for long at the sight of simple, unselfish love in deep distress. As the minutes dripped away in a silence broken only by the rustling of papers and the scraping of chairs, his pity grew almost to an obsession.

What was their story, he wondered? The boy had sensitive, intelligent features; he might have been an artist, a scientist, a musician—there was no way of telling. The girl was pregnant; she had one of those homely peasant faces so common among Russian women. She was far from beautiful, but sorrow and love had given her features a luminous sweetness. Steelman found it hard to take his eyes from her—for somehow, though there was not the slightest physical resemblance, she reminded him of Diana. Thirty years ago, as they had walked from the church together, he had seen that same glow in the eyes of his wife. He had almost forgotten it; was the fault his, or hers, that it had faded so soon?

Without any warning, his chair vibrated beneath him. A swift, sudden tremor had swept through the building, as if a giant hammer had smashed against the ground, many miles away. An earthquake? Steelman wondered; then he remembered where he was, and started counting seconds.

He gave up when he reached sixty; presumably the sound-proofing was so good that the slower, air-borne noise had not reached him, and only the shock wave through the ground recorded the fact that a thousand tons had just leapt into the sky. Another minute passed before he heard, distant but clear, a sound as of a thunderstorm raging below the edge of the world. It was even more miles away than he had dreamed; what the noise must be like at the launching site was beyond imagination.

Yet that thunder would not trouble him, he knew, when he also rose into the sky; the speeding rocket would leave it far behind. Nor would the thrust of acceleration be able to touch his body, as it rested in its bath of warm water—more comfortable even than this deeply padded chair.

That distant rumble was still rolling back from the edge of space when the door of the waiting room opened and the nurse beckoned to him. Though he felt many eyes following him, he did not look back as he walked out to receive his sentence.

The news services tried to get in contact with him all the way back from Moscow, but he refused to accept the calls. "Say I'm sleeping and mustn't be disturbed," he told the stewardess. He wondered who had tipped them off, and felt annoyed at this invasion of his privacy. Yet privacy was something he had avoided for years, and had learned to appreciate only in the last few weeks. He could not blame the reporters and commentators if they assumed that he had reverted to type.

They were waiting for him when the ramjet touched down at Washington. He knew most of them by name, and some were old friends, genuinely glad to hear the news that had raced ahead of him.

"What does it feel like, Senator," said Macauley, of the *Times*, "to know you're back in harness? I take it that it's true—the Russians can cure you?"

"They *think* they can," he answered cautiously. "This

is a new field of medicine, and no one can promise anything."

"When do you leave for space?"

"Within the week, as soon as I've settled some affairs here."

"And when will you be back—if it works?"

"That's hard to say. Even if everything goes smoothly, I'll be up there at least six months."

Involuntarily, he glanced at the sky. At dawn or sunset—even during the daytime, if one knew where to look—the Mechnikov Station was a spectacular sight, more brilliant than any of the stars. But there were now so many satellites of which this was true that only an expert could tell one from another.

"Six months," said a newsman thoughtfully. "That means you'll be out of the picture for seventy-six."

"But nicely in it for 1980," said another.

"*And* 1984," added a third. There was a general laugh; people were already making jokes about 1984, which had once seemed so far in the future, but would soon be a date no different from any other . . . it was hoped.

The ears and the microphones were waiting for his reply. As he stood at the foot of the ramp, once more the focus of attention and curiosity, he felt the old excitement stirring in his veins. What a comeback it would be, to return from space a new man! It would give him a glamour that no other candidate could match; there was something Olympian, almost godlike, about the prospect. Already he found himself trying to work it into his election slogans. . . .

"Give me time to make my plans," he said. "It's going to take me a while to get used to this. But I promise you a statement before I leave Earth."

Before I leave Earth. Now, there was a fine, dramatic phrase. He was still savoring its rhythm with his mind when he saw Diana coming toward him from the airport buildings.

Already she had changed, as he himself was changing; in her eyes was a wariness and reserve that had not been there two days ago. It said, as clearly as any words: "Is it going to happen, all over again?" Though the day was warm, he felt suddenly cold, as if he had caught a chill on those far Siberian plains.

But Joey and Susan were unchanged, as they ran to greet him. He caught them up in his arms, and buried his face in their hair, so that the cameras would not see the tears that had started from his eyes. As they clung to him in the innocent, unself-conscious love of childhood, he knew what his choice would have to be.

They alone had known him when he was free from the itch for power; that was the way they must remember him, if they remembered him at all.

"Your conference call, Mr. Steelman," said his secretary. "I'm routing it on to your private screen."

He swiveled round in his chair and faced the gray panel on the wall. As he did so, it split into two vertical sections. On the right half was a view of an office much like his own, and only a few miles away. But on the left—

Professor Stanyukovitch, lightly dressed in shorts and singlet, was floating in mid-air a good foot above his seat. He grabbed it when he saw that he had company, pulled himself down, and fastened a webbed belt around his waist. Behind him were ranged banks of communications equipment; and behind those, Steelman knew, was space.

Dr. Harkness spoke first, from the right-hand screen.

"We were expecting to hear from you, Senator. Professor Stanyukovitch tells me that everything is ready."

"The next supply ship," said the Russian, "comes

up in two days. It will be taking me back to Earth, but I hope to see you before I leave the station."

His voice was curiously high-pitched, owing to the thin oxyhelium atmosphere he was breathing. Apart from that, there was no sense of distance, no background of interference. Though Stanyukovitch was thousands of miles away, and racing through space at four miles a second, he might have been in the same office. Steelman could even hear the faint whirring of electric motors from the equipment racks behind him.

"Professor," answered Steelman, "there are a few things I'd like to ask before I go."

"Certainly."

Now he could tell that Stanyukovitch was a long way off. There was an appreciable time lag before his reply arrived; the station must be above the far side of the Earth.

"When I was at Astrograd, I noticed many other patients at the clinic. I was wondering—on what basis do you select those for treatment?"

This time the pause was much greater than the delay due to the sluggish speed of radio waves. Then Stanyukovitch answered: "Why, those with the best chance of responding."

"But your accommodation must be very limited. You must have many other candidates besides myself."

"I don't quite see the point—" interrupted Dr. Harkness, a little too anxiously.

Steelman swung his eyes to the right-hand screen. It was quite difficult to recognize, in the man staring back at him, the witness who had squirmed beneath his needling only a few years ago. That experience had tempered Harkness, had given him his baptism in the art of politics. Steelman had taught him much, and he had applied his hard-won knowledge.

His motives had been obvious from the first. Harkness would have been less than human if he did not relish this sweetest of revenges, this triumphant vindication of his faith. And as Space Administration Director, he was well aware that half his budget battles would be over when all the world knew that a potential President of the United States was in a Russian space hospital . . . because his own country did not possess one.

"Dr. Harkness," said Steelman gently, "this is *my* affair. I'm still waiting for your answer, Professor."

Despite the issues involved, he was quite enjoying this. The two scientists, of course, were playing for identical stakes. Stanyukovitch had his problems too; Steelman could guess the discussions that had taken place at Astrograd and Moscow, and the eagerness with which the Soviet astronauts had grasped this opportunity—which, it must be admitted, they had richly earned.

It was an ironic situation, unimaginable only a dozen years before. Here were NASA and the USSR Commission of Astronautics working hand in hand, using him as a pawn for their mutual advantage. He did not resent this, for in their place he would have done the same. But he had no wish to be a pawn: he was an individual who still had some control of his own destiny.

"It's quite true," said Stanyukovitch, very reluctantly, "that we can only take a limited number of patients here in Mechnikov. In any case, the station's a research laboratory, not a hospital."

"How many?" asked Steelman relentlessly.

"Well—fewer than ten," admitted Stanyukovitch, still more unwillingly.

It was an old problem, of course, though he had never imagined that it would apply to him. From the depths of memory there flashed a newspaper item he had come across long ago. When penicillin had been first discovered, it was so rare that if both Churchill and Roosevelt had been dying for lack of it, only one could have been treated. . . .

Fewer than ten. He had seen a dozen waiting at Astrograd, and how many were there in the whole world? Once again, as it had done so often in the last few days, the memory of those desolate lovers in the reception room came back to haunt him. Perhaps they were beyond his aid; he would never know.

But one thing he did know. He bore a responsibility that he could not escape. It was true that no man could foresee the future, and the endless consequences of his actions. Yet if it had not been for him, by this time his own country might have had a space hospital circling beyond the atmosphere. How many American lives were upon his conscience? Could he accept the help he had denied to others? Once he might have done so—but not now.

"Gentlemen," he said, "I can speak frankly with you both, for I know your interests are identical." (His mild irony, he saw, did not escape them.) "I appreciate your help and the trouble you have taken; I am sorry it has been wasted. No—don't protest; this isn't a sudden, quixotic decision on my part. If I was ten years younger, it might be different. Now I feel that this opportunity should be given to someone else— especially in view of my record." He glanced at Dr. Harkness, who gave an embarrassed smile. "I also have other, personal reasons, and there's no chance that I will change my mind. Please don't think me rude or ungrateful, but I don't wish to discuss the matter any further. Thank you again, and good-by."

He broke the circuit; and as the image of the two astonished scientists faded, peace came flooding back into his soul.

Imperceptibly, spring merged into summer. The eagerly awaited Bicentenary celebrations came and went;

for the first time in years, he was able to enjoy Independence Day as a private citizen. Now he could sit back and watch the others perform—or he could ignore them if he wished.

Because the ties of a lifetime were too strong to break, and it would be his last opportunity to see many old friends, he spent hours looking in on both conventions and listening to the commentators. Now that he saw the whole world beneath the light of Eternity, his emotions were no longer involved; he understood the issues, and appreciated the arguments, but already he was as detached as an observer from another planet. The tiny, shouting figures on the screen were amusing marionettes, acting out roles in a play that was entertaining, but no longer important—at least, to him.

But it was important to his grandchildren, who would one day move out onto this same stage. He had not forgotten that; they were his share of the future, whatever strange form it might take. And to understand the future, it was necessary to know the past.

He was taking them into that past, as the car swept along Memorial Drive. Diana was at the wheel, with Irene beside her, while he sat with the children, pointing out the familiar sights along the highway. Familiar to him, but not to them; even if they were not old enough to understand all that they were seeing, he hoped they would remember.

Past the marble stillness of Arlington (the thought again of Martin, sleeping on the other side of the world) and up into the hills the car wound its effortless way. Behind them, like a city seen through a mirage, Washington danced and trembled in the summer haze, until the curve of the road hid it from view.

It was quiet at Mount Vernon; there were few visitors so early in the week. As they left the car and walked toward the house, Steelman wondered what the first President of the United States would have thought could he have seen his home as it was today. He could never have dreamed that it would enter its second century still perfectly preserved, a changeless island in the hurrying river of time.

They walked slowly through the beautifully proportioned rooms, doing their best to answer the children's endless questions, trying to assimilate the flavor of an infinitely simpler, infinitely more leisurely mode of life. (But had it seemed simple or leisurely to those who lived it?) It was so hard to imagine a world without electricity, without radio, without any power save that of muscle, wind, and water. A world where nothing moved faster than a running horse, and most men died within a few miles of the place where they were born.

The heat, the walking, and the incessant questions proved more tiring than Steelman had expected. When they had reached the Music Room, he decided to rest. There were some attractive benches out on the porch, where he could sit in the fresh air and feast his eyes upon the green grass of the lawn.

"Meet me outside," he explained to Diana, "when you've done the kitchen and the stables. I'd like to sit down for a while."

"You're sure you're quite all right?" she said anxiously.

"I never felt better, but I don't want to overdo it. Besides, the kids have drained me dry—I can't think of any more answers. You'll have to invent some; the kitchen's your department, anyway."

Diana smiled.

"I was never much good in it, was I? But I'll do my best—I don't suppose we'll be more than thirty minutes."

When they had left him, he walked slowly out onto the lawn. Here Washington must have stood, two centuries ago, watching the Potomac wind its way to the sea, thinking of past wars and future problems. And here Martin Steelman, thirty-eighth President of the United States, might have stood a few months hence, had the fates ruled otherwise.

He could not pretend that he had no regrets, but they were very few. Some men could achieve both power and happiness, but that gift was not for him. Sooner or later, his ambition would have consumed him. In the last few weeks he had known contentment, and for that no price was too great.

He was still marveling at the narrowness of his escape when his time ran out and Death fell softly from the summer sky.

Trouble with Time

"We don't have much crime on Mars," said Detective Inspector Rawlings, a little sadly. "In fact, that's the chief reason I'm going back to the Yard. If I stayed here much longer, I'd get completely out of practice."

We were sitting in the main observation lounge of the Phobos Spaceport, looking out across the jagged, sun-drenched crags of the tiny moon. The ferry rocket that had brought us up from Mars had left ten minutes ago, and was now beginning the long fall back to the ocher-tinted globe hanging there against the stars. In half an hour we would be boarding the liner for Earth—a world upon which most of the passengers had never set foot, but which they still called "home."

"At the same time," continued the Inspector, "now and then there's a case that makes life interesting. You're an art dealer, Mr. Maccar; I'm sure you heard about that spot of bother at Meridian City a couple of months ago."

"I don't think so," replied the plump, olive-skinned little man I'd taken for just another returning tourist. Presumably the Inspector had already checked through the passenger list; I wondered how much he knew about me, and tried to reassure myself that my conscience was—well—reasonably clear. After all, everybody took *something* out through Martian Customs—

"It's been rather well hushed up," said the Inspector, "but you can't keep these things quiet for long. Anyway, a jewel thief from Earth tried to steal Meridian Museum's greatest treasure—the Siren Goddess."

"But that's absurd!" I objected.. "It's priceless, of course—but it's only a lump of sandstone. You couldn't sell it to anyone—you might just as well steal the Mona Lisa."

The Inspector grinned, rather mirthlessly. *"That's* happened once," he said. "Maybe the motive was the same. There are collectors who would give a fortune for such an object, even if they could only look at it themselves. Don't you agree, Mr. Maccar?"

"That's perfectly true. In my business, you meet all sorts of crazy people."

"Well, this chappie—name's Danny Weaver—had been well paid by one of them. And if it hadn't been for a piece of fantastically bad luck, he might have brought it off."

The Spaceport P.A. system apologized for a further slight delay owing to final fuel checks, and asked a number of passengers to report to Information. While we were waiting for the announcement to finish, I recalled what little I knew about the Siren Goddess. Though I'd never seen the original, like most other departing tourists I had a replica in my baggage. It bore the certificate of the Mars Bureau of Antiquities, guaranteeing that "this full-scale reproduction is an exact copy of the so-called Siren Goddess, discovered in the Mare Sirenium by the Third Expedition, A.D. 2012 (A.M. 23)."

It's quite a tiny thing to have caused so much controversy. Only eight or nine inches high—you wouldn't look at it twice if you saw it in a museum on Earth.

The head of a young woman, with slightly oriental features, elongated earlobes, hair curled in tight ringlets close to the scalp, lips half parted in an expression of pleasure or surprise—that's all. But it's an enigma so baffling that it's inspired a hundred religious sects, and driven quite a few archaeologists round the bend. For a perfectly human head has no right whatsoever to be found on Mars, whose only intelligent inhabitants were crustaceans—"educated lobsters," as the newspapers are fond of calling them. The aboriginal Martians never came near to achieving space flight, and in any event their civilization died before men existed on Earth. No wonder the Goddess is the solar system's number-one mystery; I don't suppose we'll find the answer in my lifetime—if we ever do.

"Danny's plan was beautifully simple," continued the Inspector. "You know how absolutely dead a Martian city gets on Sunday, when everything closes down and the colonists stay home to watch the TV from Earth. Danny was counting on this, when he checked into the hotel in Meridian West, late Friday afternoon. He'd have Saturday for reconnoitering the Museum, an undisturbed Sunday for the job itself, and on Monday morning he'd be just another tourist leaving town. . . .

"Early Saturday he strolled through the little park and crossed over into Meridian East, where the Museum stands. In case you don't know, the city gets its name because it's exactly on longitude one hundred and eighty degrees; there's a big stone slab in the park with the prime meridian engraved on it, so that visitors can get themselves photographed standing in two hemispheres at once. Amazing what simple things amuse some people.

"Danny spent the day going over the Museum, exactly like any other tourist determined to get his money's worth. But at closing time he didn't leave; he'd holed up in one of the galleries not open to the public, where the Museum had been arranging a Late Canal Period reconstruction but had run out of money before the job could be finished. He stayed there until about midnight, just in case there were any enthusiastic researchers still in the building. Then he emerged and got to work."

"Just a minute," I interrupted. "What about the night watchman?"

The Inspector laughed.

"My dear chap! They don't have such luxuries on Mars. There weren't even any alarms, for who would bother to steal lumps of stone? True, the Goddess was sealed up neatly in a strong glass-and-metal cabinet, just in case some souvenir hunter took a fancy to her. But even if she were stolen, there was nowhere the thief could hide, and of course all outgoing traffic would be searched as soon as the statue was missed."

That was true enough. I'd been thinking in terms of Earth, forgetting that every city on Mars is a closed little world of its own beneath the force-field that protects it from the freezing near-vacuum. Beyond those electronic shields is the utterly hostile emptiness of the Martian Outback, where a man will die in seconds without protection. That makes law enforcement very easy; no wonder there's so little crime on Mars. . . .

"Danny had a beautiful set of tools, as specialized as a watchmaker's. The main item was a microsaw no bigger than a soldering iron; it had a wafer-thin blade, driven at a million cycles a second by an ultrasonic power pack. It would go through glass or metal like butter—and left a cut only about as thick as a hair. Which was very important for Danny, since he had to leave no traces of his handiwork.

"I suppose you've guessed how he intended to operate. He was going to cut through the base of the cabinet, and substitute one of those souvenir replicas for the real Goddess. It might be a couple of years before some inquisitive expert discovered the awful truth; long before then the original would have traveled back to Earth, perfectly disguised as a copy of itself, with a genuine certificate of authenticity. Pretty neat, eh?

"It must have been a weird business, working in that darkened gallery with all those million-year-old carvings and unexplainable artifacts around him. A museum on Earth is bad enough at night, but at least it's—well—*human*. And Gallery Three, which houses the Goddess, is particularly unsettling. It's full of bas-reliefs showing quite incredible animals fighting each other; they look rather like giant beetles, and most paleontologists flatly deny that they could ever have existed. But imaginary or not, they belonged to this world, and they didn't disturb Danny as much as the Goddess, staring at him across the ages and defying him to explain her presence here. She gave him the creeps. How do I know? He told me.

"Danny set to work on that cabinet as carefully as any diamond cutter preparing to cleave a gem. It took most of the night to slice out the trap door, and it was nearly dawn when he relaxed and put down the saw. There was still a lot of work to do, but the hardest part was over. Putting the replica into the case, checking its appearance against the photos he'd thoughtfully brought with him, and covering up his traces might take most of Sunday, but that didn't worry him in the least. He had another twenty-four hours, and would positively welcome Monday's first visitors so that he could mingle with them and make his inconspicuous exit.

It was a perfectly horrible shock to his nervous system, therefore, when the main doors were noisily unbarred at eight thirty and the museum staff—all six of them—started to open up for the day. Danny bolted for the emergency exit, leaving everything behind— tools, Goddesses, the lot. He had another big surprise when he found himself in the street; it should have been completely deserted at this time of day, with everyone at home reading the Sunday papers. But here were the citizens of Meridian East, as large as life, heading for plant or office on what was obviously a normal working day.

"By the time poor Danny got back to his hotel, we were waiting for him. We couldn't claim much credit for deducing that only a visitor from Earth—and a very recent one at that—could have overlooked Meridian City's chief claim to fame. And I presume you know what *that* is."

"Frankly, I don't," I answered. "You can't see much of Mars in six weeks, and I never went east of the Syrtis Major."

"Well, it's absurdly simple, but we shouldn't be too hard on Danny; even the locals occasionally fall into the same trap. It's something that doesn't bother us on Earth, where we've been able to dump the problem in the Pacific Ocean. But Mars, of course, is all dry land; and that means that *somebody* has to live with the International Date Line. . . .

"Danny, you see, had worked from Meridian West. It was Sunday over there all right—and it was still Sunday when we picked him up back at the hotel. But over in Meridian East, half a mile away, it was only Saturday. That little trip across the park had made all the difference; I told you it was rotten luck."

There was a long moment of silent sympathy; then I asked, "What did he get?"

"Three years," said Inspector Rawlings.

"That doesn't seem very much."

"Mars years; that makes it almost six of ours. And a whacking fine which, by an odd coincidence, came to just the refund value of his return ticket to Earth. He isn't in jail, of course; Mars can't afford that kind of nonproductive luxury. Danny has to work for a living, under discreet surveillance. I told you that the Meridian Museum couldn't afford a night watchman. Well, it has one now. Guess who."

"All passengers prepare to board in ten minutes! Please collect your hand baggage!" ordered the loud-speakers.

As we started to move toward the air lock, I couldn't help asking one more question.

"What about the people who put Danny up to it? There must have been a lot of money behind him. Did you get them?"

"Not yet; they'd covered their tracks pretty thoroughly, and I believe Danny was telling the truth when he said he couldn't give us any leads. Still, it's not my case; as I told you, I'm going back to my old job at the Yard. But a policeman always keeps his eyes open—like an art dealer, eh, Mr. Maccar? Why, you look a bit green about the gills. Have one of my space-sickness tablets."

"No, thank you," answered Mr. Maccar, "I'm quite all right."

His tone was distinctly unfriendly; the social temperature seemed to have dropped below zero in the last few minutes. I looked at Mr. Maccar, and I looked at the Inspector. And suddenly I realized that we were going to have a very interesting trip.

Before Eden

"I guess," said Jerry Garfield, cutting the engines, "that this is the end of the line." With a gentle sigh, the underjets faded out; deprived of its air cushion, the scout car *Rambling Wreck* settled down upon the twisted rocks of the Hesperian Plateau.

There was no way forward; neither on its jets nor its tractors could S.5—to give the *Wreck* its official name—scale the escarpment that lay ahead. The South Pole of Venus was only thirty miles away, but it might have been on another planet. They would have to turn back, and retrace their four-hundred-mile journey through this nightmare landscape.

The weather was fantastically clear, with visibility of almost a thousand yards. There was no need of radar to show the cliffs ahead; for once, the naked eye was good enough. The green auroral light, filtering down through clouds that had rolled unbroken for a million years, gave the scene an underwater appearance, and the way in which all distant objects blurred into the haze added to the impression. Sometimes it was easy to believe that they were driving across a shallow sea bed, and more than once Jerry had imagined that he had seen fish floating overhead.

"Shall I call the ship, and say we're turning back?" he asked.

"Not yet," said Dr. Hutchins. "I want to think."

Jerry shot an appealing glance at the third member of the crew, but found no moral support there. Coleman was just as bad; although the two men argued furiously half the time, they were both scientists and therefore, in the opinion of a hardheaded engineer-navigator, not wholly responsible citizens. If Cole and Hutch had bright ideas about going forward, there was nothing he could do except register a protest.

Hutchins was pacing back and forth in the tiny cabin, studying charts and instruments. Presently he swung the car's searchlight toward the cliffs, and began to examine them carefully with binoculars. Surely, thought Jerry, he doesn't expect me to drive up there! S.5 was a hovertrack, not a mountain goat. . . .

Abruptly, Hutchins found something. He released his breath in a sudden explosive gasp, then turned to Coleman.

"Look!" he said, his voice full of excitement. "Just to the left of that black mark! Tell me what you see."

He handed over the glasses, and it was Coleman's turn to stare.

"Well I'm damned," he said at length. "You were right. There *are* rivers on Venus. That's a dried-up waterfall."

"So you owe me one dinner at the Bel Gourmet when we get back to Cambridge. With champagne."

"No need to remind me. Anyway, it's cheap at the price. But this still leaves your other theories strictly on the crackpot level."

"Just a minute," interjected Jerry. "What's all this about rivers and waterfalls? Everyone knows they can't exist on Venus. It never gets cold enough on this steam bath of a planet for the clouds to condense."

"Have you looked at the thermometer lately?" asked Hutchins with deceptive mildness.

"I've been slightly too busy driving."

"Then I've news for you. It's down to two hundred and thirty, and still falling. Don't forget—we're almost at the Pole, it's wintertime, and we're sixty thousand feet above the lowlands. All this adds up to a distinct nip in the air. If the temperature drops a few more degrees, we'll have rain. The water will be boiling, of course—but it will be water. And though George won't admit it yet, this puts Venus in a completely different light."

"Why?" asked Jerry, though he had already guessed.

"Where there's water, there may be life. We've been in too much of a hurry to assume that Venus is sterile, merely because the average temperature's over five hundred degrees. It's a lot colder here, and that's why I've been so anxious to get to the Pole. There are lakes up here in the highlands, and I want to look at them."

"But *boiling* water!" protested Coleman. "Nothing could live in that!"

"There are algae that manage it on Earth. And if we've learned one thing since we started exploring the planets, it's this: wherever life has the slightest chance of surviving, you'll find it. This is the only chance it's ever had on Venus."

"I wish we could test your theory. But you can see for yourself—we can't go up that cliff."

"Perhaps not in the car. But it won't be too difficult to climb those rocks, even wearing thermosuits. All we need do is walk a few miles toward the Pole; according to the radar maps, it's fairly level once you're over the rim. We could manage in—oh, twelve hours at the most. Each of us has been out for longer than that, in much worse conditions."

That was perfectly true. Protective clothing that had been designed to keep men alive in the Venusian lowlands would have an easy job here, where it was only a hundred degrees hotter than Death Valley in midsummer.

"Well," said Coleman, "you know the regulations. You can't go by yourself, and someone has to stay here to keep contact with the ship. How do we settle it this time—chess or cards?"

"Chess takes too long," said Hutchins, "especially when you two play it." He reached into the chart table and produced a well-worn pack. "Cut them, Jerry."

"Ten of spades. Hope you can beat it, George."

"So do I. Damn—only five of clubs. Well, give my regards to the Venusians."

Despite Hutchins' assurance, it was hard work climbing the escarpment. The slope was not too steep, but the weight of oxygen gear, refrigerated thermosuit, and scientific equipment came to more than a hundred pounds per man. The lower gravity—thirteen per cent weaker than Earth's—gave a little help, but not much, as they toiled up screes, rested on ledges to regain breath, and then clambered on again through the submarine twilight. The emerald glow that washed around them was brighter than that of the full moon on Earth. A moon would have been wasted on Venus, Jerry told himself; it could never have been seen from the surface, there were no oceans for it to rule—and the incessant aurora was a far more constant source of light.

They had climbed more than two thousand feet before the ground leveled out into a gentle slope, scarred here and there by channels that had clearly been cut by running water. After a little searching, they came across a gulley wide and deep enough to merit the name of river bed, and started to walk along it.

"I've just thought of something," said Jerry after they had traveled a few hundred yards. "Suppose there's a storm up ahead of us? I don't feel like facing a tidal wave of boiling water."

"If there's a storm," replied Hutchins a little impatiently, "we'll hear it. There'll be plenty of time to reach high ground."

He was undoubtedly right, but Jerry felt no happier as they continued to climb the gently shelving watercourse. His uneasiness had been growing ever since they had passed over the brow of the cliff and had lost radio contact with the scout car. In this day and age, to be out of touch with one's fellow men was a unique and unsettling experience. It had never happened to Jerry before in all his life; even aboard the *Morning Star,* when they were a hundred million miles from Earth, he could always send a message to his family and get a reply back within minutes. But now, a few yards of rock had cut him off from the rest of mankind; if anything happened to them here, no one would ever know, unless some later expedition found their bodies. George would wait for the agreed number of hours; then he would head back to the ship—alone. I guess I'm not really the pioneering type, Jerry told himself. I like running complicated machines, and that's how I got involved in space flight. But I never stopped to think where it would lead, and now it's too late to change my mind. . . .

They had traveled perhaps three miles toward the Pole, following the meanders of the river bed, when Hutchins stopped to make observations and collect specimens. "Still getting colder!" he said. "The temperature's down to one hundred and ninety-nine. That's far and away the lowest ever recorded on Venus. I wish we could call George and let him know."

Jerry tried all the wave bands; he even attempted to raise the ship—the unpredictable ups and downs of the planet's ionosphere sometimes made such long-distance reception possible—but there was not a whisper of a carrier wave above the roar and crackle of the Venusian thunderstorms.

"This is even better," said Hutchins, and now there was real excitement in his voice. "The oxygen concentration's way up—fifteen parts in a million. It was only five back at the car, and down in the lowlands you can scarcely detect it."

"But fifteen in a *million!*" protested Jerry. "Nothing could breathe that!"

"You've got hold of the wrong end of the stick," Hutchins explained. "Nothing does breathe it. Something *makes* it. Where do you think Earth's oxygen comes from? It's all produced by life—by growing plants. Before there were plants on Earth, our atmosphere was just like this one—a mess of carbon dioxide and ammonia and methane. Then vegetation evolved, and slowly converted the atmosphere into something that animals could breathe."

"I see," said Jerry, "and you think that the same process has just started here?"

"It looks like it. *Something* not far from here is producing oxygen—and plant life is the simplest explanation."

"And where there are plants," mused Jerry, "I suppose you'll have animals, sooner or later."

"Yes," said Hutchins, packing his gear and starting up the gulley, "though it takes a few hundred million years. We may be too soon—but I hope not."

"That's all very well," Jerry answered. "But suppose we meet something that doesn't like us? We've no weapons."

Hutchins gave a snort of disgust.

"And we don't need them. Have you stopped to think what we look like? Any animal would run a mile at the sight of us."

There was some truth in that. The reflecting metal foil of their thermosuits covered them from head to foot like flexible, glittering armor. No insects had more elaborate antennas than those mounted on their helmets and back packs, and the wide lenses through which they stared out at the world looked like blank yet monstrous eyes. Yes, there were few animals on Earth that would stop to argue with such apparitions; but any Venusians might have different ideas.

Jerry was still mulling this over when they came upon the lake. Even at that first glimpse, it made him think not of the life they were seeking, but of death. Like a black mirror, it lay amid a fold of the hills; its far edge was hidden in the eternal mist, and ghostly columns of vapor swirled and danced upon its surface. All it needed, Jerry told himself, was Charon's ferry waiting to take them to the other side—or the Swan of Tuonela swimming majestically back and forth as it guarded the entrace to the Underworld. . . .

Yet for all this, it was a miracle—the first free water that men had ever found on Venus. Hutchins was already on his knees, almost in an attitude of prayer. But he was only collecting drops of the precious liquid to examine through his pocket microscope.

"Anything there?" asked Jerry anxiously.

Hutchins shook his head.

"If there is, it's too small to see with this instrument. I'll tell you more when we're back at the ship." He sealed a test tube and placed it in his collecting bag, as tenderly as any prospector who had just found a nugget laced with gold. It might be—it probably was—nothing more than plain water. But it might also be a universe of unknown, living creatures on the first stage of their billion-year journey to intelligence.

Hutchins had walked no more than a dozen yards along the edge of the lake when he stopped again, so suddenly that Garfield nearly collided with him.

"What's the matter?" Jerry asked. "Seen something?"

"That dark patch of rock over there. I noticed it before we stopped at the lake."

"What about it? It looks ordinary enough to me."

"I think it's grown bigger."

All his life, Jerry was to remember this moment. Somehow he never doubted Hutchins' statement; by this time he could believe anything, even that rocks could grow. The sense of isolation and mystery, the presence of that dark and brooding lake, the never-ceasing rumble of distant storms and the green flickering of the aurora—all these had done something to his mind, had prepared it to face the incredible. Yet he felt no fear; that would come later.

He looked at the rock. It was about five hundred feet away, as far as he could estimate. In this dim, emerald light it was hard to judge distances or dimensions. The rock—or whatever it was—seemed to be a horizontal slab of almost black material, lying near the crest of a low ridge. There was a second, much smaller, patch of similar material near it; Jerry tried to measure and memorize the gap between them, so that he would have some yardstick to detect any change.

Even when he saw that the gap was slowly shrinking, he still felt no alarm—only a puzzled excitement. Not until it had vanished completely, and he realized how his eyes had tricked him, did that awful feeling of helpless terror strike into his heart.

Here were no growing or moving rocks. What they were watching was a dark tide, a crawling carpet, sweeping slowly but inexorably toward them over the top of the ridge.

The moment of sheer, unreasoning panic lasted, mercifully, no more than a few seconds. Garfield's first terror began to fade as soon as he recognized its cause. For that advancing tide had reminded him, all too vividly, of a story he had read many years ago about the army ants of the Amazon, and the way in which they destroyed everything in their path. . . .

But whatever this tide might be, it was moving too slowly to be a real danger, unless it cut off their line of retreat. Hutchins was staring at it intently through their only pair of binoculars; he was the biologist, and he was holding his ground. No point in making a fool of myself, thought Jerry, by running like a scalded cat, if it isn't necessary.

"For heaven's sake," he said at last, when the moving carpet was only a hundred yards away and Hutchins had not uttered a word or stirred a muscle. "What *is* it?"

Hutchins slowly unfroze, like a statue coming to life.

"Sorry," he said. "I'd forgotten all about you. It's a plant, of course. At least, I suppose we'd better call it that."

"But it's *moving!*"

"Why should that surprise you? So do terrestrial plants. Ever seen speeded-up movies of ivy in action?"

"That still stays in one place—it doesn't crawl all over the landscape."

"Then what about the plankton plants of the sea? *They* can swim when they have to."

Jerry gave up; in any case, the approaching wonder had robbed him of words.

He still thought of the thing as a carpet—a deep-pile one, raveled into tassels at the edges. It varied in thickness as it moved; in some parts it was a mere film; in others, it heaped up to a depth of a foot or more. As it came closer and he could see its texture, Jerry was reminded of black velvet. He wondered what it felt like to the touch, then remembered that it would burn his fingers even if it did nothing else to them. He found himself thinking, in the lightheaded nervous reaction that often follows a sudden shock: "If there *are* any Venusians, we'll never be able to shake hands with them. They'd burn us, and we'd give them frostbite."

So far, the thing had shown no signs that it was aware of their presence. It had merely flowed forward like the mindless tide that it almost certainly was. Apart from the fact that it climbed over small obstacles, it might have been an advancing flood of water.

And then, when it was only ten feet away, the velvet tide checked itself. On the right and the left, it still flowed forward; but dead ahead it slowed to a halt.

"We're being encircled," said Jerry anxiously. "Better fall back, until we're sure it's harmless."

To his relief, Hutchins stepped back at once. After a brief hesitation, the creature resumed its slow advance and the dent in its front line straightened out.

Then Hutchins stepped forward again—and the thing slowly withdrew. Half a dozen times the biologist advanced, only to retreat again, and each time the living tide ebbed and flowed in synchronism with his movements. I never imagined, Jerry told himself, that I'd live to see a man waltzing with a plant. . . .

"Thermophobia," said Hutchins. "Purely automatic reaction. It doesn't like our heat."

"*Our* heat!" protested Jerry. "Why, we're living icicles by comparison."

"Of course—but our suits aren't, and that's all it knows about."

Stupid of me, thought Jerry. When you were snug and cool inside your thermosuit, it was easy to forget that the refrigeration unit on your back was pumping a blast of heat out into the surrounding air. No wonder the Venusian plant had shied away. . . .

"Let's see how it reacts to light," said Hutchins. He switched on his chest lamp, and the green auroral glow was instantly banished by the flood of pure white radiance. Until Man had come to this planet, no white light had ever shone upon the surface of Venus, even by day. As in the seas of Earth, there was only a green twilight, deepening slowly to utter darkness.

The transformation was so stunning that neither man could check a cry of astonishment. Gone in a flash was the deep, somber black of the thick-piled velvet carpet at their feet. Instead, as far as their lights carried, lay a blazing pattern of glorious, vivid reds, laced with streaks of gold. No Persian prince could ever have commanded so opulent a tapestry from his weavers, yet this was the accidental product of biological forces. Indeed, until they had switched on their floods, these superb colors had not even existed, and they would vanish once more when the alien light of Earth ceased to conjure them into being.

"Tikov was right," murmured Hutchins. "I wish he could have known."

"Right about what?" asked Jerry, though it seemed almost a sacrilege to speak in the presence of such loveliness.

"Back in Russia, fifty years ago, he found that plants living in very cold climates tended to be blue and violet, while those from hot ones were red or orange. He predicted that the Martian vegetation would be violet, and said that if there were plants on Venus they'd be red. Well, he was right on both counts. But we can't stand here all day—we've work to do."

"You're sure it's quite safe?" asked Jerry, some of his caution reasserting itself.

"Absolutely—it can't touch our suits even if it wants to. Anyway, it's moving past us."

That was true. They could see now that the entire creature—if it was a single plant, and not a colony—covered a roughly circular area about a hundred yards across. It was sweeping over the ground, as the shadow of a cloud moves before the wind—and where it had rested, the rocks were pitted with innumerable tiny holes that might have been etched by acid.

"Yes," said Hutchins, when Jerry remarked about this. "That's how some lichens feed; they secrete acids that dissolve rock. But no questions, please—not till we get back to the ship. I've several lifetimes' work here, and a couple of hours to do it in."

This was botany on the run. . . . The sensitive edge of the huge plant-thing could move with surprising speed when it tried to evade them. It was as if they were dealing with an animated flapjack, an acre in extent. There was no reaction—apart from the automatic avoidance of their exhaust heat—when Hutchins snipped samples or took probes. The creature flowed steadily onward over hills and valleys, guided by some strange vegetable instinct. Perhaps it was following some vein of mineral; the geologists could decide that, when they analyzed the rock samples that Hutchins had collected both before and after the passage of the living tapestry.

There was scarcely time to think or even to frame the countless questions that their discovery had raised. Presumably these creatures must be fairly common, for them to have found one so quickly. How did they reproduce? By shoots, spores, fission, or some other means? Where did they get their energy? What relatives, rivals, or parasites did they have? This could not be the only form of life on Venus—the very idea was absurd, for if you had one species, you must have thousands. . . .

Sheer hunger and fatigue forced them to a halt at last. The creature they were studying could eat its way around Venus—though Hutchins believed that it never went very far from the lake, as from time to time it approached the water and inserted a long, tubelike tendril into it—but the animals from Earth had to rest.

It was a great relief to inflate the pressurized tent, climb in through the air lock, and strip off their thermosuits. For the first time, as they relaxed inside their tiny plastic hemisphere, the true wonder and importance of the discovery forced itself upon their minds. This world around them was no longer the same; Venus was no longer dead—it had joined Earth and Mars.

For life called to life, across the gulfs of space. Everything that grew or moved upon the face of any planet was a portent, a promise that Man was not alone in this universe of blazing suns and swirling nebulae. If as yet he had found no companions with whom he could speak, that was only to be expected, for the light-years and the ages still stretched before him, waiting to be explored. Meanwhile, he must guard and cherish the life he found, whether it be upon Earth or Mars or Venus.

So Graham Hutchins, the happiest biologist in the solar system, told himself as he helped Garfield collect their refuse and seal it into a plastic disposal bag. When they deflated the tent and started on the homeward journey, there was no sign of the creature they had been examining. That was just as well; they might have been tempted to linger for more experiments, and already it was getting uncomfortably close to their deadline.

No matter; in a few months they would be back with a team of assistants, far more adequately equipped and with the eyes of the world upon them. Evolution had labored for a billion years to make this meeting possible; it could wait a little longer.

For a while nothing moved in the greenly glimmering, fog-bound landscape; it was deserted by man and crimson carpet alike. Then, flowing over the wind-carved hills, the creature reappeared. Or perhaps it was another of the same strange species; no one would ever know.

It flowed past the little cairn of stones where Hutchins and Garfield had buried their wastes. And then it stopped.

It was not puzzled, for it had no mind. But the chemical urges that drove it relentlessly over the polar plateau were crying: Here, here! Somewhere close at hand was the most precious of all the foods it needed—phosphorous, the element without which the spark of life could never ignite. It began to nuzzle the rocks, to ooze into the cracks and crannies, to scratch and scrabble with probing tendrils. Nothing that it did was beyond the capacity of any plant or tree on Earth—but it moved a thousand times more quickly, requiring only minutes to reach its goal and pierce through the plastic film.

And then it feasted, on food more concentrated than any it had ever known. It absorbed the carbohydrates and the proteins and the phosphates, the nicotine from the cigarette ends, the cellulose from the paper cups and spoons. All these it broke down and assimilated into its strange body, without difficulty and without harm.

Likewise it absorbed a whole microcosmos of living creatures—the bacteria and viruses which, upon an older planet, had evolved into a thousand deadly strains. Though only a very few could survive in this heat and this atmosphere, they were sufficient. As the carpet crawled back to the lake, it carried contagion to all its world.

Even as the Morning Star *set course for her distant*

home, Venus was dying. The films and photographs and specimens that Hutchins was carrying in triumph were more precious even than he knew. They were the only record that would ever exist of life's third attempt to gain a foothold in the solar system.

Beneath the clouds of Venus, the story of Creation was ended.

A Slight Case of Sunstroke

Someone else should be telling this story—someone who understands the funny kind of football they play down in South America. Back in Moscow, Idaho, we grab the ball and run with it. In the small but prosperous republic which I'll call Perivia, they kick it around with their feet. And that is nothing to what they do to the referee.

Hasta la Vista, the capital of Perivia, is a fine, modern town up in the Andes, almost two miles above sea level. It is very proud of its magnificent football stadium, which can hold a hundred thousand people. Even so, it's hardly big enough to pack in all the fans who turn up when there's a really important game—such as the annual one with the neighboring republic of Panagura.

One of the first things I learned when I got to Perivia, after various distressing adventures in the less democratic parts of South America, was that last year's game had been lost because of the knavish dishonesty of the ref. He had, it seemed, penalized most of the players on the team, disallowed a goal, and generally made sure that the best side wouldn't win. This diatribe made me quite homesick, but remembering where I was, I merely commented, "You should have paid him more money." "We did," was the bitter reply, "but the Panagurans got at him later." "Too bad," I answered. "It's hard nowadays to find an honest man who stays bought." The Customs Inspector who'd just taken my last hundred-dollar bill had the grace to blush beneath his stubble as he waved me across the border.

The next few weeks were tough, which isn't the only reason why I'd rather not talk about them. But presently I was back in the agricultural-machinery business—though none of the machines I imported ever went near a farm, and it now cost a good deal more than a hundred dollars a time to get them over the frontier without some busybody looking into the packing cases. The last thing I had time to bother about was football; I knew that my expensive imports were going to be used at any moment, and wanted to make sure that *this* time my profits went with me when I left the country.

Even so, I could hardly ignore the excitement as the day for the return game drew nearer. For one thing, it interfered with business. I'd go to a conference, arranged with great difficulty and expense at a safe hotel or in the house of some reliable sympathizer, and half the time everyone would be talking about football. It was maddening, and I began to wonder if the Perivians took their politics as seriously as their sports. "Gentlemen!" I'd protest. "Our next consignment of rotary drills is being unloaded tomorrow, and unless we get that permit from the Minister of Agriculture, someone may open the cases and then . . ."

"Don't worry, my boy," General Sierra or Colonel Pedro would answer airily, "that's already taken care of. Leave it to the Army."

I knew better than to retort "Which army?", and

for the next ten minutes I'd have to listen while an argument raged about football tactics and the best way of dealing with recalcitrant referees. I never dreamed—and I'm sure that no one else did—that this topic was intimately bound up with our particular problem.

Since then, I've had the leisure to work out what really happened, though it was very confusing at the time. The central figure in the whole improbable drama was undoubtedly Don Hernando Días—millionaire playboy, football fan, scientific dilettante, and, I am sure, future President of Perivia. Owing to his fondness for racing cars and Hollywood beauties, which has made him one of his country's best-known exports, most people assume that the "playboy" label describes Don Hernando completely. Nothing, but nothing, could be farther from the truth.

I knew that Don Hernando was one of us, but at the same time he was a considerable favorite of President Ruiz, which placed him in a powerful yet delicate position. Naturally, I'd never met him; he had to be very particular about his friends, and there were few people who cared to meet *me*, unless they had to. His interest in science I didn't discover until much later; it seems that he has a private observatory which is in frequent use on clear nights, though rumor has it that its functions are not entirely astronomical.

It must have taken all Don Hernando's charm and powers of persuasion to talk the President into it; if the old boy hadn't been a football fan too, and smarting under last year's defeat like every other patriotic Perivian, he would never have agreed. But the sheer originality of the scheme must have appealed to him even though he may not have been too happy about having half his troops out of action for the best part of an afternoon. Still, as Don Hernando undoubtedly reminded him, what better way of ensuring the loyalty of the Army than by giving it fifty thousand seats for the game of the year?

I knew nothing about all this when I took my place in the stadium on that memorable day. If you think I had no wish to be there, you are quite correct. But Colonel Pedro had given me a ticket, and it was unhealthy to hurt his feelings by not using it. So there I was, under the sweltering sun, fanning myself with the program and listening to the commentary over my portable radio while we waited for the game to begin.

The stadium was packed, its great oval bowl a solid sea of faces. There had been a slight delay in admitting the spectators; the police had done their best, but it takes time to search a hundred thousand people for concealed firearms. The visiting team had insisted on this, to the great indignation of the locals. The protests faded swiftly enough, however, as the artillery accumulated at the check points.

It was easy to tell the exact moment the referee drove up in his armor-plated Cadillac; you could follow his progress by the booing of the crowd. "Surely," I said to my neighbor—a young lieutenant so junior that it was safe for him to be seen out with me—"you could change the ref if you feel that way about him?"

He shrugged resignedly. "The visitors have the right to choose. There's nothing we can do about it."

"Then at least you ought to win the games you play in Panagura."

"True," he agreed. "But last time we were overconfident. We played so badly that even our ref couldn't save us."

I found it hard to feel much sympathy for either side, and settled down to a couple of hours of noisy boredom. Seldom have I been more mistaken.

Admittedly, the game took some time to get started. First a sweating band played the two national anthems, then the teams were presented to El Presidente and his lady, then the Cardinal blessed everybody, then there was a pause while the two captains had some obscure argument over the size or shape of the ball. I spent the waiting period reading my program, an expensive and beautifully produced affair that had been given to me by the lieutenant. It was tabloid size, printed on art paper, lavishly illustrated, and looked as if it had been bound in silver. It seemed unlikely that the publishers would get their money back, but this was obviously a matter of prestige rather than economics. In any event there was an impressive list of subscribers, headed by the President, to this "Special Victory Souvenir Issue." Most of my friends were on it, and I noted with amusement that the bill for presenting fifty thousand free copies to our gallant fighting men had been met by Don Hernando. It seemed a somewhat naïve bid for popularity, and I doubted if the good will was worth the considerable cost. The "Victory" also struck me as a trifle premature, not to say tactless.

These reflections were interrupted by the roar of the enormous crowd as play started. The ball slammed into action, but had barely zigzagged halfway down the field when a blue-jerseyed Perivian tripped a black-striped Panaguran. They don't waste much time, I told myself; what's the ref going to do? To my surprise, he did nothing, and I wondered if this match we'd got him to accept C.O.D. terms.

"Wasn't that a foul, or whatever you call it?" I said to my companion.

"Pfui!" he answered, not taking his eyes off the game. "Nobody bothers about *that* sort of thing. Besides, the coyote never saw it."

That was true. The referee was a long way down the field, and seemed to be finding it hard to keep up with the game. His movements were distinctly labored, and that puzzled me until I guessed the reason. Have you ever seen a man trying to run in a bulletproof vest? Poor devil, I thought, with the detached sympathy of one crook for another; you're earning your bribe. *I* was finding it hot enough merely sitting still.

For the first ten minutes, it was a pretty open game, and I don't think there were more than three fights. The Perivians just missed one goal; the ball was headed out so neatly that the frantic applause from the Panaguran supporters (who had a special police guard and a fortified section of the stadium all to themselves) went quite unbooed. I began to feel disappointed. Why, if you changed the shape of the ball this might be a good-natured game back home.

Indeed, there was no real work for the Red Cross until nearly half time, when three Perivians and two Panagurans (or it may have been the other way around) fused together in a magnificent melee from which only one survivor emerged under his own power. The casualties were carted off the field of battle amid much pandemonium, and there was a short break while replacements were brought up. This started the first major incident: the Perivians complained that the other side's wounded were shamming so that fresh reserves could be poured in. But the ref was adamant, the new men came on, and the background noise dropped to just below the threshold of pain as the game resumed.

The Panagurans promptly scored, and though none of my neighbors actually committed suicide, several seemed close to it. The transfusion of new blood had apparently pepped up the visitors, and things looked bad for the home team. Their opponents were passing the ball with such skill that the Perivian defenses were as porous as a sieve. At this rate, I told myself, the ref can afford to be honest; his side will win anyway. And to give him his due, I'd seen no sign of any obvious bias so far.

I didn't have long to wait. A last-minute rally by the home team blocked a threatened attack on their goal, and a mighty kick by one of the defenders sent the ball rocketing toward the other end of the field. Before it had reached the apex of its flight, the piercing shriek of the referee's whistle brought the game to a halt. There was a brief consultation between ref and captains, which almost at once broke up in disorder. Down there on the field everyone was gesticulating violently, and the crowd was roaring its disapproval. "What's happening now?" I asked plaintively.

"The ref says our man was off side."

"But how can he be? He's on top of his own goal!"

"Shush!" said the lieutenant, unwilling to waste time enlightening my ignorance. I don't shush easily, but this time I let it go, and tried to work things out for myself. It seemed that the ref had awarded the Panagurans a free kick at our goal, and I could understand the way everybody felt about it.

The ball soared through the air in a beautiful parabola, nicked the post—and cannoned in despite a flying leap by the goalie. A mighty roar of anguish rose from the crowd, then died abruptly to a silence that was even more impressive. It was as if a great animal had been wounded—and was biding the time for its revenge. Despite the heat pouring down from the not-far-from-vertical sun, I felt a sudden chill, as if a cold wind had swept past me. Not for all the wealth of the Incas would I have changed places with the man sweating out there on the field in his bulletproof vest.

We were two down, but there was still hope—it was not yet half time and a lot could happen before the end of the game. The Perivians were on their mettle now, playing with almost demonic intensity, like men who had accepted a challenge and were going to show that they could meet it.

The new spirit paid off promptly. The home team scored one impeccable goal within a couple of minutes, and the crowd went wild with joy. By this time I was shouting like everyone else, and telling that referee things I didn't know I could say in Spanish. One to two now, and a hundred thousand people praying and cursing for the goal that would bring us level again.

It came just before half time. In a matter that had such grave consequences, I want to be perfectly fair. The ball had been passed to one of our forwards, he ran about fifty feet with it, evaded a couple of the defenders with some neat footwork, and kicked it cleanly into the goal. It had scarcely dropped down from the net when that whistle went again.

Now what? I wondered. He can't disallow *that*.

But he did. The ball, it seemed, had been handled. I've got pretty good eyes, and I never saw it. So I cannot honestly say that I blame the Perivians for what happened next.

The police managed to keep the crowd off the field, though it was touch and go for a minute. The two teams drew apart, leaving the center of the field bare except for the stubbornly defiant figure of the referee. He was probably wondering how he could make his escape from the stadium, and was consoling himself with the thought that when this game was over he could retire for good.

The thin, high bugle call took everyone completely by surprise—everyone, that is, except the fifty thousand well-trained men who had been waiting for it with mounting impatience. The whole arena became instantly silent, so silent that I could hear the noise of the traffic outside the stadium. A second time that bugle sounded—and all the vast acreage of faces opposite me vanished in a blinding sea of fire.

- I cried out and covered my eyes; for one horrified moment I thought of atomic bombs and braced myself uselessly for the blast. But there was no concussion— only that flickering veil of flame that beat even through my closed eyelids for long seconds, then vanished as swiftly as it had come when the bugle blared out for the third and last time.

Everything was just as it had been before, except for one minor item. Where the referee had been standing there was a small, smoldering heap, from which a thin column of smoke curled up into the still air.

What in heaven's name had happened? I turned to my companion, who was as shaken as I was. *"Madre de Dios,"* I heard him mutter, "I never knew it would do *that."* He was staring, not at the small funeral pyre down there on the field, but at the handsome souvenir program spread across his knees. And then, in a flash of incredulous comprehension, I understood.

Yet even now, when it's all been explained to me, I still find it hard to credit what I saw with my own eyes. It was so simple, so logical—so unbelievable.

Have you ever annoyed anyone by flicking a pocket mirror across his eyes? I guess every kid has; I remember doing it to a teacher once, and getting duly paddled. But I'd never imagined what would happen if fifty thousand well-trained men did the same trick, each using a tin-foil reflector a couple of feet square.

A mathematically minded friend of mine has worked it out—not that I needed any further proof, but I always like to get to the bottom of things. I never knew, until then, just how much energy there is in sunlight; it's well over a horsepower on every square yard facing the sun. Most of the heat falling on one side of that enormous stadium had been diverted into the single small area occupied by the late ref. Even allowing for all the programs that weren't aimed in the right direction, he must have intercepted at least a thousand horsepower of raw heat. He couldn't have felt much; it was as if he had been dropped into a blast furnace.

I'm sure that no one except Don Hernando realized what was likely to happen; his well-drilled fans had been told that the ref would merely be blinded and put out of action for the rest of the game. But I'm also equally sure that no one had any regrets. They play football for keeps in Perivia.

Likewise politics. While the game was continuing to its now-predictable end, beneath the benign gaze of a new and understandably docile referee, my friends were hard at work. When our victorious team had marched off the field (the final score was fourteen to two), everything had been settled. There had been practically no shooting, and as the President emerged from the stadium he was politely informed that a seat had been reserved for him on the morning flight to Mexico City.

As General Sierra remarked to me when I boarded the same plane as his late chief, "We let the Army win the football match, and while it was busy we won the country. So everybody's happy."

Though I was too polite to voice any doubts, I could not help thinking that this was a rather shortsighted attitude. Several million Panagurans were very unhappy indeed, and sooner or later there would be a day of reckoning.

I suspect that it's not far away. Last week a friend of mine, who is one of the world's top experts in his specialized field but prefers to work on a free-lance basis under an assumed name, indiscreetly blurted out one of his problems to me.

"Joe," he said, "why the devil should anyone want me to build a guided rocket that can fit inside a football?"

Dog Star

When I heard Laika's frantic barking, my first reaction was one of annoyance. I turned over in my bunk and murmured sleepily, "Shut up, you silly bitch." That dreamy interlude lasted only a fraction of a second; then consciousness returned—and, with it, fear. Fear of loneliness, and fear of madness.

For a moment I dared not open my eyes; I was afraid of what I might see. Reason told me that no dog had ever set foot upon this world, that Laika was separated from me by a quarter of a million miles of space—and, far more irrevocably, five years of time.

"You've been dreaming," I told myself angrily. "Stop being a fool—open your eyes! You won't see anything except the glow of the wall paint."

That was right, of course. The tiny cabin was empty, the door tightly closed. I was alone with my memories, overwhelmed by the transcendental sadness that often comes when some bright dream fades into drab reality. The sense of loss was so desolating that I longed to return to sleep. It was well that I failed to do so, for at that moment sleep would have been death. But I did not know this for another five seconds, and during that eternity I was back on Earth, seeking what comfort I could from the past.

No one ever discovered Laika's origin, though the Observatory staff made a few enquiries and I inserted several advertisements in the Pasadena newspapers. I found her, a lost and lonely ball of fluff, huddled by the roadside one summer evening when I was driving up to Palomar. Though I have never liked dogs, or indeed any animals, it was impossible to leave this helpless little creature to the mercy of the passing cars. With some qualms, wishing that I had a pair of gloves, I picked her up and dumped her in the baggage compartment. I was not going to hazard the upholstery of my new '92 Vik, and felt that she could do little damage there. In this, I was not altogether correct.

When I had parked the car at the Monastery—the astronomers' residential quarters, where I'd be living for the next week—I inspected my find without much enthusiasm. At that stage, I had intended to hand the puppy over to the janitor; but then it whimpered and opened its eyes. There was such an expression of helpless trust in them that—well, I changed my mind.

Sometimes I regretted that decision, though never for long. I had no idea how much trouble a growing dog could cause, deliberately and otherwise. My cleaning and repair bills soared; I could never be sure of finding an unravaged pair of socks or an unchewed copy of the *Astrophysical Journal*. But eventually Laika was both house-trained and Observatory-trained: she must have been the only dog ever to be allowed inside the two-hundred-inch dome. She would lie there quietly in the shadows for hours, while I was up in the cage making adjustments, quite content if she could hear my voice from time to time. The other astronomers became equally fond of her (it was old Dr. Anderson who suggested her name), but from the begin-

ning she was my dog, and would obey no one else.
Not that she would always obey me.

She was a beautiful animal, about ninety-five per
cent Alsatian. It was that missing five per cent, I
imagine, that led to her being abandoned. (I still feel a
surge of anger when I think of it, but since I shall
never know the facts, I may be jumping to false con-
clusions.) Apart from two dark patches over the eyes,
most of her body was a smoky gray, and her coat was
soft as silk. When her ears were pricked up, she looked
incredibly intelligent and alert; sometimes I would be
discussing spectral types of stellar evolution with my
colleagues, and it would be hard to believe that she
was not following the conversation.

Even now, I cannot understand why she became so
attached to me, for I have made very few friends
among human beings. Yet when I returned to the
Observatory after an absence, she would go almost
frantic with delight, bouncing around on her hind legs
and putting her paws on my shoulders—which she
could reach quite easily—all the while uttering small
squeaks of joy which seemed highly inappropriate from
so large a dog. I hated to leave her for more than a
few days at a time, and though I could not take her
with me on overseas trips, she accompanied me on
most of my shorter journeys. She was with me when I
drove north to attend that ill-fated seminar at Berkeley.

We were staying with university acquaintances; they
had been polite about it, but obviously did not look
forward to having a monster in the house. However, I
assured them that Laika never gave the slightest trouble, and rather reluctantly they let her sleep in the
living room. "You needn't worry about burglars tonight," I said. "We don't have any in Berkeley," they
answered, rather coldly.

In the middle of the night, it seemed that they were
wrong. I was awakened by a hysterical, high-pitched

barking from Laika which I had heard only once before—when she had first seen a cow, and did not know what on earth to make of it. Cursing, I threw off the sheets and stumbled out into the darkness of the unfamiliar house. My main thought was to silence Laika before she roused my hosts—assuming that this was not already far too late. If there had been an intruder, he would certainly have taken flight by now. Indeed, I rather hoped that he had.

For a moment I stood beside the switch at the top of the stairs, wondering whether to throw it. Then I growled, "Shut up, Laika!" and flooded the place with light.

She was scratching frantically at the door, pausing from time to time to give that hysterical yelp. "If you want out," I said angrily, "there's no need for all that fuss." I went down, shot the bolt, and she took off into the night like a rocket.

It was very calm and still, with a waning Moon struggling to pierce the San Francisco fog. I stood in the luminous haze, looking out across the water to the lights of the city, waiting for Laika to come back so that I could chastise her suitably. I was still waiting when, for the second time in the twentieth century, the San Andreas Fault woke from its sleep.

Oddly enough, I was not frightened—at first. I can remember that two thoughts passed through my mind, in the moment before I realized the danger. Surely, I told myself, the geophysicists could have given us *some* warning. And then I found myself thinking, with great surprise, "I'd no idea that earthquakes make so much noise!"

It was about then that I knew that this was no ordinary quake; what happened afterward, I would prefer to forget. The Red Cross did not take me away until quite late the next morning, because I refused to leave Laika. As I looked at the shattered house con-

taining the bodies of my friends, I knew that I owed
my life to her; but the helicopter pilots could not be
expected to understand that, and I cannot blame them
for thinking that I was crazy, like so many of the
others they had found wandering among the fires and
the debris.

After that, I do not suppose we were ever apart for
more than a few hours. I have been told—and I can
well believe it—that I became less and less interested
in human company, without being actively unsocial or
misanthropic. Between them, the stars and Laika filled
all my needs. We used to go for long walks together
over the mountains; it was the happiest time I have
ever known. There was only one flaw; I knew, though
Laika could not, how soon it must end.

We had been planning the move for more than a decade. As far back as the nineteen-sixties it was realized that Earth was no place for an astronomical
observatory. Even the small pilot instruments on the
Moon had far outperformed all the telescopes peering
through the murk and haze of the terrestrial atmosphere. The story of Mount Wilson, Palomar, Green-
wich, and the other great names was coming to an
end; they would still be used for training purposes, but
the research frontier must move out into space.

I had to move with it; indeed, I had already been
offered the post of Deputy Director, Farside Observatory. In a few months, I could hope to solve problems
I had been working on for years. Beyond the atmosphere, I would be like a blind man who had suddenly
been given sight.

It was utterly impossible, of course, to take Laika
with me. The only animals on the Moon were those
needed for experimental purposes; it might be another
generation before pets were allowed, and even then it
would cost a fortune to carry them there—and to keep
them alive. Providing Laika with her usual two pounds

of meat a day would, I calculated, take several times my quite comfortable salary.

The choice was simple and straightforward. I could stay on Earth and abandon my career. Or I could go to the Moon—and abandon Laika.

After all, she was only a dog. In a dozen years, she would be dead, while I should be reaching the peak of my profession. No sane man would have hesitated over the matter; yet I did hesitate, and if by now you do not understand why, no further words of mine can help.

In the end, I let matters go by default. Up to the very week I was due to leave, I had still made no plans for Laika. When Dr. Anderson volunteered to look after her, I accepted numbly, with scarcely a word of thanks. The old physicist and his wife had always been fond of her, and I am afraid that they considered me indifferent and heartless—when the truth was just the opposite. We went for one more walk together over the hills; then I delivered her silently to the Andersons, and did not see her again.

Take-off was delayed almost twenty-four hours, until a major flare storm had cleared the Earth's orbit; even so, the Van Allen belts were still so active that we had to make our exit through the North Polar Gap. It was a miserable flight; apart from the usual trouble with weightlessness, we were all groggy with antiradiation drugs. The ship was already over Farside before I took much interest in the proceedings, so I missed the sight of Earth dropping below the horizon. Nor was I really sorry; I wanted no reminders, and intended to think only of the future. Yet I could not shake off that feeling of guilt; I had deserted someone who loved and trusted me, and was no better than those who had abandoned Laika when she was a puppy, beside the dusty road to Palomar.

The news that she was dead reached me a month

later. There was no reason that anyone knew; the Andersons had done their best, and were very upset. She had just lost interest in living, it seemed. For a while, I think I did the same; but work is a wonderful anodyne, and my program was just getting under way. Though I never forgot Laika, in a little while the memory ceased to hurt.

Then why had it come back to haunt me, five years later, on the far side of the Moon? I was searching my mind for the reason when the metal building around me quivered as if under the impact of a heavy blow. I reacted without thinking, and was already closing the helmet of my emergency suit when the foundations slipped and the wall tore open with a short-lived scream of escaping air. Because I had automatically pressed the General Alarm button, we lost only two men, despite the fact that the tremor—the worst ever recorded on Farside—cracked all three of the Observatory's pressure domes.

It is hardly necessary for me to say that I do not believe in the supernatural; everything that happened has a perfectly rational explanation, obvious to any man with the slightest knowledge of psychology. In the second San Francisco earthquake, Laika was not the only dog to sense approaching disaster; many such cases were reported. And on Farside, my own memories must have given me that heightened awareness, when my never-sleeping subconscious detected the first faint vibrations from within the Moon.

The human mind has strange and labyrinthine ways of going about its business; it knew the signal that would most swiftly rouse me to the knowledge of danger. There is nothing more to it than that; though in a sense one could say that Laika woke me on both occasions, there is no mystery about it, no miraculous warning across the gulf that neither man nor dog can ever bridge.

Of that I am sure, if I am sure of anything. Yet sometimes I wake now, in the silence of the Moon, and wish that the dream could have lasted a few seconds longer—so that I could have looked just once more into those luminous brown eyes, brimming with an unselfish, undemanding love I have found nowhere else on this or on any other world.

The Road to the Sea

The first leaves of autumn were falling when Durven
met his brother on the headland beside the Golden
Sphinx. Leaving his flyer among the shrubs by the
roadside, he walked to the brow of the hill and looked
down upon the sea. A bitter wind was toiling across
the moors, bearing the threat of early frost, but down
in the valley Shastar the Beautiful was still warm and
sheltered in its crescent of hills. Its empty quays lay
dreaming in the pale, declining sunlight, the deep blue
of the sea washing gently against their marble flanks.
As he looked down once more into the hauntingly
familiar streets and gardens of his youth, Durven felt
his resolution failing. He was glad he was meeting
Hannar here, a mile from the city, and not among the
sights and sounds that would bring his childhood crowding back upon him.

Hannar was a small dot far down the slope, climbing
in his old unhurried, leisurely fashion. Durven could
have met him in a moment with the flyer, but he knew
he would receive little thanks if he did. So he waited
in the lee of the great Sphinx, sometimes walking
briskly to and fro to keep warm. Once or twice he

went to the head of the monster and stared up at the still face brooding upon the city and the sea. He remembered how as a child in the gardens of Shastar he had seen the crouching shape upon the sky line, and had wondered if it was alive.

Hannar looked no older than he had seemed at their last meeting, twenty years before. His hair was still dark and thick, and his face unwrinkled, for few things ever disturbed the tranquil life of Shastar and its people. It seemed bitterly unfair, and Durven, gray with the years of unrelenting toil, felt a quick spasm of envy stab through his brain.

Their greetings were brief, but not without warmth. Then Hannar walked over to the ship, lying in its bed of heather and crumpled gorse bushes. He rapped his stick upon the curving metal and turned to Durven.

"It's very small. Did it bring you all the way?"

"No: only from the Moon. I came back from the Project in a liner a hundred times the size of this."

"And where is the Project—or don't you want us to know?"

"There's no secret about it. We're building the ships out in space beyond Saturn, where the sun's gravitational gradient is almost flat and it needs little thrust to send them right out of the solar system."

Hannar waved his stick toward the blue waters beneath them, the colored marble of the little towers, and the wide streets with their slowly moving traffic.

"Away from all this, out into the darkness and loneliness—in search of what?"

Durven's lips tightened into a thin, determined line.

"Remember," he said quietly, "I have already spent a lifetime away from Earth."

"And has it brought you happiness?" continued Hannar remorselessly.

Durven was silent for a while.

"It has brought me more than that," he replied at

last. "I have used my powers to the utmost, and have tasted triumphs that you can never imagine. The day when the First Expedition returned to the solar system was worth a lifetime in Shastar."

"Do you think," asked Hannar, "that you will build fairer cities than this beneath those strange suns, when you have left our world forever?"

"If we feel that impulse, yes. If not, we will build other things. But build we must; and what have your people created in the last hundred years?"

"Because we have made no machines, because we have turned our backs upon the stars and are content with our own world, don't think we have been completely idle. Here in Shastar we have evolved a way of life that I do not think has ever been surpassed. We have studied the art of living; ours is the first aristocracy in which there are no slaves. That is our achievement, by which history will judge us."

"I grant you this," replied Durven, "but never forget that your paradise was built by scientists who had to fight as we have done to make their dreams come true."

"They have not always succeeded. The planets defeated them once; why should the worlds of other suns be more hospitable?"

It was a fair question. After five hundred years, the memory of the first failure was still bitter. With what hopes and dreams had Man set out for the planets, in the closing years of the twentieth century—only to find them not merely barren and lifeless, but fiercely hostile! From the sullen fires of the Mercurian lava seas to Pluto's creeping glaciers of solid nitrogen, there was nowhere that he could live unprotected beyond his own world; and to his own world, after a century of fruitless struggle, he had returned.

Yet the vision had not wholly died; when the planets had been abandoned, there were still some who dared to dream of the stars. Out of that dream had come at last the Transcendental Drive, the First Expedition—and now the heady wine of long-delayed success.

"There are fifty solar-type stars within ten years' flight of Earth," Durven replied, "and almost all of them have planets. We believe now that the possession of planets is almost as much a characteristic of a G-type star as its spectrum, though we don't know why. So the search for worlds like Earth was bound to be successful in time; I don't think that we were particularly lucky to find Eden so soon."

"Eden? Is that what you've called your new world?"

"Yes; it seemed appropriate."

"What incurable romantics you scientists are! Perhaps the name's too well chosen; all the life in that first Eden wasn't friendly to Man, if you remember."

Durven gave a bleak smile.

"That, again, depends on one's viewpoint," he replied. He pointed toward Shastar, where the first lights had begun to glimmer. "Unless our ancestors had eaten deeply from the Tree of Knowledge, you would never have had this."

"And what do you suppose will happen to it now?" asked Hannar bitterly. "When you have opened the road to the stars, all the strength and vigor of the race will ebb away from Earth as from an open wound."

"I do not deny it. It has happened before, and it will happen again. Shastar will go the way of Babylon and Carthage and New York. The future is built on the rubble of the past; wisdom lies in facing that fact, not in fighting against it. I have loved Shastar as much as you have done—so much so that now, though I shall never see it again, I dare not go down once more into its streets. You ask me what will become of it, and I will tell you. What we are doing will merely hasten the end. Even twenty years ago, when I was last here, I felt my will being sapped by the aimless ritual of your lives. Soon it will be the same in all the cities of Earth, for every one of them apes Shastar. I think the Drive has come none too soon; perhaps even you would believe me if you had spoken to the men who have come back from the stars, and felt the blood stirring in your veins once more after all these centuries of sleep. For your world is dying, Hannar; what you have now you may hold for ages yet, but in the end it will slip from your fingers. The future belongs to us; we will leave you to your dreams. We also have dreamed, and now we go to make our dreams come true."

The last light was catching the brow of the Sphinx as the sun sank into the sea and left Shastar to night but not to darkness. The wide streets were luminous rivers carrying a myriad of moving specks; the towers and pinnacles were jeweled with colored lights, and there came a faint sound of wind-borne music as a pleasure boat put slowly out to sea. Smiling a little, Durven watched it draw away from the curving quay. It had been five hundred years or more since the last merchant ship had unloaded its cargo, but while the sea remained, men would still sail upon it.

There was little more to say; and presently Hannar stood alone upon the hill, his head tilted up toward the stars. He would never see his brother again; the sun, which for a few hours had gone from his sight, would soon have vanished from Durven's forever as it shrank into the abyss of space.

Unheeding, Shastar lay glittering in the darkness along the edge of the sea. To Hannar, heavy with foreboding, its doom seemed already almost upon it. There was truth in Durven's words; the exodus was about to begin.

Ten thousand years ago other explorers had set out from the first cities of mankind to discover new lands. They had found them, and had never returned, and

Time had swallowed their deserted homes. So must it be with Shastar the Beautiful.

Leaning heavily on his stick, Hannar walked slowly down the hillside toward the lights of the city. The Sphinx watched him dispassionately as his figure vanished into the distance and the darkness.

It was still watching, five thousand years later.

Brant was not quite twenty when his people were expelled from their homes and driven westward across two continents and an ocean, filling the ether with piteous cries of injured innocence. They received scant sympathy from the rest of the world, for they had only themselves to blame, and could scarcely pretend that the Supreme Council had acted harshly. It had sent them a dozen preliminary warnings and no fewer than four positively final ultimatums before reluctantly taking action. Then one day a small ship with a very large acoustic radiator had suddenly arrived a thousand feet above the village and started to emit several kilowatts of raw noise. After a few hours of this, the rebels had capitulated and begun to pack their belongings. The transport fleet had called a week later and carried them, still protesting shrilly, to their new homes on the other side of the world.

And so the Law had been enforced, the Law which ruled that no community could remain on the same spot for more than three lifetimes. Obedience meant change, the destruction of traditions, and the uprooting of ancient and well-loved homes. That had been the very purpose of the Law when it was framed, four thousand years ago; but the stagnation it had sought to prevent could not be warded off much longer. One day there would be no central organization to enforce it, and the scattered villages would remain where they were until Time engulfed them as it had the earlier civilizations of which they were the heirs.

It had taken the people of Chaldis the whole of three months to build new homes, remove a square mile of forest, plant some unnecessary crops of exotic and luxurious fruits, re-lay a river, and demolish a hill which offended their aesthetic sensibilities. It was quite an impressive performance, and all was forgiven when the local Supervisor made a tour of inspection a little later. Then Chaldis watched with great satisfaction as the transports, the digging machines, and all the paraphernalia of a mobile and mechanized civilization climbed away into the sky. The sound of their departure had scarcely faded when, as one man, the village relaxed once more into the sloth that it sincerely hoped nothing would disturb for another century at least.

Brant had quite enjoyed the whole adventure. He was sorry, of course, to lose the home that had shaped his childhood; and now he would never climb the proud, lonely mountain that had looked down upon the village of his birth. There were no mountains in this land—only low, rolling hills and fertile valleys in which forests had run rampant for millennia, since agriculture had come to an end. It was warmer, too, than in the old country, for they were nearer the equator and had left behind them the fierce winters of the North. In almost every respect the change was for the good; but for a year or two the people of Chaldis would feel a comfortable glow of martyrdom.

These political matters did not worry Brant in the least. The entire sweep of human history from the dark ages into the unknown future was considerably less important at the moment than the question of Yradne and her feelings toward him. He wondered what Yradne was doing now, and tried to think of an excuse for going to see her. But that would mean meeting her parents, who would embarrass him by their hearty pretense that his call was simply a social one.

He decided to go to the smithy instead, if only to make a check on Jon's movements. It was a pity about Jon; they had been such good friends only a short while ago. But love was friendship's deadliest enemy, and until Yradne had chosen between them they would remain in a state of armed neutrality.

The village sprawled for about a mile along the valley, its neat, new houses arranged in calculated disorder. A few people were moving around in no particular hurry, or gossiping in little groups beneath the trees. To Brant it seemed that everyone was following him with their eyes and talking about him as he passed—an assumption that, as it happened, was perfectly correct. In a closed community of fewer than a thousand highly intelligent people, no one could expect to have any private life.

The smithy was in a clearing at the far end of the village, where its general untidiness would cause as little offense as possible. It was surrounded by broken and half-dismantled machines that Old Johan had not got around to mending. One of the community's three flyers was lying, its bare ribs exposed to the sunlight, where it had been dumped weeks ago with a request for immediate repair. Old Johan would fix it one day, but in his own time.

The wide door of the smithy was open, and from the brilliantly lit interior came the sound of screaming metal as the automatic machines fashioned some new shape to their master's will. Brant threaded his way carefully past the busy slaves and emerged into the relative quiet at the back of the shop.

Old Johan was lying in an excessively comfortable chair, smoking a pipe and looking as if he had never done a day's work in his life. He was a neat little man with a carefully pointed beard, and only his brilliant, ceaselessly roaming eyes showed any signs of animation. He might have been taken for a minor poet—as indeed he fancied himself to be—but never for a village blacksmith.

"Looking for Jon?" he said between puffs. "He's around somewhere, making something for that girl. Beats me what you two see in her."

Brant turned a slight pink and was about to make some sort of reply when one of the machines started calling loudly for attention. In a flash Old Johan was out of the room, and for a minute strange crashings and bangings and much bad language floated through the doorway. Very soon, however, he was back again in his chair, obviously not expecting to be disturbed for quite a while.

"Let me tell you something, Brant," he continued, as if there had been no interruption. "In twenty years she'll be exactly like her mother. Ever thought of that?"

Brant hadn't, and quailed slightly. But twenty years is an eternity to youth; if he could win Yradne in the present, the future could take care of itself. He told Johan as much.

"Have it your own way," said the smith, not unkindly. "I suppose if we'd all looked that far ahead the human race would have died out a million years ago. Why don't you play a game of chess, like sensible people, to decide who'll have her first?"

"Brant would cheat," answered Jon, suddenly appearing in the entrance and filling most of it. He was a large, well-built youth, in complete contrast to his father, and was carrying a sheet of paper covered with engineering sketches. Brant wondered what sort of present he was making for Yradne.

"What are you doing?" he asked, with a far from disinterested curiosity.

"Why should I tell you?" asked Jon good-naturedly. "Give me one good reason."

Brant shrugged his shoulders.

"I'm sure it's not important—I was only being polite."

"Don't overdo it," said the smith. "The last time you were polite to Jon, you had a black eye for a week. Remember?" He turned to his son, and said brusquely: "Let's see those drawings, so I can tell you why it can't be done."

He examined the sketches critically, while Jon showed increasing signs of embarrassment. Presently Johan snorted disapprovingly and said: "Where are you going to get the components? They're all nonstandard, and most of them are submicro."

Jon looked hopefully around the workshop.

"There aren't very many of them," he said. "It's a simple job, and I was wondering . . ."

". . . if I'd let you mess up the integrators to try to make the pieces? Well, we'll see about that. My talented son, Brant, is trying to prove that he possesses brains as well as brawn, by making a toy that's been obsolete for about fifty centuries. I hope you can do better than that. Now when I was your age . . ."

His voice and his reminiscences trailed off into silence. Yradne had drifted in from the clangorous bustle of the machine shop, and was watching them from the doorway with a faint smile on her lips.

It is probable that if Brant and Jon had been asked to describe Yradne, it would have seemed as if they were speaking of two entirely different people. There would have been superficial points of resemblance, of course. Both would have agreed that her hair was chestnut, her eyes large and blue, and her skin that rarest of colors—an almost pearly white. But to Jon she seemed a fragile little creature, to be cherished and protected; while to Brant her self-confidence and complete assurance were so obvious that he despaired of ever being of any service to her. Part of that differ-

ence in outlook was due to Jon's extra six inches of
height and nine inches of girth, but most of it came
from profounder psychological causes. The person one
loves never really exists, but is a projection focused
through the lens of the mind onto whatever screen it
fits with least distortion. Brant and Jon had quite
different ideals, and each believed that Yradne em-
bodied them. This would not have surprised her in the
least, for few things ever did.

"I'm going down to the river," she said. "I called
for you on the way, Brant, but you were out."

That was a blow at Jon, but she quickly equalized.

"I thought you'd gone off with Lorayne or some
other girl, but I knew I'd find Jon at home."

Jon looked very smug at this unsolicited and quite
inaccurate testimonial. He rolled up his drawings and
dashed off into the house, calling happily over his
shoulder: "Wait for me—I won't be long!"

Brant never took his eyes off Yradne as he shifted
uncomfortably from one foot to the other. She hadn't
actually invited *anyone* to come with her, and until
definitely ordered off, he was going to stand his ground.
But he remembered that there was a somewhat ancient saying to the effect that if two were company,
three were the reverse.

Jon returned, resplendent in a surprising green cloak
with diagonal explosions of red down the sides. Only a
very young man could have got away with it, and even
Jon barely succeeded. Brant wondered if there was
time for him to hurry home and change into something
still more startling, but that would be too great a risk
to take. It would be flying in the face of the enemy;
the battle might be over before he could get his
reinforcements.

"Quite a crowd," remarked Old Johan unhelpfully
as they departed. "Mind if I come along too?" The
boys looked embarrassed, but Yradne gave a gay little

laugh that made it hard for him to dislike her. He stood in the outer doorway for a while, smiling as they went away through the trees and down the long, grass-covered slope to the river. But presently his eyes ceased to follow them, as he lost himself in dreams as vain as any that can come to man—the dreams of his own departed youth. Very soon he turned his back upon the sunlight and, no longer smiling now, disappeared into the busy tumult of the workshop.

Now the northward-climbing sun was passing the equator, the days would soon be longer than the nights, and the rout of winter was complete. The countless villages throughout the hemisphere were preparing to greet the spring. With the dying of the great cities and the return of man to the fields and woods, he had returned also to many of the ancient customs that had slumbered through a thousand years of urban civilization. Some of those customs had been deliberately revived by the anthropologists and social engineers of the third millennium, whose genius had sent so many patterns of human culture safely down the ages. So it was that the spring equinox was still welcomed by rituals which, for all their sophistication, would have seemed less strange to primitive man than to the people of the industrial cities whose smoke had once stained the skies of Earth.

The arrangements for the Spring Festival were always the subject of much intrigue and bickering between neghboring villages. Although it involved the disruption of all other activities for at least a month, any village was greatly honored to be chosen as host for the celebrations. A newly settled community, still recovering from transplantation, would not, of course, be expected to take on such a responsibility. Brant's people, however, had thought of an ingenious way to regaining favor and wiping out the stain of their recent disgrace. There were five other villages within a hundred miles, and all had been invited to Chaldis for the Festival.

The invitation had been very carefully worded. It hinted delicately that, for obvious reasons, Chaldis couldn't hope to arrange as elaborate a ceremonial as it might have wished, and thereby implied that if the guests wanted a really good time they had better go elsewhere. Chaldis expected one acceptance at the most, but the inquisitiveness of its neighbors had overcome their sense of moral superiority. They had all said that they would be delighted to come; and there was no possible way in which Chaldis could now evade its responsibilities.

There was no night and little sleep in the valley. High above the trees a row of artificial suns burned with a steady, blue-white brilliance, banishing the stars and the darkness and throwing into chaos the natural routine of all the wild creatures for miles around. Through lengthening days and shortening nights, men and machines were battling to make ready the great amphitheater needed to hold some four thousand people. In one respect at least, they were lucky: there was no need for a roof or any artificial heating in this climate. In the land they had so reluctantly left, the snow would still be thick upon the ground at the end of March.

Brant woke early on the great day to the sound of aircraft falling down from the skies above him. He stretched himself wearily, wondering when he would get to bed again, and then climbed into his clothes. A kick with his foot at a concealed switch and the rectangle of yielding foam rubber, an inch below floor level, was completely covered by a rigid plastic sheet that had unrolled from within the wall. There was no bed linen to worry about because the room was kept auto-

matically at body temperature. In many such ways
Brant's life was simpler than those of his remote
ancestors—simpler through the ceaseless and almost
forgotten efforts of five thousand years of science.

The room was softly lit by light pouring through one
translucent wall, and was quite incredibly untidy. The
only clear floor space was that concealing the bed, and
probably this would have to be cleared again by nightfall. Brant was a great hoarder and hated to throw
anything away. This was a very unusual characteristic
in a world where few things were of value because
they could be made so easily, but the objects Brant
collected were not those that the integrators were used
to creating. In one corner a small tree trunk was
propped against the wall, partly carved into a vaguely
anthropomorphic shape. Large lumps of sandstone and
marble were scattered elsewhere over the floor, until
such time as Brant decided to work on them. The
walls were completely covered with paintings, most of
them abstract in character. It would have needed very
little intelligence to deduce that Brant was an artist; it
was not so easy to decide if he was a good one.

He picked his way through the debris and went in
search of food. There was no kitchen; some historians
maintained that it had survived until as late as A.D.
2500, but long before then most families made their
own meals about as often as they made their own
clothes. Brant walked into the main living room and
went across to a metal box set in the wall at chest
level. At its center was something that would have
been quite familiar to every human being for the last
fifty centuries—a ten-digit impulse dial. Brant called a
four-figure number and waited. Nothing whatsoever
happened. Looking a little annoyed, he pressed a concealed button and the front of the apparatus slid open,
revealing an interior which should, by all the rules,

have contained an appetizing breakfast. It was completely empty.

Brant could call up the central food machine to demand an explanation, but there would probably be no answer. It was quite obvious what had happened—the catering department was so busy preparing for the day's overload that he'd be lucky if he got any breakfast at all. He cleared the circuit, then tried again with a little-used number. This time there was a gentle purr, a dull click, and the doors slid open to reveal a cup of some dark, steaming beverage, a few not-very-exciting-looking sandwiches, and a large slice of melon. Wrinkling up his nose, and wondering how long mankind would take to slip back to barbarism at this rate, Brant started on his substitute meal and very soon polished it off.

His parents were still asleep as he went quietly out of the house into the wide, grass-covered square at the center of the village. It was still very early and there was a slight chill in the air, but the day was clear and fine, with that freshness which seldom lingers after the last dew has gone. Several aircraft were lying on the green, disgorging passengers, who were milling around in circles or wandering off to examine Chaldis with critical eyes. As Brant watched, one of the machines went humming briskly up into the sky, leaving a faint trail of ionization behind it. A moment later the others followed; they could carry only a few-dozen passengers and would have to make many trips before the day was out.

Brant strolled over to the visitors, trying to look self-assured yet not so aloof as to discourage all contacts. Most of the strangers were about his own age—the older people would be arriving at a more reasonable time.

They looked at him with a frank curiosity which he

returned with interest. Their skins were much darker than his, he noticed, and their voices were softer and less modulated. Some of them even had a trace of accent, for despite a universal language and instantaneous communication, regional variations still existed. At least, Brant assumed that they were the ones with accents; but once or twice he caught them smiling a little as he spoke.

Throughout the morning the visitors gathered in the square and made their way to the great arena that had been ruthlessly carved out of the forest. There were tents and bright banners here, and much shouting and laughter, for the morning was for the amusement of the young. Though Athens had swept like a dwindling but never-dying beacon for ten thousand years down the river of time, the pattern of sport had scarcely changed since those first Olympic days. Men still ran and jumped and wrestled and swam; but they did all these things a good deal better now than their ancestors. Brant was a fair sprinter over short distances and managed to finish third in the hundred meters. His time was just over eight seconds, which was not very good, because the record was less than seven. Brant would have been much amazed to learn that there was a time when no one in the world could have approached this figure.

Jon enjoyed himself hugely, bouncing youths even larger than himself onto the patient turf, and when the morning's results were added up, Chaldis had scored more points than any of the visitors, although it had been first in relatively few events.

As noon approached, the crowd began to flow amoebalike down to Five Oaks Glade, where the molecular synthesizers had been working since the early hours to cover hundreds of tables with food. Much skill had gone into preparing the prototypes which were being reproduced with absolute fidelity down to the last atom; for though the mechanics of food production had altered completely, the art of the chef had survived, and had even gone forward to victories in which Nature had played no part at all.

The main feature of the afternoon was a long poetic drama—a pastiche put together with considerable skill from the works of poets whose very names had been forgotten ages since. On the whole Brant found it boring, though there were some fine lines here and there that had stuck in his memory:

> For winter's rains and ruins are over,
> And all the season of snows and sins . . .

Brant knew about snow, and was glad to have left it behind. Sin, however, was an archaic word that had dropped out of use three or four thousand years ago; but it had an ominous and exciting ring.

He did not catch up with Yradne until it was almost dusk, and the dancing had begun. High above the valley, floating lights had started to burn, flooding the woods with ever-changing patterns of blue and red and gold. In twos and threes and then in dozens and hundreds, the dancers moved out into the great oval of the amphitheater, until it became a sea of laughing, whirling forms. Here at last was something at which Brant could beat Jon handsomely, and he let himself be swept away on the tide of sheer physical enjoyment.

The music ranged through the whole spectrum of human culture. At one moment the air pulsed to the throb of drums that might have called from some primeval jungle when the world was young; and a little later, intricate tapestries of quarter tones were being woven by subtle electronic skills. The stars peered down wanly as they marched across the sky, but no one saw them and no one gave any thought to the passage of time.

Brant had danced with many girls before he found Yradne. She looked very beautiful, brimming over with the enjoyment of life, and she seemed in no hurry to join him when there were so many others to choose from. But at last they were circling together in the whirlpool, and it gave Brant no small pleasure to think that Jon was probably watching them glumly from afar.

They broke away from the dance during a pause in the music because Yradne announced that she was a little tired. This suited Brant admirably, and presently they were sitting together under one of the great trees, watching the ebb and flow of life around them with that detachment that comes in moments of complete relaxation.

It was Brant who broke the spell. It had to be done, and it might be a long time before such an opportunity came again.

"Yradne," he said, "why have you been avoiding me?"

She looked at him with innocent, open eyes.

"Oh, Brant," she replied, "what an unkind thing to say; you know it isn't true! I wish you weren't so jealous: you can't expect me to be following you around *all* the time."

"Oh, very well!" said Brant weakly, wondering if he was making a fool of himself. But he might as well go on now he had started.

"You know, *some* day you'll have to decide between us. If you keep putting it off, perhaps you'll be left high and dry like those two aunts of yours."

Yradne gave a tinkling laugh and tossed her head with great amusement at the thought that she could ever be old and ugly.

"Even if you're too impatient," she replied, "I think I can rely on Jon. Have you seen what he's given me?"

"No," said Brant, his heart sinking.

"You *are* observant, aren't you! Haven't you noticed this necklace?"

On her breast Yradne was wearing a large group of jewels, suspended from her neck by a thin golden chain. It was quite a fine pendant, but there was nothing particularly unusual about it, and Brant wasted no time in saying so. Yradne smiled mysteriously and her fingers flickered toward her throat. Instantly the air was suffused with the sound of music, which first mingled with the background of the dance and then drowned it completely.

"You see," she said proudly, "wherever I go now I can have music with me. Jon says there are so many thousands of hours of it stored up that I'll never know when it repeats itself. Isn't it clever?"

"Perhaps it is," said Brant grudgingly, "but it isn't exactly new. Everyone used to carry this sort of thing once, until there was no silence anywhere on Earth and they had to be forbidden. Just think of the chaos if we all had them!"

Yradne broke away from him angrily.

"There you go again—always jealous of something you can't do yourself. What have you ever given me that's half as clever or useful as this? I'm going—and don't try to follow me!"

Brant stared open-mouthed as she went, quite taken aback by the violence of her reaction. Then he called after her, "Hey, Yradne, I didn't mean . . ." But she was gone.

He made his way out of the amphitheater in a very bad temper. It did him no good at all to rationalize the cause of Yradne's outburst. His remarks, though rather spiteful, had been true, and sometimes there is nothing more annoying than the truth. Jon's gift was an ingenious but trivial toy, interesting only because it now happened to be unique.

One thing she had said still rankled in his mind. What *was* there he had ever given Yradne? He had nothing but his paintings, and they weren't really very good. She had shown no interest in them at all when he had offered her some of his best, and it had been very hard to explain that he wasn't a portrait painter and would rather not try to make a picture of her. She had never really understood this, and it had been very difficult not to hurt her feelings. Brant liked taking his inspiration from Nature, but he never copied what he saw. When one of his pictures was finished (which occasionally happened), the title was often the only clue to the original source.

The music of the dance still throbbed around him, but he had lost all interest; the sight of other people enjoying themselves was more than he could stand. He decided to get away from the crowd, and the only peaceful place he could think of was down by the river, at the end of the shining carpet of freshly planted glow-moss that led through the wood.

He sat at the water's edge, throwing twigs into the current and watching them drift downstream. From time to time other idlers strolled by, but they were usually in pairs and took no notice of him. He watched them enviously and brooded over the unsatisfactory state of his affairs.

It would almost be better, he thought, if Yradne did make up her mind to choose Jon, and so put him out of his misery. But she showed not the slightest sign of preferring one to the other. Perhaps she was simply enjoying herself at their expense, as some people— particularly Old Johan—maintained; though it was just as likely that she was genuinely unable to choose. What was wanted, Brant thought morosely, was for one of them to do something really spectacular which the other could not hope to match.

"Hello," said a small voice behind him. He twisted

around and looked over his shoulder. A little girl of eight or so was staring at him with her head slightly on one side, like an inquisitive sparrow.

"Hello," he replied without enthusiasm. "Why aren't you watching the dance?"

"Why aren't you in it?" she replied promptly.

"I'm tired," he said, hoping that this was an adequate excuse. "You shouldn't be running around by yourself. You might get lost."

"I am lost," she replied happily, sitting down on the bank beside him. "I like it that way." Brant wondered which of the other villages she had come from; she was quite a pretty little thing, but would look prettier with less chocolate on her face. It seemed that his solitude was at an end.

She stared at him with that disconcerting directness which, perhaps fortunately, seldom survives childhood. "*I* know what's the matter with you," she said suddenly.

"Indeed?" queried Brant with polite skepticism.

"You're in love!"

Brant dropped the twig he was about to throw into the river, and turned to stare at his inquisitor. She was looking at him with such solemn sympathy that in a moment all his morbid self-pity vanished in a gale of laughter. She seemed quite hurt, and he quickly brought himself under control.

"How could you tell?" he asked with profound seriousness.

"I've read all about it," she replied solemnly. "And once I saw a picture play and there was a man in it and he came down to a river and sat there just like you and presently he jumped into it. There was some awful pretty music then."

Brant looked thoughtfully at this precocious child and felt relieved that she didn't belong to his own community.

"I'm sorry I can't arrange the music," he said gravely, "but in any case the river isn't really deep enough."

"It is farther along," came the helpful reply. "This is only a baby river here—it doesn't grow up until it leaves the woods. I saw it from the flyer."

"What happens to it then?" asked Brant, not in the least interested, but thankful that the conversation had taken a more innocuous turn. "I suppose it reaches the sea?"

She gave an unladylike sniff of disgust.

"Of course not, silly. All the rivers this side of the hills go to the Great Lake. I know that's as big as a sea, but the *real* sea is on the other side of the hills."

Brant had learned very little about the geographical details of his new home, but he realized that the child was quite correct. The ocean as less than twenty miles to the north, but separated from them by a barrier of low hills. A hundred miles inland lay the Great Lake, bringing life to lands that had been desert before the geological engineers had reshaped this continent.

The child genius was making a map out of twigs and patiently explaining these matters to her rather dull pupil.

"Here we are," she said, "and here's the river, and the hills, and the lake's over there by your foot. The sea goes along here—and I'll tell you a secret."

"What's that?"

"You'll never guess!"

"I don't suppose I will."

Her voice dropped to a confidential whisper. "If you go along the coast—it isn't very far from here—you'll come to Shastar."

Brant tried to look impressed, but failed.

"I don't believe you've ever heard of it!" she cried, deeply disappointed.

"I'm sorry," replied Brant. "I suppose it was a city,

and I know I've heard of it somewhere. But there were such a lot of them, you know—Carthage and Chicago and Babylon and Berlin—you simply can't remember them all. And they've all gone now, anyway."

"Not Shastar. It's still there."

"Well, some of the later ones are still standing, more or less, and people often visit them. About five hundred miles from my old home there was quite a big city once, called . . ."

"Shastar isn't just *any* old city," interrupted the child mysteriously. "My grandfather told me about it: he's been there. It hasn't been spoiled at all and it's still full of wonderful things that no one has any more."

Brant smiled inwardly. The deserted cities of Earth had been the breeding places of legends for countless centuries. It would be four—no, nearer five—thousand years since Shastar had been abandoned. If its buildings were still standing, which was of course quite possible, they would certainly have been stripped of all valuables ages ago. It seemed that Grandfather had been inventing some pretty fairy stories to entertain the child. He had Brant's sympathy.

Heedless of his skepticism, the girl prattled on. Brant gave only half his mind to her words, interjecting a polite "Yes" or "Fancy that" as occasion demanded. Suddenly, silence fell.

He looked up and found that his companion was staring with much annoyance toward the avenue of trees that overlooked the view.

"Good-by," she said abruptly. "I've got to hide somewhere else—here comes my sister."

She was gone as suddenly as she had arrived. Her family must have a busy time looking after her, Brant decided: but she had done him a good turn by dispelling his melancholy mood.

Within a few hours, he realized that she had done very much more than that.

*　　*　　*

Simon was leaning against his doorpost watching the world go by when Brant came in search of him. The world usually accelerated slightly when it had to pass Simon's door, for he was an interminable talker and once he had trapped a victim there was no escape for an hour or more. It was most unusual for anyone to walk voluntarily into his clutches, as Brant was doing now.

The trouble with Simon was that he had a first-class mind, and was too lazy to use it. Perhaps he might have been luckier had he been born in a more energetic age; all he had ever been able to do in Chaldis was to sharpen his wits at other people's expense, thereby gaining more fame than popularity. But he was quite indispensable, for he was a storehouse of knowledge, the greater part of it perfectly accurate.

"Simon," began Brant without any preamble. "I want to learn something about this country. The maps don't tell me much—they're too new. What was here, back in the old days?"

Simon scratched his wiry beard.

"I don't suppose it was very different. How long ago do you mean?"

"Oh, back in the time of the cities."

"There weren't so many trees, of course. This was probably agricultural land, used for food production. Did you see that farming machine they dug up when the amphitheater was being built? It must have been old; it wasn't even electric."

"Yes," said Brant impatiently. "I saw it. But tell me about the cities around here. According to the map, there was a place called Shastar a few hundred miles west of us along the coast. Do you know anything about it?"

"Ah, Shastar," murmured Simon, stalling for time.

"A very interesting place; I think I've even got a picture of it around somewhere. Just a moment while I go and see."

He disappeared into the house and was gone for nearly five minutes. In that time he made a very extensive library search, though a man from the age of books would hardly have guessed this from his actions. All the records Chaldis possessed were in a metal case a meter on a side; it contained, locked perpetually in subatomic patterns, the equivalent of a billion volumes of print. Almost all the knowledge of mankind, and the whole of its surviving literature, lay here concealed.

It was not merely a passive storehouse of wisdom, for it possessed a librarian. As Simon signaled his request to the tireless machine, the search went down, layer by layer, through the almost infinite network of circuits. It took only a fraction of a second to locate the information he needed, for he had given the name and the approximate date. Then he relaxed as the mental images came flooding into his brain, under the lightest of self-hypnosis. The knowledge would remain in his possession for a few hours only—long enough for his purpose—and would then fade away. Simon had no desire to clutter up his well-organized mind with irrelevancies, and to him the whole story of the rise and fall of the great cities was a historical digression of no particular importance. It was an interesting, if a regrettable, episode, and it belonged to a past that had irretrievably vanished.

Brant was still waiting patiently when he emerged, looking very wise.

"I couldn't find any pictures," he said. "My wife has been tidying up again. But I'll tell you what I can remember about Shastar."

Brant settled himself down as comfortably as he could; he was likely to be here for some time.

"Shastar was one of the very last cities that man

ever built. You know, of course, that cities arose quite late in human culture—only about twelve thousand years ago. They grew in number and importance for several thousand years, until at last there were some containing millions of people. It is very hard for us to imagine what it must have been like to live in such places—deserts of steel and stone with not even a blade of grass for miles. But they were necessary, before transport and communication had been perfected, and people had to live near each other to carry out all the intricate operations of trade and manufacture upon which their lives depended.

"The really great cities began to disappear when air transport became universal. The threat of attack in those far-off, barbarous days also helped to disperse them. But for a long time . . ."

"I've studied the history of that period," interjected Brant, not very truthfully. "I know all about . . ."

". . . for a long time there were still many small cities which were held together by cultural rather than commercial links. They had populations of a few score thousand and lasted for centuries after the passing of the giants. That's why Oxford and Princeton and Heidelberg still mean something to us, while far larger cities are no more than names. But even these were doomed when the invention of the integrator made it possible for any community, however small, to manufacture without effort everything it needed for civilized living.

"Shastar was built when there was no longer any need, technically, for cities, but before people realized that the culture of cities was coming to its end. It seems to have been a conscious work of art, conceived and designed as a whole, and those who lived there were mostly artists of some kind. But it didn't last very long; what finally killed it was the exodus."

Simon became suddenly quiet, as if brooding on

those tumultuous centuries when the road to the stars had been opened up and the world was torn in twain. Along that road the flower of the race had gone, leaving the rest behind; and thereafter it seemed that history had come to an end on Earth. For a thousand years or more the exiles had returned fleetingly to the solar system, wistfully eager to tell of strange suns and far planets and the great empire that would one day span the galaxy. But there are gulfs that even the swiftest ships can never cross; and such a gulf was opening now between Earth and her wandering children. They had less and less in common; the returning ships became ever more infrequent, until at last generations passed between the visits from outside. Simon had not heard of any such for almost three hundred years.

It was unusual when one had to prod Simon into speech, but presently Brant remarked: "Anyway, I'm more interested in the place itself than its history. Do you think it's still standing?"

"I was coming to that," said Simon, emerging from his reverie with a start. "Of course it is; they built well in those days. But why are you so interested, may I ask? Have you suddenly developed an overwhelming passion for archaeology? Oh, I think I understand!"

Brant knew perfectly well the uselessness of trying to conceal anything from a professional busybody like Simon.

"I was hoping," he said defensively, "that there might still be things there worth going to find, even after all this time."

"Perhaps," said Simon doubtfully. "I must visit it one day. It's almost on our doorstep, as it were. But how are *you* going to manage? The village will hardly let you borrow a flyer! And you can't walk. It would take you at least a week to get there."

But that was exactly what Brant intended to do. As,

during the next few days, he was careful to point out to almost everyone in the village, a thing wasn't worth doing unless one did it the hard way. There was nothing like making a virtue out of a necessity.

Brant's preparations were carried out in an unprecedented blaze of secrecy. He did not wish to be too specific about his plans, such as they were, in case any of the dozen or so people in Chaldis who had the right to use a flyer decided to look at Shastar first. It was, of course, only a matter of time before this happened, but the feverish activity of the past months had prevented such explorations. Nothing would be more humiliating than to stagger into Shastar after a week's journey, only to be coolly greeted by a neighbor who had made the trip in ten minutes.

On the other hand, it was equally important that the village in general, and Yradne in particular, should realize that he was making some exceptional effort. Only Simon knew the truth, and he had grudgingly agreed to keep quiet for the present. Brant hoped that he had managed to divert attention from his true objective by showing a great interest in the country to the *east* of Chaldis, which also contained several archaeological relics of some importance.

The amount of food and equipment one needed for a two or three weeks' absence was really astonishing, and his first calculations had thrown Brant into a state of considerable gloom. For a while he had even thought of trying to beg or borrow a flyer, but the request would certainly not be granted—and would indeed defeat the whole object of his enterprise. Yet it was quite impossible for him to carry everything he needed for the journey.

The solution would have been perfectly obvious to anyone from a less-mechanized age, but it took Brant some little time to think of it. The flying machine had killed all forms of land transport save one, the oldest and most versatile of all—the only one that was self-perpetuating and could manage very well, as it had done before, with no assistance at all from man.

Chaldis possessed six horses, rather a small number for a community of its size. In some villages the horses outnumbered the humans, but Brant's people, living in a wild and mountainous region, had so far had little opportunity for equitation. Brant himself had ridden a horse only two or three times in his life, and then for exceedingly short periods.

The stallion and five mares were in the charge of Treggor, a gnarled little man who had no discernible interest in life except animals. His was not one of the oustanding intellects of Chaldis, but he seemed perfectly happy running his private menagerie, which included dogs of many shapes and sizes, a couple of beavers, several monkeys, a lion cub, two bears, a young crocodile, and other beasts more usually admired from a distance. The only sorrow that had ever clouded his placid life arose from the fact that he had so far failed to obtain an elephant.

Brant found Treggor, as he expected, leaning on the gate of the paddock. There was a stranger with him, who was introduced to Brant as a horse fancier from a neighboring village. The curious similarity between the two men, extending from the way they dressed even to their facial expressions, made this explanation quite unnecessary.

One always feels a certain nervousness in the presence of undoubted experts, and Brant outlined his problem with some diffidence. Treggor listened gravely and paused for a long time before replying.

"Yes," he said slowly, jerking his thumb toward the mares, "any of them would do—if you knew how to handle 'em." He looked rather doubtfully at Brant.

"They're like human beings, you know; if they don't like you, you can't do a thing with them."

"Not a thing," echoed the stranger, with evident relish.

"But surely you could teach me how to handle them?"

"Maybe yes, maybe no. I remember a young fellow just like you, wanted to learn to ride. Horses just wouldn't let him get near them. Took a dislike to him—and that was that."

"Horses can *tell*," interjected the other darkly.

"That's right," agreed Treggor. "You've got to be sympathetic. Then you've nothing to worry about."

There was, Brant decided, quite a lot to be said for the less-temperamental machine after all.

"I don't want to ride," he answered with some feeling. "I only want a horse to carry my gear. Or would it be likely to object to that?"

His mild sarcasm was quite wasted. Treggor nodded solemnly.

"That wouldn't be any trouble," he said. "They'll all let you lead them with a halter—all except Daisy, that is. You'd never catch *her*."

"Then do you think I could borrow one of the—er, more amenable ones—for a while?"

Treggor shuffled around uncertainly, torn between two conflicting desires. He was pleased that someone wanted to use his beloved beasts, but nervous lest they come to harm. Any damage that might befall Brant was of secondary importance.

"Well," he began doubtfully, "it's a bit awkward at the moment. . . ."

Brant looked at the mares more closely, and realized why. Only one of them was accompanied by a foal, but it was obvious that this deficiency would soon be rectified. Here was another complication he had overlooked.

"How long will you be away?" asked Treggor.

"Three weeks, at the most: perhaps only two."

Treggor did some rapid gynaecological calculations.

"Then you can have Sunbeam," he concluded. "She won't give you any trouble at all—best-natured animal I've ever had."

"Thank you very much," said Brant. "I promise I'll look after her. Now would you mind introducing us?"

"I don't see why I should do this," grumbled Jon good-naturedly, as he adjusted the panniers on Sunbeam's sleek sides, "especially since you won't even tell me where you're going or what you expect to find."

Brant couldn't have answered the last question even had he wished. In his more rational moments he knew that he would find nothing of value in Shastar. Indeed, it was hard to think of anything that his people did not already possess, or could not obtain instantly if they wished. But the journey itself would be the proof—the most convincing he could imagine—of his love for Yradne.

There was no doubt that she was quite impressed by his preparations, and he had been careful to underline the dangers he was about to face. It would be very uncomfortable sleeping in the open, and he would have a most monotonous diet. He might even get lost and never be seen again. Suppose there were still wild beasts—dangerous ones—up in the hills or the forests?

Old Johan, who had no feeling for historical traditions, had protested at the indignity of a blacksmith having anything to do with such a primitive survival as a horse. Sunbeam had nipped him delicately for this, with great skill and precision, while he was bending to examine her hoofs. But he had rapidly manufactured a set of panniers in which Brant could put everything he needed for the journey—even his drawing materials, from which he refused to be separated. Treggor had advised on the technical details of the harness, producing ancient prototypes consisting largely of string.

It was still early morning when the last adjustments had been completed; Brant had intended making his departure as unobtrusive as possible, and his complete success was slightly mortifying. Only Jon and Yradne came to see him off.

They walked in thoughtful silence to the end of the village and crossed the slim metal bridge over the river. Then Jon said gruffly: "Well, don't go and break your silly neck," shook hands, and departed, leaving him alone with Yradne. It was a very nice gesture, and Brant appreciated it.

Taking advantage of her master's preoccupation, Sunbeam began to browse among the long grass by the river's edge. Brant shifted awkwardly from foot to foot for a moment, then said halfheartedly:

"I suppose I'd better be going."

"How long will you be away?" asked Yradne. She wasn't wearing Jon's present: perhaps she had grown tired of it already. Brant hoped so—then realized she might lose interest equally quickly in anything he brought back for her.

"Oh, about a fortnight—if all goes well," he added darkly.

"Do be careful," said Yradne, in tones of vague urgency, "and don't do anything rash."

"I'll do my best," answered Brant, still making no move to go, "but one has to take risks sometimes."

This disjointed conversation might have lasted a good deal longer had Sunbeam not taken charge. Brant's arm received a sudden jerk and he was dragged away at a brisk walk. He had regained his balance and was about to wave farewell when Yradne came flying up to him, gave him a large kiss, and disappeared toward the village before he could recover.

She slowed down to a walk when Brant could no longer see her. Jon was still a good way ahead, but she made no attempt to overtake him. A curiously solemn feeling, out of place on this bright spring morning, had overcome her. It was very pleasant to be loved, but it had its disadvantages if one stopped to look beyond the immediate moment. For a fleeting instant Yradne wondered if she had been fair to Jon, to Brant—even to herself. One day the decision would have to be made; it could not be postponed forever. Yet she could not for the life of her decide which of the boys she liked the better; and she did not know if she loved either.

No one had ever told her, and she had not yet discovered, that when one has to ask "Am I really in love?" the answer is always "No."

Beyond Chaldis the forest stretched for five miles to the east, then faded out into the great plain which spanned the remainder of the continent. Six thousand years ago this land had been one of the mightiest deserts in the world, and its reclamation had been among the first achievements of the Atomic Age.

Brant intended to go east until he was clear of the forest, and then to turn toward the high land of the North. According to the maps, there had once been a road along the spine of the hills, linking together all the cities on the coast in a chain that ended at Shastar. It should be easy to follow its track, though Brant did not expect that much of the road itself would have survived the centuries.

He kept close to the river, hoping that it had not changed its path since the maps were made. It was both his guide and his highway through the forest; when the trees were too thick, he and Sunbeam could always wade in the shallow water. Sunbeam was quite co-operative; there was no grass here to distract her, so she plodded methodically along with little prompting.

Soon after midday the trees began to thin out. Brant had reached the frontier that, century by century, had been on the march across the lands that Man no longer wished to hold. A little later the forest was behind him and he was out in the open plain.

He checked his position from the map, and noted that the trees had advanced an appreciable distance eastward since it was drawn. But there was a clear route north to the low hills along which the ancient road had run, and he should be able to reach them before evening.

At this point certain unforeseen difficulties of a technical nature arose. Sunbeam, finding herself surrounded by the most appetizing grass she had seen for a long time, was unable to resist pausing every three or four steps to collect a mouthful. As Brant was attached to her bridle by a rather short rope, the resulting jerk almost dislocated his arm. Lengthening the rope made matters even worse, because he then had no control at all.

Now Brant was quite fond of animals, but it soon became apparent to him that Sunbeam was simply imposing on his good nature. He put up with it for half a mile, and then steered a course toward a tree which seemed to have particularly slender and lissom branches. Sunbeam watched him warily out of the corners of her limpid brown eyes as he cut a fine, resilient switch and attached it ostentatiously to his belt. Then she set off so briskly that he could scarcely keep pace with her.

She was undoubtedly, as Treggor had claimed, a singularly intelligent beast.

The range of hills that was Brant's first objective was less than two thousand feet high, and the slope was very gentle. But there were numerous annoying foothills and minor valleys to be surmounted on the

way to the crest, and it was well toward evening before they had reached the highest point. To the south
Brant could see the forest through which he had come,
and which could now hinder him no more. Chaldis was
somewhere in the midst, though he had only a rough
idea of its location; he was surprised to find that he
could see no signs of the great clearings that his people
had made. To the southeast the plain stretched end-
lessly away, a level sea of grass dotted with little
clumps of trees. Near the horizon Brant could see tiny
creeping specks, and guessed that some great herd of
wild animals was on the move.

Northward lay the sea, only a dozen miles away
down the long slope and across the lowlands. It seemed
almost black in the falling sunlight, except where tiny
breakers dotted it with flecks of foam.

Before nightfall Brant found a hollow out of the
wind, anchored Sunbeam to a stout bush, and pitched
the little tent that Old Johan had contrived for him.
This was, in theory, a very simple operation, but, as a
good many people had found before, it was one that
could tax skill and temper to the utmost. At last everything was finished, and he settled down for the night.

There are some things that no amount of pure intelligence can anticipate, but which can only be learned by
bitter experience. Who would have guessed that the
human body was so sensitive to the almost impercepti-
ble slope on which the tent had been pitched? More
uncomfortable still were the minute thermal differ-
ences between one point and another, presumably
caused by the draughts that seemed to wander through
the tent at will. Brant could have endured a uniform
temperature gradient, but the unpredictable variations
were maddening.

He woke from his fitful sleep a dozen times, or so it
seemed, and toward dawn his morale had reached its

lowest ebb. He felt cold and miserable and stiff, as if he had not slept properly for days, and it would have needed very little persuasion to have made him abandon the whole enterprise. He was prepared—even willing—to face danger in the cause of love; but lumbago was a different matter.

The discomforts of the night were soon forgotten in the glory of the new day. Here on the hills the air was fresh with the tang of salt, borne by the wind that came climbing up from the sea. The dew was everywhere, hanging thickly on each bent blade of grass—but so soon to be destroyed beyond all trace by the steepening sun. It was good to be alive; it was better to be young; it was best of all to be in love.

They came upon the road very soon after they had started the day's journey. Brant had missed it before because it had been farther down the seaward slope, and he had expected to find it on the crest of the hill. It had been superbly built, and the millennia had touched it lightly. Nature had tried in vain to obliterate it; here and there she had succeeded in burying a few meters with a light blanket of earth, but then her servants had turned against her and the wind and the rain had scoured it clean once more. In a great jointless band, skirting the edge of the sea for more than a thousand miles, the road still linked the cities that Man had loved in his childhood.

It was one of the great roads of the world. Once it had been no more than a footpath along which savage tribes had come down to the sea, to barter with wily, bright-eyed merchants from distant lands. Then it had known new and more exacting masters; the soldiers of a mighty empire had shaped and hewn the road so skillfully along the hills that the path they gave it had remained unchanged down all the ages. They had paved it with stone so that their armies could move more swiftly than any that the world had known; and along the road their legions had been hurled like thunderbolts at the bidding of the city whose name they bore. Centuries later, that city had called them home in its last extremity; and the road had rested then for five hundred years.

But other wars were still to come; beneath crescent banners the armies of the Prophet were yet to storm westward into Christendom. Later still—centuries later—the tide of the last and greatest of conflicts was to turn here, as steel monsters clashed together in the desert, and the sky itself rained death.

The centurions, the paladins, the armored divisions—even the desert—all were gone. But the road remained, of all man's creations the most enduring. For ages enough it had borne his burdens; and now along its whole thousand miles it carried no more traffic than one boy and a horse.

Brant followed the road for three days, keeping always in sight of the sea. He had grown used to the minor discomforts of a nomadic existence, and even the nights were no longer intolerable. The weather had been perfect—long, warm days and mild nights—but the fine spell was coming to an end.

He estimated that he was less than five miles from Shastar on the evening of the fourth day. The road was now turning away from the coast to avoid a great headland jutting out to sea. Beyond this was the sheltered bay along whose shores the city had been built; when it had bypassed the high ground, the road would sweep northward in a great curve and come down upon Shastar from the hills.

Toward dusk it was clear that Brant could not hope to see his goal that day. The weather was breaking, and thick, angry clouds had been gathering swiftly from the west. He was climbing now—for the road was rising slowly as it crossed the last ridge—in the teeth of a gale. He would have pitched camp for the night if he could have found a sheltered spot, but the hill was bare for miles behind him and there was nothing to do but to struggle onward.

Far ahead, at the very crest of the ridge, something low and dark was silhouetted against the threatening sky. The hope that it might provide shelter drove Brant onward: Sunbeam, head well down against the wind, plodded steadily beside him with equal determination.

They were still a mile from the summit when the rain began to fall, first in single, angry drops and then in blinding sheets. It was impossible to see more than a few paces ahead, even when one could open one's eyes against the stinging rain. Brant was already so wet that any additional moisture could add nothing to his discomfort; indeed, he had reached that sodden state when the continuing downpour almost gave him a masochistic pleasure. But the sheer physical effort of fighting against the gale was rapidly exhausting him.

It seemed ages before the road leveled out and he knew he had reached the summit. He strained his eyes into the gloom and could see, not far ahead, a great dark shape, which for a moment he thought might be a building. Even if it was in ruins, it would give him shelter from the storm.

The rain began to slacken as he approached the object; overhead, the clouds were thinning to let through the last fading light of the western sky. It was just sufficient to show Brant that what lay ahead of him was no building at all, but a great stone beast, crouching upon the hilltop and staring out to sea. He had no time to examine it more closely, but hurriedly pitched his tent in its shelter, out of reach of the wind that still raved angrily overhead.

It was completely dark when he had dried himself and prepared a meal. For a while he rested in his warm little oasis, in that state of blissful exhaustion that comes after hard and successful effort. Then he roused himself, took a hand-torch, and went out into the night.

The storm had blown away the clouds and the night was brilliant with stars. In the west a thin crescent moon was sinking, following hard upon the footsteps of the sun. To the north Brant was aware—though how, he could not have said—of the sleepless presence of the sea. Down there in the darkness Shastar was lying, the waves marching forever against it; but strain his eyes as he might, he could see nothing at all.

He walked along the flanks of the great statue, examining the stonework by the light of his torch. It was smooth and unbroken by any joints or seams, and although time had stained and discolored it, there was no sign of wear. It was impossible to guess its age; it might be older than Shastar or it might have been made only a few centuries ago. There was no way of telling.

The hard, blue-white beam of the torch flickered along the monster's wetly gleaming sides and came to rest upon the great, calm face and the empty eyes. One might have called it a human face, but thereafter words faltered and failed. Neither male nor female, it seemed at first sight utterly indifferent to all the passions of mankind; then Brant saw that the storms of ages had left their mark behind them. Countless raindrops had coursed down those adamantine cheeks, until they bore the stains of Olympian tears—tears, perhaps, for the city whose birth and death now seemed almost equally remote.

Brant was so tired that when he awoke the sun was already high. He lay for a moment in the filtered half-light of the tent, recovering his senses and remembering where he was. Then he rose to his feet and

went blinking into the daylight, shielding his eyes from
the dazzling glare.

The Sphinx seemed smaller than by night, though it
was impressive enough. It was colored, Brant saw for
the first time, a rich, autumnal gold, the color of no
natural rock. He knew from this that it did not belong,
as he had half suspected, to any prehistoric culture. It
had been built by science from some inconceivably
stubborn, synthetic substance, and Brant guessed that
its creation must lie almost midway in time between
him and the fabulous original which had inspired it.

Slowly, half afraid of what he might discover, he
turned his back upon the Sphinx and looked to the
north. The hill fell away at his feet and the road went
sweeping down the long slope as if impatient to greet
the sea; and there at its end lay Shastar.

It caught the sunlight and tossed it back to him,
tinted with all the colors of its makers' dreams. The
spacious buildings lining the wide streets seemed un-
ravished by time; the great band of marble that held
the sea at bay was still unbreached; the parks and
gardens, though long overgrown with weeds, were not
yet jungles. The city followed the curve of the bay for
perhaps two miles, and stretched half that distance
inland; by the standards of the past, it was very small
indeed. But to Brant it seemed enormous, a maze of
streets and squares intricate beyond unraveling. Then
he began to discern the underlying symmetry of its
design, to pick out the main thoroughfares, and to see
the skill with which its makers had avoided both monotony and discord.

For a long time Brant stood motionless on the hilltop, conscious only of the wonder spread beneath his
eyes. He was alone in all that landscape, a tiny figure
lost and humble before the achievements of greater
men. The sense of history, the vision of the long slope
up which Man had been toiling for a million years or

more, was almost overwhelming. In that moment it seemed to Brant that from his hilltop he was looking over Time rather than Space: and in his ears there whispered the soughing of the winds of eternity as they sweep into the past.

Sunbeam seemed very nervous as they approached the outskirts of the city. She had never seen anything like this before in her life, and Brant could not help sharing her disquiet. However unimaginative one may be, there is something ominous about buildings that have been deserted for centuries—and those of Shastar had been empty for the better part of five thousand years.

The road ran straight as an arrow between two tall pillars of white metal; like the Sphinx, they were tarnished but unworn. Brant and Sunbeam passed beneath these silent guardians and found themselves before a long, low building which must have served as some kind of reception point for visitors to the city.

From a distance it had seemed that Shastar might have been abandoned only yesterday, but now Brant could see a thousand signs of desolation and neglect. The colored stone of the buildings was stained with the patina of age; the windows were gaping, skull-blank eyes, with here and there a miraculously preserved fragment of glass.

Brant tethered Sunbeam outside the first building and made his way to the entrance across the rubble and thickly piled dirt. There was no door, if indeed there had ever been one, and he passed through the high, vaulted archway into a hall which seemed to run the full length of the structure. At regular intervals there were openings into further chambers, and immediately ahead of him a wide flight of stairs rose to the single floor above.

It took him almost an hour to explore the building,

and when he left he was infinitely depressed. His careful search had revealed absolutely nothing. All the rooms, great and small, were completely empty; he had felt like an ant crawling through the bones of a clean-picked skeleton.

Out in the sunlight, however, his spirits revived a little. This building was probably only some sort of administrative office and would never have contained anything but records and information machines; elsewhere in the city, things might be different. Even so, the magnitude of the search appalled him.

Slowly he made his way toward the sea front, moving awe-struck through the wide avenues and admiring the towering façades on either side. Near the center of the city he came upon one of its many parks. It was largely overgrown with weeds and shrubs, but there were still considerable areas of grass, and he decided to leave Sunbeam here while he continued his explorations. She was not likely to move very far away while there was plenty to eat.

It was so peaceful in the park that for a while Brant was loath to leave it to plunge again into the desolation of the city. There were plants here unlike any that he had ever seen before, the wild descendants of those which the people of Shastar had cherished ages since. As he stood among the high grasses and unknown flowers, Brant heard for the first time, stealing through the calm stillness of the morning, the sound he was always to link with Shastar. It came from the sea, and though he had never heard it before in all his life, it brought a sense of aching recognition into his heart. Where no other voices sounded now, the lonely sea gulls were still calling sadly across the waves.

It was quite clear that many days would be needed to make even the most superficial examination of the city, and the first thing to do would be to find somewhere to live. Brant spent several hours searching for the residential district before it began to dawn on him that there was something very peculiar about Shastar. All the buildings he entered were, without exception, designed for work, entertainment, or similar purposes; but none of them had been designed *to live in*. The solution came to him slowly. As he grew to know the pattern of the city, he noticed that at almost every street intersection there were low, single-storied structures of nearly identical form. They were circular or oval, and had many openings leading into them from all directions. When Brant entered one of them, he found himself facing a line of great metal gates, each with a vertical row of indicator lamps by its side. And so he knew where the people of Shastar had lived.

At first the idea of underground homes was completely repellent to him. Then he overcame his prejudice, and realized how sensible, as well as how inevitable, this was. There was no need to clutter up the surface, and to block the sunlight, with buildings designed for the merely mechanical processes of sleeping and eating. By putting all these things underground, the people of Shastar had been able to build a noble and spacious city—and yet keep it so small that one could walk its whole length within an hour.

The elevators were, of course, useless, but there were emergency stairways winding down into the darkness. Once all this underworld must have been a blaze of light, but Brant hesitated now before he descended the steps. He had his torch, but he had never been underground before and had a horror of losing his way in some subterranean catacombs. Then he shrugged his shoulders and started down the steps; after all, there was no danger if he took the most elementary precautions—and there were hundreds of other exits even if he did lose his way.

He descended to the first level and found himself in

a long, wide corridor stretching as far as his beam could penetrate. On either side were rows of numbered doors, and Brant tried nearly a dozen before he found one that opened. Slowly, even reverently, he entered the little home that had been deserted for almost half the span of recorded history.

It was clean and tidy, for there had been no dust or dirt to settle here. The beautifully proportioned rooms were bare of furniture; nothing of value had been left behind in the leisurely, age-long exodus. Some of the semipermanent fittings were still in position; the food distributor, with its familiar selector dial, was so strikingly like the one in Brant's own home that the sight of it almost annihilated the centuries. The dial still turned, though stiffly, and he would scarcely have been surprised to see a meal appear in the materialization chamber.

Brant explored several more homes before he returned to the surface. Though he found nothing of value, he felt a growing sense of kinship toward the people who had lived here. Yet he still thought of them as his inferiors, for to have lived in a city—however beautiful, however brilliantly designed—was to Brant one of the symbols of barbarism.

In the last home he entered he came across a brightly colored room with a fresco of dancing animals around the walls. The pictures were full of a whimsical humor that must have delighted the hearts of the children for whom they had been drawn. Brant examined the paintings with interest, for they were the first works of representative art he had found in Shastar. He was about to leave when he noticed a tiny pile of dust in one corner of the room, and bending down to investigate found himself looking at the still-recognizable fragments of a doll. Nothing solid remained save a few colored buttons, which crumbled to powder in his hand when he picked them up. He wondered why this sad little

relic had been left behind by its owner; then he tiptoed away and returned to the surface and the lonely
but sunlit streets. He never went to the underground
city again.

Toward evening he revisited the park to see that
Sunbeam had been up to no mischief, and prepared to
spend the night in one of the numerous small buildings
scattered through the gardens. Here he was surrounded
by flowers and trees, and could almost imagine he was
home again. He slept better than he had done since he
had left Chaldis, and for the first time for many days,
his last waking thoughts were not of Yradne. The
magic of Shastar was already working upon his mind;
the infinite complexity of the civilization he had af-
fected to despise was changing him more swiftly than
he could imagine. The longer he stayed in the city, the
more remote he would become from the naïve yet
self-confident boy who had entered it only a few hours
before.

The second day confirmed the impressions of the
first. Shastar had not died in a year, or even in a
generation. Slowly its people had drifted away as the
new—yet how old!—pattern of society had been evolved
and humanity had returned to the hills and the forests.
They had left nothing behind them, save these marble
monuments to a way of life that was gone forever.
Even if anything of value had remained, the thousands
of curious explorers who had come here in the fifty
centuries since would have taken it long ago. Brant
found many traces of his predecessors; their names
were carved on walls throughout the city, for this is
one kind of immortality that men have never been
able to resist.

Tired at last by his fruitless search, he went down to
the shore and sat on the wide stonework of the break-
water. The sea lying a few feet beneath him was utterly calm and of a cerulean blue; it was so still and

clear that he could watch the fish swimming in its depths, and at one spot could see a wreck lying on its side with the seaweed streaming straight up from it like long, green hair. Yet there must be times, he knew, when the waves came thundering over the massive walls; for behind him the wide parapet was strewn with a thick carpet of stones and shells, tossed there by the gales of centuries.

The enervating peacefulness of the scene, and the unforgettable object lesson in the futility of ambition that surrounded him on every side, took away all sense of disappointment or defeat. Though Shastar had given him nothing of material value, Brant did not regret his journey. Sitting here on the sea wall, with his back to the land and his eyes dazzled by that blinding blue, he already felt remote from his old problems, and could look back with no pain at all, but only a dispassionate curiosity, on all the heartache and the anxiety that had plagued him these last few months.

He went slowly back into the city, after walking a little way along the sea front so that he could return by a new route. Presently he found himself before a large circular building whose roof was a shallow dome of some translucent material. He looked at it with little interest, for he was emotionally exhausted, and decided that it was probably yet another theater or concert hall. He had almost passed the entrance when some obscure impulse diverted him and he went through the open doorway.

Inside, the light filtered through the ceiling with such little hindrance that Brant almost had the impression of being in the open air. The entire building was divided into numerous large halls whose purpose he realized with a sudden stir of excitement. The telltale rectangles of discoloration showed that the walls had once been almost covered with pictures; it was just possible that some had been left behind, and it would be interesting to see what Shastar could offer in the way of serious art. Brant, still secure in his consciousness of superiority, did not expect to be unduly impressed; and so the shock was all the greater when it came.

The blaze of color along the whole length of the great wall smote him like a fanfare of trumpets. For a moment he stood paralyzed in the doorway, unable to grasp the pattern or meaning of what he saw. Then, slowly, he began to unravel the details of the tremendous and intricate mural that had burst suddenly upon his vision.

It was nearly a hundred feet long, and was incomparably the most wonderful thing that Brant had ever seen in his life. Shastar had awed and overwhelmed him, yet its tragedy had left him curiously unmoved. But this struck straight at his heart and spoke in a language he could understand; and as it did so, the last vestiges of his condescension toward the past were scattered like leaves before a gale.

The eye moved naturally from left to right across the painting, to follow the curve of tension to its moment of climax. On the left was the sea, as deep a blue as the water that beat against Shastar; and moving across its face was a fleet of strange ships, driven by tiered banks of oars and by billowing sails that strained toward the distant land. The painting covered not only miles of space but perhaps years of time; for now the ships had reached the shore, and there on the wide plain an army lay encamped, its banners and tents and chariots dwarfed by the walls of the fortress city it was beleaguering. The eye scaled those still inviolate walls and came to rest, as it was meant to do, upon the woman who stood upon them, looking down at the army that had followed her across the ocean.

She was leaning forward to peer over the battlements, and the wind was catching her hair so that it formed a golden mist about her head. Upon her face was written a sadness too deep for words, yet one that did nothing to mar the unbelievable beauty of her face—a beauty that held Brant spellbound, for long unable to tear away his eyes. When at last he could do so, he followed her gaze down those seemingly impregnable walls to the group of soldiers toiling in their shadow. They were gathered around something so foreshortened by perspective that it was some time before Brant realized what it was. Then he saw that it was an enormous image of a horse, mounted on rollers so that it could be easily moved. It roused no echoes in his mind, and he quickly returned to the lonely figure on the wall, around whom, as he now saw, the whole great design was balanced and pivoted. For as the eye moved on across the painting, taking the mind with it into the future, it came upon ruined battlements, the smoke of the burning city staining the sky, and the fleet returning homeward, its mission done.

Brant left only when the light was so poor that he could no longer see. When the first shock had worn off, he had examined the great painting more closely; and for a while he had searched, but in vain, for the signature of the artist. He also looked for some caption or title, but it was clear that there had never been one—perhaps because the story was too well known to need it. In the intervening centuries, however, some other visitor to Shastar had scratched two lines of poetry on the wall:

> Is this the face that launched a thousand ships
> And burned the topless towers of Ilium?

Ilium! It was a strange and magical name; but it meant nothing to Brant. He wondered whether it belonged to history or to fable, not knowing how many before him had wrestled with that same problem.

As he emerged into the luminous twilight, he still carried the vision of that sad, ethereal loveliness before his eyes. Perhaps if Brant had not himself been an artist, and had been in a less susceptible state of mind, the impression would not have been so overwhelming. Yet it was the impression that the unknown master had set out to create, Phoenix-like, from the dying embers of a great legend. He had captured, and held for all future ages to see, that beauty whose service is the purpose of life, and its sole justification.

For a long time Brant sat under the stars, watching the crescent moon sink behind the towers of the city, and haunted by questions to which he could never know the answers. All the other pictures in these galleries had gone, scattered beyond tracing, not merely throughout the world, but throughout the universe. How had they compared with the single work of genius that now must represent forever the art of Shastar?

In the morning Brant returned, after a night of strange dreams. A plan had been forming in his mind; it was so wild and ambitious that at first he tried to laugh it away, but it would give him no peace. Almost reluctantly, he set up his little folding easel and prepared his paints. He had found one thing in Shastar that was both unique and beautiful; perhaps he had the skill to carry some faint echo of it back to Chaldis.

It was impossible, of course, to copy more than a fragment of the vast design, but the problem of selection was easy. Though he had never attempted a portrait of Yradne, he would now paint a woman who, if indeed she had ever existed, had been dust for five thousand years.

Several times he stopped to consider this paradox, and at last thought he had resolved it. He had never painted Yradne because he doubted his own skill, and was afraid of her criticism. That would be no problem here, Brant told himself. He did not stop to ask how Yradne would react when he returned to Chaldis carrying as his only gift the portrait of another woman.

In truth, he was painting for himself, and for no one else. For the first time in his life he had come into direct contact with a great work of classic art, and it had swept him off his feet. Until now he had been a dilettante; he might never be more than this, but at least he would make the effort.

He worked steadily all through the day, and the sheer concentration of his labors brought him a certain peace of mind. By evening he had sketched in the palace walls and battlements, and was about to start on the portrait itself. That night, he slept well.

He lost most of his optimism the next morning. His food supply was running low, and perhaps the thought that he was working against time had unsettled him. Everything seemed to be going wrong; the colors would not match, and the painting, which had shown such promise the day before, was becoming less and less satisfactory every minute.

To make matters worse, the light was failing, though it was barely noon, and Brant guessed that the sky outside had become overcast. He rested for a while in the hope that it might clear again, but since it showed no signs of doing so, he recommenced work. It was now or nothing; unless he could get that hair right he would abandon the whole project. . . .

The afternoon waned rapidly, but in his fury of concentration Brant scarcely noticed the passage of time. Once or twice he thought he noticed distant sounds and wondered if a storm was coming up, for the sky was still very dark.

There is no experience more chilling than the sudden, the utterly unexpected knowledge that one is no longer alone. It would be hard to say what impulse made Brant slowly lay down his brush and turn, even more slowly, toward the great doorway forty feet behind him. The man standing there must have entered almost soundlessly, and how long he had been watching him Brant had no way of guessing. A moment later he was joined by two companions, who also made no attempt to pass the doorway.

Brant rose slowly to his feet, his brain whirling. For a moment he almost imagined that ghosts from Shastar's past had come back to haunt him. Then reason reasserted itself. After all, why should he not meet other visitors here, when he was one himself?

He took a few paces forward, and one of the strangers did likewise. When they were a few yards apart, the other said in a very clear voice, speaking rather slowly: "I hope we haven't disturbed you."

It was not a very dramatic conversational opening, and Brant was somewhat puzzled by the man's accent —or, more accurately, by the exceedingly careful way he was pronouncing his words. It almost seemed that he did not expect Brant to understand him otherwise.

"That's quite all right," Brant replied, speaking equally slowly. "But you gave me a surprise—I hardly expected to meet anyone here."

"Neither did we," said the other with a slight smile. "We had no idea that anyone still lived in Shastar."

"But I don't," explained Brant. "I'm just a visitor like you."

The three exchanged glances, as if sharing some secret joke. Then one of them lifted a small metal object from his belt and spoke a few words into it, too softly for Brant to overhear. He assumed that other members of the party were on the way, and felt annoyed that his solitude was to be so completely shattered.

Two of the strangers had walked over to the great

mural and begun to examine it critically. Brant wondered what they were thinking; somehow he resented sharing his treasure with those who would not feel the same reverence toward it—those to whom it would be nothing more than a pretty picture. The third man remained by his side comparing, as unobtrusively as possible, Brant's copy with the original. All three seemed to be deliberately avoiding further conversation. There was a long and embarrassing silence: then the other two men rejoined them.

"Well, Erlyn, what do you think of it?" said one, waving his hand toward the painting. They seemed for the moment to have lost all interest in Brant.

"It's a very fine late third-millennium primitive, as good as anything we have. Don't you agree, Latvar?"

"Not exactly. I wouldn't say it's late third. For one thing, the subject . . ."

"Oh, you and your theories! But perhaps you're right. It's too good for the last period. On second thoughts, I'd date it around 2500. What do you say, Trescon?"

"I agree. Probably Aroon or one of his pupils."

"Rubbish!" said Latvar.

"Nonsense!" snorted Erlyn.

"Oh, very well," replied Trescon good-naturedly. "I've only studied this period for thirty years, while you've just looked it up since we started. So I bow to your superior knowledge."

Brant had followed this conversation with growing surprise and a rapidly mounting sense of bafflement.

"Are all three of you artists?" he blurted out at last.

"Of course," replied Trescon grandly. "Why else would we be here?"

"Don't be a damned liar," said Erlyn, without even raising his voice. "You won't be an artist if you live a thousand years. You're merely an expert, and you know it. Those who can—do: those who can't—criticize."

"Where have you come from?" asked Brant, a little faintly. He had never met anyone quite like these extraordinary men. They were in late middle age, yet seemed to have an almost boyish gusto and enthusiasm. All their movements and gestures were just a little larger than life, and when they were talking to each other they spoke so quickly that Brant found it difficult to follow them.

Before anyone could reply, there was a further interruption. A dozen men appeared in the doorway—and were brought to a momentary halt by their first sight of the great painting. Then they hurried to join the little group around Brant, who now found himself the center of a small crowd.

"Here you are, Kondar," said Trescon, pointing to Brant. "We've found someone who can answer your questions."

The man who had been addressed looked at Brant closely for a moment, glanced at his unfinished painting, and smiled a little. Then he turned to Trescon and lifted his eyebrows in interrogation.

"No," said Trescon succinctly.

Brant was getting annoyed. Something was going on that he didn't understand, and he resented it.

"Would you mind telling me what this is all about?" he said plaintively.

Kondar looked at him with an unfathomable expression. Then he said quietly: "Perhaps I could explain things better if you came outside."

He spoke as if he never had to ask twice for a thing to be done; and Brant followed him without a word, the others crowding close behind him. At the outer entrance Kondar stood aside and waved Brant to pass.

It was still unnaturally dark, as if a thundercloud

had blotted out the sun; but the shadow that lay the full length of Shastar was not that of any cloud.

A dozen pairs of eyes were watching Brant as he stood staring at the sky, trying to gauge the true size of the ship floating above the city. It was so close that the sense of perspective was lost; one was conscious only of sweeping metal curves that dwindled away to the horizon. There should have been some sound, some indication of the energies holding that stupendous mass at rest above Shastar; but there was only a silence deeper than any that Brant had ever known. Even the crying of the sea gulls had ceased, as if they, too, were overawed by the intruder who had usurped their skies.

At last Brant turned toward the men gathered behind him. They were waiting, he knew, for his reactions; and the reason for their curiously aloof yet not unfriendly behavior became suddenly clear. To these men, rejoicing in the powers of gods, he was little more than a savage who happened to speak the same language—a survival from their own half-forgotten past, reminding them of the days when their ancestors had shared the Earth with his.

"Do you understand, now, who we are?" asked Kondar.

Brant nodded. "You have been gone a long time," he said. "We had almost forgotten you."

He looked up again at the great metal arch spanning the sky, and thought how strange it was that the first contact after so many centuries should be here, in this lost city of mankind. But it seemed that Shastar was well remembered among the stars, for certainly Trescon and his friends had appeared perfectly familiar with it.

And then, far to the north, Brant's eye was caught by a sudden flash of reflected sunlight. Moving purposefully across the band of sky framed beneath the ship was another metal giant that might have been its twin, dwarfed though it was by distance. It passed swiftly across the horizon and within seconds was gone from sight.

So this was not the only ship; and how many more might there be? Somehow the thought reminded Brant of the great painting he had just left, and of the invading fleet moving with such deadly purpose toward the doomed city. And with that thought there came into his soul, creeping out from the hidden caves of racial memory, the fear of strangers that once had been the curse of all mankind. He turned to Kondar and cried accusingly:

"You're invading Earth!"

For a moment no one spoke. Then Trescon said, with a slight touch of malice in his voice:

"Go ahead, Commander—you've got to explain it sooner or later. Now's a good time to practice."

Commander Kondar gave a worried little smile that first reassured Brant, then filled him with yet deeper forebodings.

"You do us an injustice, young man," he said gravely. "We're not invading Earth. We're evacuating it."

"I hope," said Trescon, who had taken a patronizing interest in Brant, "that *this* time the scientists have learned a lesson—though I doubt it. They just say, 'Accidents will happen,' and when they've cleaned up one mess, they go on to make another. The Sigma Field is certainly their most spectacular failure so far, but progress never ceases."

"And if it does hit Earth—what will happen?"

"The same thing that happened to the control apparatus when the Field got loose—it will be scattered uniformly throughout the cosmos. And so will you be, unless we get you out in time."

"Why?" asked Brant.

"You don't really expect a technical answer, do

you? It's something to do with Uncertainty. The Ancient Greeks—or perhaps it was the Egyptians—discovered that you can't define the position of any atom with absolute accuracy; it has a small but finite probability of being anywhere in the universe. The people who set up the Field hoped to use it for propulsion. It would change the atomic odds, as it were, so that a spaceship orbiting Vega would suddenly decide that it really ought to be circling Betelgeuse.

"Well, it seems that the Sigma Field does only half the job. It merely *multiplies* probabilities—it doesn't organize them. And now it's wandering at random through the stars, feeding on interstellar dust and the occasional sun. No one's been able to devise a way of neutralizing it—though there's a horrible suggestion that a twin should be created and a collision arranged. If they try that, I know just what will happen."

"I don't see why we should worry," said Brant. "It's still ten light-years away."

"Ten light-years is much too close for a thing like the Sigma Field. It's zigzagging at random, in what the mathematicians call the Drunkard's Walk. If we're unlucky, it'll be here tomorrow. But the chances are twenty to one that the Earth will be untouched; in a few years, you'll be able to go home again, just as if nothing had ever happened."

"As if nothing had ever happened!" Whatever the future brought, the old way of life was gone forever. What was taking place in Shastar must now be occurring in one form or another, over all the world. Brant watched wide-eyed as strange machines rolled down the splendid streets, clearing away the rubble of ages and making the city fit for habitation again. As an almost extinct star may suddenly blaze up in one last hour of glory, so for a few months Shastar would be one of the capitals of the world, housing the army of

scientists, technicians, and administrators that had descended upon it from space.

Brant was growing to know the invaders very well.
Their vigor, the lavishness of everything they did, and
the almost childlike delight they took in their superhu-
man powers never ceased to astonish him. These, his
cousins, were the heirs to all the universe; and they
had not yet begun to exhaust its wonders or to tire of
its mystery. For all their knowledge, there was still a
feeling of experimentation, even of cheerful irrespon-
sibility, about many of the things they did. The Sigma
Field itself was an example of this; they had made a
mistake, they did not seem to mind in the least, and
they were quite sure that sooner or later they would
put things right.

Despite the tumult that had been loosed upon
Shastar, as indeed upon the entire planet, Brant had
remained stubbornly at his task. It gave him something fixed and stable in a world of shifting values, and
as such he clung to it desperately. From time to time
Trescon or his colleagues would visit him and proffer
advice—usually excellent advice, though he did not
always take it. And occasionally, when he was tired
and wished to rest his eyes or brain, he would leave
the great empty galleries and go out into the trans-
formed streets of the city. It was typical of its new
inhabitants that, though they would be here for no
more than a few months, they had spared no efforts to
make Shastar clean and efficient, and to impose upon
it a certain stark beauty that would have surprised its
first builders.

At the end of four days—the longest time he had
ever devoted to a single work—Brant slowed to a halt.
He could go on tinkering indefinitely, but if he did he
would only make things worse. Not at all displeased
with his efforts, he went in search of Trescon.

He found the critic, as usual, arguing with his col-

leagues over what should be saved from the accumulated art of mankind. Latvar and Erlyn had threatened
violence if one more Picasso was taken aboard, or
another Fra Angelico thrown out. Not having heard of
either, Brant had no compunction in pressing his own
claim.

Trescon stood in silence before the painting, glancing at the original from time to time. His first remark
was quite unexpected.

"Who's the girl?" he said.

"You told me she was called Helen—" Brant started
to answer.

"I mean the one you've *really* painted."

Brant looked at his canvas, then back at the original. It was odd that he hadn't noticed those differ-
ences before, but there were undoubtedly traces of
Yradne in the woman he had shown on the fortress
walls. This was not the straightforward copy he had set
out to make. His own mind and heart had spoken
through his fingers.

"I see what you mean," he said slowly. "There's a
girl back in my village; I really came here to find a
present for her—something that would impress her."

"Then you've been wasting your time," Trescon
answered bluntly. "If she really loves you, she'll tell
you soon enough. If she doesn't, you can't make her.
It's as simple as that."

Brant did not consider that at all simple, but decided not to argue the point.

"You haven't told me what you think about it," he
complained.

"It shows promise," Trescon answered cautiously.
"In another thirty—well, twenty—years you may get
somewhere, if you keep at it. Of course the brushwork
is pretty crude, and that hand looks like a bunch of
bananas. But you have a nice bold line, and I think
more of you for not making a carbon copy. Any fool

can do that—this shows you've some originality. What you need now is more practice—and above all, more experience. Well, I think we can provide you with that."

"If you mean going away from Earth," said Brant, "that's not the sort of experience I want."

"It will do you good. Doesn't the thought of traveling out to the stars arouse any feelings of excitement in your mind?"

"No; only dismay. But I can't take it seriously, because I don't believe you'll be able to make us go."

Trescon smiled, a little grimly.

"You'll move quickly enough when the Sigma Field sucks the starlight from the sky. And it may be a good thing when it comes: I have a feeling we were just in time. Though I've often made fun of the scientists, they've freed us forever from the stagnation that was overtaking your race.

"You have to get away from Earth, Brant; no man who has lived all his life on the surface of a planet has ever seen the stars, only their feeble ghosts. Can you imagine what it means to hang in space amid one of the great multiple systems, with colored suns blazing all around you? I've done that; and I've seen stars floating in rings of crimson fire, like your planet Saturn, but a thousand times greater. And can you imagine night on a world near the heart of the Galaxy, where the whole sky is luminous with star mist that has not yet given birth to suns? Your Milky Way is only a scattered handful of third-rate suns; wait until you see the Central Nebula!

"These are the great things, but the small ones are just as wonderful. Drink your fill of all that the universe can offer; and if you wish, return to Earth with your memories. *Then* you can begin to work; then, and no sooner, you'll know if you are an artist."

Brant was impressed, but not convinced.

"According to *that* argument," he said "real art couldn't have existed before space travel."

"There's a whole school of criticism based on that thesis; certainly space travel was one of the best things that ever happened to art. Travel, exploration, contact with other cultures—that's the great stimulus for all intellectual activity." Trescon waved at the mural blazing on the wall behind them. "The people who created that legend were seafarers, and the traffic of half a world came through their ports. But after a few thousand years, the sea was too small for inspiration or adventure, and it was time to go into space. Well, the time's come for you, whether you like it or not."

"I don't like it. I want to settle down with Yradne."

"The things that people want and the things that are good for them are very different. I wish you luck with your painting; I don't know whether to wish you luck in your other endeavor. Great art and domestic bliss are mutually incompatible. Sooner or later, you'll have to make your choice."

Sooner or later, you'll have to make your choice. Those words still echoed in Brant's mind as he trudged toward the brow of the hill, and the wind came down the great road to meet him. Sunbeam resented the termination of her holiday, so they moved even more slowly than the gradient demanded. But gradually the landscape widened around them, and the horizon moved farther out to sea, and the city began to look more and more like a toy built from colored bricks—a toy dominated by the ship that hung effortlessly, motionlessly above it.

For the first time Brant was able to see it as a whole, for it was now floating almost level with his eyes and he could encompass it at a glance. It was roughly cylindrical in shape, but ended in complex polyhedral structures whose functions were beyond conjecture. The great curving back bristled with equally mysterious bulges, flutings, and cupolas. There was power and purpose here, but nothing of beauty, and Brant looked upon it with distaste.

This brooding monster usurping the sky—if only it would vanish, like the clouds that drifted past its flanks!

But it would not disappear because he willed it; against the forces that were gathering now, Brant knew that he and his problems were of no importance. This was the pause when history held its breath, the hushed moment between the lightning flash and the advent of the first concussion. Soon the thunder would be rolling round the world; and soon there might be no world at all, while he and his people would be homeless exiles among the stars. That was the future he did not care to face—the future he feared more deeply than Trescon and his fellows, to whom the universe had been a plaything for five thousand years, could ever understand.

It seemed unfair that this should have happened in his time, after all these centuries of rest. But men cannot bargain with Fate, and choose peace or adventure as they wish. Adventure and Change had come to the world again, and he must make the best of it—as his ancestors had done when the age of space had opened, and their first frail ships had stormed the stars.

For the last time he saluted Shastar, then turned his back upon the sea. The sun was shining in his eyes, and the road before him seemed veiled with a bright, shimmering mist, so that it quivered like a mirage, or the track of the Moon upon troubled waters. For a moment Brant wondered if his eyes had been deceiving him; then he saw that it was no illusion.

As far as the eye could see, the road and the land on either side of it were draped with countless strands of gossamer, so frail and fine that only the glancing sunlight revealed their presence. For the last quarter-mile he had been walking through them, and they had resisted his passage no more than coils of smoke.

Throughout the morning, the wind-borne spiders must have been falling in millions from the sky; and as he stared up into the blue, Brant could still catch momentary glimpses of sunlight upon drifting silk as belated voyagers went sailing by. Not knowing whither they would travel, these tiny creatures had ventured forth into an abyss more friendless and more fathomless than any he would face when the time came to say farewell to Earth. It was a lesson he would remember in the weeks and months ahead.

Slowly the Sphinx sank into the sky line as it joined Shastar beyond the eclipsing crescent of the hills. Only once did Brant look back at the crouching monster, whose agelong vigil was now drawing to its close. Then he walked slowly forward into the sun, while ever and again impalpable fingers brushed his face, as the strands of silk came drifting down the wind that blew from home.